I0547993

No Substitute for

Misinformation

Carolyn J. Rose

No Substitute for Misinformation

Copyright © 2017 Carolyn J. Rose

www.deadlyduomysteries.com

All rights reserved. No part of this book may be used or reproduced by any means, graphic, electronic, or mechanical, including photocopying, recording, taping, or by any other means, without the written permission of the author, except in the case of brief quotations used in articles and reviews.

This novel is a work of fiction. Names, characters, places, incidents, and dialogues are products of the author's imagination and are not to be construed as real. Any resemblance to actual events or persons, living or dead, is entirely coincidental.

Cover design by Dorion D. Rose, Broken Cork Photography

Interior design for print edition by Boulevard Photografica/Patty G. Henderson

Digital editions (epub and mobi) produced by Booknook.biz

Paperback edition ISBN: 978-0-9968645-5-8

Mobi edition ISBN: 978-0-9968645-6-5

Epub edition ISBN: 978-0-9968645-7-2

2017

Cheese Puff thanks all of you who, despite his stubborn entitlement, seem to find him more amusing than annoying

Chapter 1

"I was NOT a stripper."

Muriel Ballantine, my elegant, refined, and wealthy neighbor, slammed her fist on my dining room table with enough force to make the salt and pepper shakers jump. "I was a *showgirl*. I made that perfectly clear to Rick Rivers when he recorded the interview at the radio station. You know I did, Barbara. You were sitting right next to me."

She was correct. I'd been right beside her. And I'd hated every minute of being in the same room with the slimeball who downsized me from my former position as the producer for his talk show. "You even explained the difference to him. Twice."

"*And* I wrote it down. He can't say he misunderstood. So why does he insist on calling me a stripper every time he mentions that my interview will run next weekend?"

Half a dozen responses leaped to my lips, chief among them being the fact that Rick Rivers, the self-proclaimed "Voice of Reckless River, Washington," had no filter. He said whatever he thought might increase his ratings, or whatever was on his mind. That usually wasn't much, and it wasn't of fine quality. Rick wasn't given to deep thought. And his intelligence-impaired brain was small—so miniscule even a fruit fly wouldn't consider swapping without bargaining for a ripe peach to sweeten the deal.

Mrs. B pounded the table again, drawing a yip from Cheese Puff, my ten-pound entitled mutt. Lola, the drug-sniffing Golden Retriever partnered with my live-in detective boyfriend Dave Martin, answered with a whine. "I ought to sue him for everything he's got."

That amounted to a collection of shoes with lifts, tasteless jackets with fat shoulder pads, and puffy hairpieces designed to add another inch of height. The only thing big about Rick Rivers was his ego. It was more inflated than the average blimp. As his former producer, an unwritten job requirement had been to stoke and stroke his ego.

I gagged, remembering the advice from coworkers—heap praise on him in the interest of job security.

I hadn't heaped all that much, which could be why, when the recession hit, Rick tossed me to the wolves and manfully told management he could go it alone. His ratings indicated that where he was going was downhill at a slow and steady pace, but he retained a core group of opinionated and vocal listeners. They kept the phone lines hot, and that kept management cool on the concept of canceling his show.

"If you sue, he'll milk the legal situation for publicity," I told Mrs. B. "And if the suit goes to court, who knows what kind of slant his attorneys will put on, well, lots of things. Your career. Your marriage. Your finances. Dario."

Mrs. B frowned, her sapphire eyes growing darker. The diamond rings on her fingers flashed as she clenched her fists.

I wasn't bothered by her past, even though it could best be described as "colorful." Mrs. B is the widow of Marco Ballantine, a reputed mobster she met in Las Vegas in years gone by—about half a century's worth of years. Claiming to be on the run from the mob, Marco carried her off on a series of around-the-world adventures that lasted decades before they settled here in Reckless River. Dave swore Marco had only played the part of a made man in order to seem daring and dangerous and woo her away from a horde of suitors. But others claimed that where there was smoke, there was fire.

Dario O'Brien, a man I thought of as a thug with a heart of gold, was also a source of smoke. He'd been a friend in her showgirl days and was now an assistant producer of *Still Got That Strut*, a Vegas-themed reality show on which Mrs. B was slated to appear in two weeks. The show featured former showgirls competing for a hefty financial prize by attempting to wow judges with their early routines as well as new ones.

Dave hadn't decided whether Dario's aura of danger was genuine or an act, but we'd both decided we liked him. In a dicey situation, it was a plus to have him on the team. But what really tipped the balance was this—he was the only one brave enough to give driving lessons to Dave's teenage daughter Allison.

Mrs. B raised her fist to thump the table once more. I scrambled to rescue the moose and squirrel salt and pepper shakers before they went over the edge.

"Sorry, dear." She sighed and massaged her hand. "You're right. And I can't say you didn't warn me about Rick Rivers." She ran her fingers through her feathery silver hair. "But Dario insisted the interview would be good publicity for the show."

"And it will be." I patted her arm. "Sadly, probably even better publicity because he called you a stripper."

Mrs. B's sapphire eyes shot sparks.

Big sparks.

I raised my hands and made a cross with my index fingers. "Just sayin'."

The sparks didn't fade.

"Of course, when people watch *Still Got That Strut* and see your costumes and routines, they'll know you weren't a—"

"Don't say it. I don't want to hear that word again. Ever."

"Got it." I put my right hand over my heart. "You won't hear it from me."

"Thank you, dear." Mrs. B carried her coffee cup to the sink and headed for the sliding glass door that opened onto the large deck created when she removed the privacy panels between our condo units. "Come on, Cheese Puff. We have work to do."

That work was practicing a dance for the second routine she'd present in Las Vegas. What the moves were, only Mrs. B and Cheese Puff knew. And neither had dropped even a hint of the role my orange scruffball of a dog would play.

Cheese Puff bounced from his favorite chair—the one with enough space between the seat cushion and the side for him to wedge himself in like taco filling in a corn tortilla shell—and followed her out the door. Sticking to my pledge to work on being less resentful about the way he obeyed Mrs. B and ignored me, I didn't scowl or stick out my tongue. Mentally, however, I did both. I mean, I rescued him from hungry homelessness. I took him in. I—

"I knew Mrs. Ballantine wasn't just a showgirl!" a voice boomed from the hallway.

Crap.

My sister.

Saying Indigo Zephyr—better known as Iz—was overbearing, was like saying it could get a little chilly in Antarctica.

"I knew there was more to the story."

Her cast thumping the floor, Lola slunk to the tiny downstairs bathroom and nosed the door shut behind her. I scanned the living room and kitchen for possible hiding places, but knew I was doomed. And I had no one to blame but myself.

4

I hadn't locked the door to the parking lot after I took the garbage out. If the knob turned and the door swung on its hinges, Iz wasn't the type who bothered to knock. And she wasn't the type to ask if she was welcome. Probably because she usually wasn't.

"Rick Rivers says she was a stripper," my sister proclaimed as she barreled in.

(For the record, if you imagine an actual barrel of the 55-gallon variety, give it legs and arms, short brown hair and squinty eyes, and dress it in cargo pants and a baggy trench coat, you have a pretty good idea of what my sister looks like. When we were young, an elderly aunt kindly described her as "sturdy." My friend Paulette charitably refers to her as "stocky." But Allison, never one to pull a punch, calls her "hulking." Allison is, however, savvy enough not to do that if Iz can hear.)

"Rick Rivers said it on the air. He said she was a stripper. So it must be true."

I didn't inquire whether Iz made a habit of believing everything that was broadcast or printed. And I didn't utter any of the many responses percolating to the surface of my brain, especially those questioning the integrity of Rick Rivers. My sister, who held the opinion that I seldom did anything right, believed I'd been let go because I wasn't up to the job of producing his show. She'd see my negative comments as sour grapes.

"I hope you have something to eat besides cheese snacks." Iz opened the refrigerator, studied the contents for a few moments, and liberated a can of cola and a package of sliced Hawaiian ham. "I guess I'll make do with this. I like honey ham better. Or turkey. The kind with the pepper crust, not the herb or tomato."

She turned to shoot me an accusatory scowl. "You know that."

5

And you know you don't live here.

I didn't say a word, but I made a mental note to steer clear of honey ham and sliced turkey with pepper crust for as long as I was able to stand upright and push a grocery cart unassisted.

Iz pulled a loaf of artisan whole wheat bread from the freezer. "Is this it? No sourdough?"

I stared into my empty coffee cup, imagining it was a deep well and Iz was at the bottom, ordering me to toss her a rope. With a secret smile, I imagined myself walking—no, skipping—away, skipping the rope I didn't toss to her. As I went, I'd whistle an annoying tune that would be stuck in her head for hours while her skin turned prune-like and her demands gave way to begging and bargaining.

Not that I'd *really* leave her at the bottom of a well.

I owed my sister one of those debts that can never be repaid. So, I might dawdle before I tossed the rope. I might even ask her how long she could tread water. But, because Iz stepped in to get me raised after my brother died and my parents checked out emotionally, eventually I *would* toss the dang rope. And when she got a grip, I'd heave with every bit of strength I had to get her out of the well.

"I'll pass on the bread," Iz said with a lung-emptying sigh. "I'm not supposed to have it, anyway. Penelope has us on a low-carb diet."

Penelope, an electrician who had—inexplicably as far as I'm concerned—fallen for my sister, needed to diet about as much as a Mexican Hairless needed to hit the barber shop for a little off the top. But if she was using that ploy to get my sister to shed a few pounds, I'd back her play. "Better put that cola away and get a diet drink."

Chewing a slice of ham, Iz studied the can for a few seconds, then popped the top. "There probably isn't enough sugar in here to have any effect."

6

Want to bet?

"And if I drink it all at once, it will be out of my system in no time."

(For the record, I'd heard a lot of dieting "theories" during my college days, and this was right up there with the most ridiculous of them. In case you're wondering, that was the cream-cheese-as-a-blood-thinner theory.)

I clamped my jaw and stuck to the policy of silence, even though not responding came with perils of its own.

"I know what you're thinking." Iz skewered me with a malevolent gaze. "I know every catty comment passing through your little mind. But at least *I'm* taking a proactive stand. Unlike *some* people, *I'm* on a diet."

See what I mean about the perils of silence?

"At least *I'm* doing something about my few extra pounds. I'm not just talking endlessly about trimming a ton of lard from my hips."

Difficult as it was not to challenge the word "few" or the "ton" part of that statement, I gnawed on the insides of both cheeks and kept silent. First, unless the word "few" can be expanded to mean about 40, Iz has more than a "few extra pounds." Second, while it's a known fact my skin is wrapped around 10 pounds I'd love to part with, they're distributed in a way that usually makes Dave smile when we manage a few moments of alone time.

Unfortunately, those moments had been few and far between recently, thanks to his broken arm, his drama-queen daughter, my oppressive substitute teaching schedule, our friends and neighbors, and miscellaneous misadventures involving murder and mayhem. For that reason, I'd been snacking more than usual. To make things worse, the supermarket I frequent had introduced a new line of cheesy snacks. To say those were my downfall was like saying Achilles had a little issue with his heel.

I carried my coffee cup to the sink and waited until Iz finished glugging the cola and delivered a belch that reminded me of a performing seal calling for the trainer to toss another fish. Then I went on the offensive. "Did you sleep in that trench coat after you rolled in the mud?"

Iz shot me a glare and brushed at her lapel. Paulette had bought the coat at a thrift store when we enlisted my sister to play the part of a private detective in order to trap the woman who murdered a former mobster and framed Mrs. Ballantine. Although our venture was a success and justice was done, the day will live in infamy for many reasons, one being that Iz decided investigating crime was a piece of cake. Shortly afterward, she applied for a PI license. Given her many past arrests for leading protests that lacked the necessary permitting and/or got out of hand, her application was in permanent limbo. But my sister, never one to restrict herself to coloring within the legal lines, had decided a license wasn't necessary as long as she didn't advertise and operated on a cash basis.

"How's flying below the radar working out? Got any clients yet?"

"For your information, this morning I met with a woman who suspects her husband is cheating on her." Iz plopped on the sofa, making the cushions wheeze. "Talk about a no-brainer of a case. He's a man. Of course he's cheating."

That statement, broad as it might be, applied to 50% of my husbands. And, lest you think I've made a career of matrimony, the husband total is two—Albert Peters and Jake Stranahan. Albert, a mild-mannered birder, never so much as looked at another female unless she had feathers and wings. Jake, an egotistical con man, spent almost every waking hour on the hunt for females of the human variety.

To head her off before she reviewed my track record and moved on to insinuating that Dave wasn't as faithful as I believed, I sat in Cheese Puff's favorite chair and slipped in a trio of questions. "What's your game plan? How will you prove he's cheating? How will you get evidence that will stand up in divorce court?"

Iz frowned.

I followed up.

"Stakeouts?   Surveillance?   Hidden   cameras   or microphones?"

"Sure."

"You have the equipment?"

Iz squirmed, making the sofa cushion gasp once more. "Not, uh, exactly."

"But you have a car, right? Penelope will need her truck for work."

"I know that! I'm not stupid."

Hmmm.

She executed another squirm, this one worthy of a worm trying to escape the beak of the early bird. Then she aimed a meaty forefinger at my head. "Your car sits at school all day. And it sits in the parking lot here most nights."

"No. No. No." For the second time in an hour I crossed my index fingers to ward her off. "You're not using my car to tail a suspect."

"Would it kill you to help me out?" Iz stood and loomed over me. "Just once?"

I folded my arms. The days when Iz could intimidate me were in the past. Not *far* in the past, but definitely a few calendar pages behind me. Rolling my eyes, I called her on the lie. "Once?"

Iz deflated like a bad tire on a hot highway. "All right, so you let me stay with you now and then. Until you met Dave."

"And?"

"And you loaned me money when I broke up with Sindie Lu and had to get rid of that tattoo."

"And?"

Her cheeks hit the sofa cushion again. It whimpered like its expiration date had come due. "And you covered for me with our parents when I flunked out of college."

"And?"

She flapped her hands. "Other stuff, okay. Lots of other stuff."

"So?"

"So I'll rent a car. Or something. But yours would have been perfect for surveillance. It's so . . . meh."

She nailed that. The late-model used car I bought to replace the one wrecked by the killer mentioned earlier took the concept of neutral to new levels. It was so beige—or maybe gray or possibly taupe—that it was practically invisible. Fine by me. It ran far better than the previous one. And the payments didn't bust my budget.

Iz stood, stretched, and checked a band around her wrist. "Well, gotta run, gotta hit 10,000. Need a few more steps."

"How many is a few?"

"Uh, 95."

This was my sister talking. And using the word "few" again. I asked the logical question, "Hundred?"

"Bah." Iz stomped toward the door.

"Wait," I called. "Tell me more about this diet."

Chapter 2

"You're not having any?" Dave scooped another helping of chicken-tortilla casserole from the pan.

"Not really hungry," I lied.

"Too bad. It's the best you ever made." He spooned sour cream on top of the steaming portion and glopped guacamole on top of that.

My salivary glands went into overdrive and I swallowed. Twice. According to Iz, in only a week of depriving myself, I could shed five pounds—maybe even more—if I stuck to the diet Penelope had found on the Internet. I hadn't had time to search it out and absorb the details yet, so I'd based my meal on what Iz said they'd had for dinner last night. That amounted to a few cubes of baked chicken sprinkled atop a small salad and dressed with lemon juice.

Even if I'd been alone, and a hundred miles from that casserole, the new nutritional program would be in trouble. Five minutes into the diet and already I longed for a slice of bread, a few crackers, even a single crouton. And already I could feel my crabbiness meter creeping toward the red zone.

Anchoring his plate with the cast on his left arm, Dave rammed his fork in the heap, loaded about 200 calories worth of casserole on the tines, deposited it between his teeth, and chewed with glazed-eyed gusto. I stabbed a tomato slice with stomach-rumbling disgust. The man could eat anything. He could devour as much as he wanted without gaining an ounce. Why couldn't the spin of the genetic roulette wheel have given me a higher metabolism?

I popped the tomato slice in my mouth and told myself to be grateful for what I had. At least the spin of the wheel had given me strong teeth and a reasonable amount of intelligence. At least it hadn't made me a duplicate of my sister. At least—

The phone rang.

"I'll get it," Allison shouted from upstairs.

In a moment she shouted again. "It's for you, Dad."

"I suppose it's pointless to ask her to explain that we're eating, or offer to take a message," I said.

Dave snorted. "Remember the last message?"

I did. An illegible scrawl littered with spelling errors and written in crayon on an empty cereal box she'd left in the middle of the hallway. We'd puzzled over it for half an hour, Dave suggesting the message had something to do with the TV series *Downton Abbey,* and me insisting it clearly referred to the delivery of an appliance—never mind that we hadn't ordered one.

Finally I'd caved and called Allison.

"OMG, are you blind?" she'd ranted. "It says to call your dentist and make an appointment."

Dave gobbled another forkful of casserole and pushed away from the table while complaining about the state of public education and the way keyboarding took precedence over penmanship. I, meanwhile, lamented written exchanges shortened to a few letters, numbers, or simply an emoji.

Pondering that led to a vow to write to my parents soon. Maybe tomorrow. Or the day after. Or over the next weekend.

That may sound cold and callous, but my parents are busy with friends and activities in their gated community in Missouri. They don't seem to need or want contact with me. Since the emotional disconnect triggered by my brother's death, we've been like sailing ships caught in divergent currents, drifting farther and farther apart. For all the response I get, I may as well drop a letter addressed to them in a trash can instead of a mailbox. And the last time I called, I could almost hear my mother reminding herself that I was her daughter.

Dave scooped up the handset from its cradle at the edge of the kitchen counter. "Dave Martin here."

Lola raised her head and thumped her tail on the carpet, signaling she was ready to go along if he needed her to sniff out drugs. But she made no effort to get to her feet. The cast on her right rear leg made standing a chore, and she'd quickly learned to conserve energy and move only when she was hungry or had to answer the call of nature.

I poked at a slice of radish and eavesdropped without feeling a single pang of guilt. Dave and I had been together for almost a year, so he knew I had a tendency toward minding other people's business. He would, I told myself, be worried if I didn't try to listen in. And if he wanted privacy, he'd have taken the call in the tiny office at the end of the hall. Or upstairs.

Unfortunately, after all that rationalization, there was almost nothing to hear. Dave emitted a series of grunts and one low whistle. Then he said, "I'll be there in a few minutes."

"You'll be where in a few minutes?"

"Downtown." He bolted another forkful of casserole, both feet pointing toward the hallway. "Chuck needs me."

"I hope he needs you only in a professional way."

Dave leered and hit me with a sloppy kiss that left a smear of sour cream on my lips. "You're the only one I need in any other way."

"And vice versa."

I'd been hoping we could demonstrate our mutual need later on, but Chuck was Detective Charles Atwell, the Reckless River Police Department's homicide honcho. When he said "jump," Dave's feet left the ground. Until his arm healed and he went back on the drug beat, he was assigned to homicide, and he was racking up experience investigating suspicious deaths.

I followed Dave to the door, peppering him with questions. "It's a homicide, isn't it? Where? Male or female? Shooting? Stabbing?"

"Definitely. In an alley. Male. Don't know yet." He kissed me again and was gone.

I licked my lips, teasing every molecule of sour cream from the corners. My stomach made squitchy sounds, signifying I should send more high-calorie stuff down my esophagus. Back at the table, I stared at my wilting salad, trying to convince myself the next bites would be better than the first. My taste buds weren't buying that. Neither was my stomach. My brain voted with them.

My gaze slid to Dave's plate and the cooling casserole. Not a full portion. Really only a half portion. Since he'd eaten some, it shouldn't go back in the pan—especially not with sour cream and guacamole on top. And besides, wasting food was, well, wasteful. Everyone knew that. And the other thing everyone knew was that there was no point in starting a diet on Sunday at dinner time. You had to start first thing Monday morning.

I reached for the plate, drew my hand back, then reached again. Tomorrow I'd be subbing in sophomore English, leading—or perhaps dragging—five classes through *Lord of the Flies*, step by tedious step. The book may be a classic, and it may be chock full of symbolism and statements about human nature and the endless battle between our loftier and baser instincts, but it wasn't among my favorites. Having to delve into it five times in one day made me deserving of the casserole *and* another dollop of sour cream.

I was loading the last glass in the dishwasher and contemplating calling out to Allison to bring down the dirty dishes in her room, when the sliding glass door to the deck opened. Damp wind gusted in. It was followed by my neighbors Verna and Sybil.

Like my sister, they hadn't bothered to knock. Unlike my sister, they were welcome. As members of the Cheese Puff Care and Comfort Committee, a group formed by Mrs. B, they'd provided dog feeding and walking services while I pursued post-graduate classes. And they continued now that I subbed nearly every day. Their visits and interactions were usually diverting—although often on the bizarre end of the diversion spectrum.

Verna, tall, dark, and angular, wore black leather pirate boots and a deep blue velvet cape with an enormous hood. Sybil, short, blond, and plump, wore a hot pink cape and a broad-brimmed vinyl hat with pink and green swirls that matched the design on her high-heeled rain boots. Halloween was in the rearview mirror and rain wasn't expected until after midnight, so I had no clue what prompted their wardrobe choices. But then, I seldom did.

I closed the dishwasher and braced myself against the counter, trying to gauge their expressions and how I might be affected by whatever they'd come here for. Both were smiling, but their smiles were directed only at me. They avoided making eye contact with each other. Experience with such body language told me I was about to be asked for an opinion. Experience had also taught me to avoid expressing one and thereby getting caught in a squeeze play. I was willing to go to

NO SUBSTITUTE FOR MISINFORMATION

almost any lengths to avoid that, even faking a seizure or setting the kitchen on fire.

Call me a coward if you must, but I was there when Jim, another neighbor, tried to mediate a dispute between these two. Verna and Sybil tore at him like ravenous sharks, and he's walked on eggshells ever since. All three serve on the Krammee's Reconstruction Committee, the group responsible for overhauling a former burger stand and converting it to the Reckless River Sandwich Shop. Given their personalities, the project hasn't been a stroll in the park—unless the park you select for the stroll is poorly lit and ground zero for a turf war between rival gangs armed with assault rifles.

"We can only stay a minute," Sybil burbled.

Verna consulted her watch. "*Masterpiece Mystery* is on soon."

Sybil clasped her pudgy hands. "It's *Foyle's War* tonight."

"I like *Wallander* better," Verna said.

"Of course you do. He's a brooder. Like you."

"I am *not* a brooder." Verna pushed back her hood and glared at Sybil. "I'm a deep thinker. Just because I don't jump in—"

"I'm fond of both shows," I said, planting my bottom firmly on the fence. "Now, what's up, ladies?"

"My income, I hope," Sybil said with a giggle.

"More like your debts." Verna snorted. She was all about the bottom line.

"You're jealous because you didn't think up this system."

"It's not a system."

"It is so. It's scientific and everything."

"Scientifically worthless, you mean."

Sybil stuck out her tongue.

Verna turned her back and folded her arms.

My, this was going well.

16

Hiding a smile and reminding myself not to try to mediate, I rinsed the sponge and went to work wiping smears from the refrigerator. Strawberry jam. Chocolate ice cream. Avocado dip. Not my smears. Some of Dave's. And a lot of Allison's. Not that either would admit culpability. No, they fell back on the time-honored tradition of blaming each other. Someday I intended to dust for prints.

"I got the idea from a movie," Sybil said.

"A surfing movie," Verna added in a tone that implied surfing and moviemaking cancelled each other out.

I scrubbed at a stubborn stain that looked a lot like dried blood but was probably salsa, or catsup, or some of that Asian sweet and hot sauce Dave had taken to squirting on sandwiches. As I scrubbed, their argument washed over me. (Pun intended.)

"See, in the ocean, the seventh waves are always the biggest."

"Except when they're not."

"But lots of times they are."

"Hmmph."

I gave the sponge another rinse and attacked a bluish dribble on the side of the door. What the heck had that been before it oozed? And why wasn't the refrigerator door made of something smooth? Why did it have a zillion tiny crevasses that served no purpose except collecting gunk?

"So when we get to Las Vegas for *Still Got That Strut,*" Sybil said, "all I have to do is count. First I find the seventh casino on the street. Then I find the seventh slot machine. Then I play seven dollars." She clapped her hands. "Then money comes pouring out and I'm rich."

"Or you're out those seven dollars." Verna turned to face her friend. "Where will you start counting from?"

"I already told you. I'll count from the first casino."

17

"The first casino on which end?"

"Which end of what?"

"The Strip."

"She did not!" Sybil stamped both feet, her rain boots sliding on the linoleum. "Muriel never took off her clothes on stage! I don't care what that nasty Rick Rivers says."

Verna grasped her elbow to hold her upright. "I wasn't talking about Muriel. The Strip is the area where a lot of the hotels and casinos are."

"Oh. I didn't know that." Sybil chewed her thumbnail. "How many casinos are there?"

"On the Strip? Thirty? Forty?" Verna shrugged. "In the whole area? Maybe 100?"

"So there would be a lot of seventh casinos." Sybil held up her hands, fingers spread. "Let's see, seven goes into ten once and carry the three—"

"And big casinos have hundreds of machines," I supplied, breaking my vow to remain on the fence.

"Hundreds?" Sybil echoed.

"And they're not all in a row." I told myself I wasn't siding with Verna, I was simply providing information. "They're in a lot of rows. And in groups and clusters."

Sybil buried her face in her hands and moaned. "I thought it was a great idea. I thought it would be so easy."

"You always do. You're always an optimist." Verna put her arm around her friend's shoulders and led her to the door. "That's one of the things I like about you. Now let's go watch Mr. Foyle and Samantha."

And they were gone. They left behind the scent of the baby powder Sybil used instead of deodorant. And they left me wondering if the energy I'd expended scrubbing would offset the calories in a cookie.

18

Chapter 3

"Who was that?" Allison plunged down the stairs, a stack of dishes clattering in her arms. "Who was here?"

"Verna and Sybil. Please be careful with those."

"Why do you always say that?" She jumped from the final step with a clank and a rattle, sauntered to the kitchen counter, and sent a cascade of crusty plates and silverware spilling across it. "I hardly *ever* break *anything*."

(For the record, the expression "hardly ever" used in that last sentence amounts to, by my tally, breaking things fewer than three times a week. Until Allison flies the nest, I'm shopping at thrift stores for replacements. And I'm not trying to match the few pieces that remain of the set I had when Dave and Allison moved in six months ago. I'm going for white, cheap, and sturdy.)

"Besides, it's not like your stuff all goes together." In a move borrowed from high jumpers, she shed her flip-flops, propelled herself backwards over the coffee table, and landed in a sprawl on the sofa. "Mrs. Ballantine's plates all match."

I refrained from explaining why that statement was true. Given the mood she'd been in for the past few days, Allison would either tell me I was wrong about the breakage, or ask why I was so hung up on material possessions. Sixteen was not shaping up to be an easy year—for any of us. And that included Frankie DeMille, director of the Reckless River Amateur Theater Company.

Last month, miffed because she hadn't been awarded the starring role in the Captain Meriwether High School winter production, Allison trotted her talents to the amateur theater downtown. Somehow, even though she'd missed the auditions, and even though she sang like a deflating balloon, Frankie took her on as the understudy for Audrey in *Little Shop of Horrors*. Since then, Allison had been surfing the Internet daily, searching out reports on the flu and other communicable diseases that might strike Reckless River, take down the lead actress, and allow her to step in.

I didn't envy Frankie DeMille. But then, she was used to managing large egos consigned to small roles. And her imposing appearance probably helped. Frankie was six feet tall, thin enough to carry off the vagaries of fashion, and blessed with a mass of long black hair shot with gray. She was also in possession of a pair of steely eyes any substitute teacher would envy, and a voice that could slice through the air like a ninja throwing star. In addition, she possessed a hot temper she alternately blamed on her Bolivian grandfather, her Hungarian grandmother, a boarding school in Spain, the years she lived in Greece, or having been done wrong by one of her many lovers. While Allison didn't exactly respect the theater director, she was certainly in awe of her, and never considered how much of Frankie's past might be fabricated for effect.

I eyed the heap on the counter and wished our dishwasher had more cycles than light, regular, and heavy. What we needed was a cycle capable of stripping paint, blasting rocks to gravel, or splitting the atom. "Are those all the dirty dishes from your room?"

20

"I guess."

Not the answer I was looking for. "How about glasses? Or mugs?"

She punched the TV remote, bringing up a comedy that seemed to have more laugh track than dialogue. "I guess."

"You guess there are? Or you guess there aren't?"

"I don't know. And why are you always bugging me?"

Not because it gets me anywhere.

I glanced at the clock. Going on 8:00. Time to select my subbing outfits for the week, collect Cheese Puff from Mrs. B, take Lola out to do her thing, and ease toward bed with a good book. It was definitely not the time to get into a discussion/argument/complainathon with Allison. That was Dave's job.

Except Dave was at the scene of a crime.

"You're always on my case. You're always picking on me."

Speaking of crime scenes, if Allison was to be believed, there was one right here. Apparently I'd been caught red-handed tormenting a teen. Not that most of the adults I knew would find me guilty. A jury of teenagers, however, would sentence me to life in prison. And, grim as that would be, it might be an improvement on life as a high school substitute teacher.

I glanced at the clock once more. 8:02.

Unless I took action, the dirty glasses—and I knew there were at least six of them—would remain in Allison's room and the dirty plates and silverware would remain on the counter. In their guilt-inducing manner, they'd call out to me, crying, "Wash me. Put me away."

Well, of course they wouldn't literally be crying out. But if you're the type who has trouble relaxing while there's a mess in the kitchen, you know what I'm talking about.

Dave would say, "Ignore the mess for now. It will be there in the morning."

And that, of course, was part of the problem. A *big* part of the problem.

I sidestepped in front of the TV where, thanks to my extra pounds, I blocked a good portion of the screen.

"Are you in my way on purpose?" Allison whined.

"I guess."

She sat up and leaned to her left.

I sidled a step to my right.

"Is this about the dishes?"

"I guess."

She punched off the remote and slammed it on the coffee table. "Why do I have to do to everything around here?"

Everything?

Pondering where to begin, I sat in Cheese Puff's favorite chair. Should I have her compile a list of what she'd done today to help out? It would be a short list, pretty much limited to bringing down the load of dishes spread on the counter. Should I enumerate the many chores I'd done? The sheets and towels I'd washed and dried and folded, the groceries I'd shopped for, the meal I'd cooked, the kitchen I'd cleaned? No, she'd claim that stupid chores like those didn't count because they had to be done over and over again.

And, darn it all, they did.

With a groan, I slumped deeper in the chair.

Being an adult was less fun than I'd thought it would be when I was Allison's age.

I glanced at the dirty dishes, thought about *Lord of the Flies* and the day of subbing ahead, groaned again, and hugged myself.

Being an adult—a halfway responsible adult—sometimes sucked.

"Are you okay?"

"I guess."

"You're imitating me." She kicked the sofa arm. "That's not funny."

I giggled. "I guess."

"It's annoying."

My giggle morphed into a laugh. "I guess."

Allison kicked the sofa arm again. "Then why are you laughing?"

"Because when I was your age I didn't want to grow up." My laugh morphed into a strangled sob. "And it happened anyway. And here I am."

The sob morphed into the hiccups. "And I can't, hic, go back."

Not that I really wanted to go back—at least not back to the way it was after Iz took off to have a life and I was left with my parents. Don't get me wrong, they didn't mistreat me, but they didn't nurture me, either. They supplied the necessities—or handed over cash and the car keys so I could make supply runs—but there were no home-cooked meals, no family game nights, no resounding applause from them when the curtain came down on the class play.

On the other hand, those take-out dinners, heat-and-eat individual meals, salads in sacks, paper plates, and plastic utensils added up to no major mess in the kitchen. *And* I had plenty of freedom. My parents seldom asked where I was going and seldom listened when I told them where I'd been. The spare change from supply runs supplemented my allowance to provide gas for the car I borrowed almost every evening after claiming I had to go to the library, study with a friend, pick up colored pens for a project, or buy a new pair of sneakers.

In a rare demonstration of compassion, Allison arose from the sofa and brought me water in the last clean glass in the cabinet. While I alternately sipped and held my breath, she perched on the arm of the chair, patted my back, and consoled me. "I hate hiccups. I hate them almost as much as I hate snorting soda through my nose when I laugh."

The back patting was a little too hard, but I didn't mention that. It's the thought that counts. Right?

"Did you have a boyfriend when you were my age?"

"Yes," I admitted, hoping she wouldn't dig for intimate details. I wasn't a great liar, and I suspected that lying while hiccupping would tax my limited skills. "But not a, hic, serious boyfriend like Josh."

"He's serious all right," Allison carped. "Serious about getting good grades, serious about being the assistant manager at the sandwich shop, serious about everything but the important stuff."

I assumed she defined "important stuff" as whatever she wanted him to do with her.

"I wanted to go to the movies tonight, but he's got a stupid test tomorrow on British government. Who cares about that? We don't live in England. And he wants me to quiz him on the way to school tomorrow. But I was gonna run my Audrey lines. That's way more important."

I sighed inwardly. I'd heard similar tales of woe before. Many times. Defending Josh would get my head bitten off. If Allison didn't reconstruct her universe soon and move away from the center of it, Josh would decide he'd had enough whining and take a hike. And this time he might not return.

The idea of Josh pulling the plug on their relationship frightened me. And it scared Dave so much he turned white around the lips at the thought. As we'd discovered during their brief relationship hiatus before school started, Allison in a breakup tailspin was 10 times more out of control than Allison on a normal day. Plus, there was the danger she might slip into a depression like the one she'd been in a year ago. If that happened, she might run away or attempt to harm herself.

I hiccupped, then hauled in a long breath and held it.

Sure, I could deliver the lecture about how important it was to be yourself and how that made you better when you became part of a relationship. But, since I'd accrued only a few months of singleness between Albert, Jake, and Dave, I could hardly point to myself as an example of a woman who lived life on her own and made a success of it. Perhaps I could prevail on my friend Paulette. Her husband, an airline pilot, was away half the time and she seemed to manage fine. More than fine, actually, since she was involved in a slew of projects and money-making enterprises.

Coward that I am, I drained the glass, took a few shallow breaths to ascertain that the hiccups were gone, then went with a change of subject and a perky, positive attitude. "Well, the grand opening of the sandwich shop is coming up, and after that Josh will have more time for fun. But in the meantime, you should keep busy. How about we go over to the motor vehicle place tomorrow after school and get your learner's permit?"

Allison scowled and picked at the orange nail polish on her toes. "What happens if I flunk again?"

"You won't. I bet you miss only one or two questions."

She skewered me with a glare. "You suck at lying."

"So I've been told." I carried the glass to the kitchen and placed it in the dishwasher, leaving the door open to provide a hint. Not that hinting had ever worked with Allison before. But if I stopped hoping, my attitude would head south faster than a snowbird with a souped-up RV.

"Okay, to be honest, I don't know what happens if you fail the test again. But I think it would be good to believe you can pass. Study hard, and tell yourself you'll ace it."

"But what if I don't?"

"If that happens, I'm sure they'll inform us what to do next. Maybe there's a waiting period. Or a class. Or maybe you'll need to get a special driving instructor."

Allison slid into the chair I'd vacated and curled into a ball. "I'll probably never get my license."

That would certainly keep the highways safer. But it would also impose a huge burden on those of us expected to act as chauffeurs. And if Josh dropped out of her life, the burden on me and Dave would go from huge to astronomical.

"Even if I get my permit, there's another test after that. And I'll never get enough practice. Your car looks like a puddle of oatmeal puke. Dad's is full of food wrappers and dog hair and he's busy hanging around with Detective Atwell. And Mrs. B is busy dancing. And everyone else is busy with the sandwich shop." She wound up with a wail. "And Dario is stuck in Las Vegas."

"When *Still Got That Strut* is over for the season," I said, "Dario will be able to spend more time here."

I crossed my fingers and made a wish. Dario O'Brien's background might be questionable, but there was no question he loved Mrs. B and, by extension, all of her friends. Dario even seemed to enjoy giving Allison lessons and recounting what he called "tales of terror in the passenger seat." But since his assistant had been arrested for murder in an attempt to frame Mrs. B and rig the outcome of the reality show competition, Dario's time off had been sliced. He'd made only one short visit to Reckless River in recent weeks.

Allison drummed her heels on the floor. "I don't get why they have to make the tests so hard."

To try to ensure drivers knew what they were doing? To protect the rest of us on the road?

"Most of the rules about driving are stupid." Allison flung an arm across her eyes in a dramatic gesture. "And really picky. And some of the signs are dumb."

Telling myself not to rise to the bait, I motioned for Lola and headed for the door to the deck.

"What does it matter what color the line in the road is? Or if it's solid? And those traffic lights are ugly. Why isn't there blue instead of yellow?" Allison raised her voice and went on with her rant. "And why is the speed limit so slow by the school? We can't get anywhere good for lunch and back in time for fourth period if we can't go faster."

I slid the door closed, wondering how long it would be before she noticed I was gone. What I didn't wonder was whether the dishes would still be on the counter when I returned.

Chapter 4

They were.

And they were there still, crustier than ever, when I came downstairs at 6:00 the next morning.

Their presence made it a challenge to find a clean space to assemble a low-carb, diet lunch for school.

So I didn't bother.

Telling myself there was no point in starting a stressful day by elevating my tension level before I left home, I spooned a healthy portion of last night's casserole into the final clean bowl, slapped a piece of foil over it, and wedged it in my briefcase. Gnawing on a slice of whole wheat toast and sipping coffee, I fed the dogs and took them out to do their thing. They crossed the damp deck at a good clip, Lola's cast thumping on the boards. When I opened the gate, they hustled down the short flight of steps to the carpet of bark mulch surrounding a few rose bushes in the narrow garden between the deck and the asphalt trail along the Columbia River.

The fast-flowing water was pewter gray and blistered with whitecaps courtesy of a vicious wind. A chevron of geese passed overhead, flapping their way to warmer climes. Leaves skittered along the trail in the wake of a lone runner. He wore black sweats and an expression of determined misery.

The dogs didn't linger and, within moments, we were all upstairs again. Lola lowered herself to a spot beside the heat vent, while Cheese Puff burrowed beneath the covers and pasted himself to Dave's side.

"Thought you were going to school," he muttered without opening his eyes.

"I am. That's Cheese Puff next to you."

"Unnggh. Rather have you."

"Thanks." I bent to kiss him. "Who got killed?"

"No ID. Shoes are worn out. Clothes have seen better days. Could be homeless."

"Like you and your daughter will be if the dirty dishes are still on the counter this afternoon."

Dave opened his eyes a few millimeters. "What dishes?"

A dozen responses leaped to mind, responses running the gamut from disbelief to outrage. I canned them in favor of a question. "What's the weather like on Planet Oblivious this morning?"

"Huh?"

I patted his pointy little head and made for the stairs. A great wailing rose up to meet me. "Where are all the clean bowls? How am I supposed to eat my cereal?"

Shakespeare himself couldn't have created tragedy on this level.

"Seriously," Allison asked as I grabbed my jacket and briefcase, "what am I supposed to do?"

"The dishes?" I asked in voice syrupy enough to pour over a tall stack of pancakes.

The wailing that followed was loud enough to be heard on Planet Oblivious.

Or so I hoped.

My morning with *Lord of the Flies* went surprisingly well—I wasn't hunted down with sharpened sticks, and my questions for the class actually elicited more than a few grunts. So, when third period ground to a close, I wasn't in dire need of decompression time. Good thing, because the group in the teachers' room where I eat lunch was wound tight.

The first thing I noticed was Brenda Waring's hair. Chopped off half an inch below her ears. And tinted a greenish orange. Or perhaps a yellowish blue. The color seemed to change as she moved her head.

I gasped, then pretended to sneeze and slid my gaze toward Gertrude Suttle. She made a lip-zipping motion. So did Ardette Johnson.

Got it.

My mission was to pretend the hair didn't register on my OMG scale.

I slid my lunch from the refrigerator and into the microwave, noting that both appliances were sparkling clean. Since she joined us a month ago, Ardette—known to her friends as Ardie—had taken on the task of badgering us about cleaning up after ourselves. She, in turn, wiped and scrubbed daily to bring conditions up to her standards.

If Ardie's standards were a cut and a half above mine, they were a mile above those of history teacher Aston Marsden. His passion was historical re-enactment, and he frequently turned out for his day at Captain Meriwether High School dressed as a fur trapper or wilderness explorer. He also frequently ate in character, bringing items for lunch that it was best not to ask about—or glance at for more than a second or two. Today, with much gnawing and masticating, he was dining on what appeared to be a large rib. Between bites of gray and grisly meat ripped from the bone, he drank yellow liquid from a cup fashioned from a chunk of horn. Apparently it hadn't been fashioned all that well, or had cracked recently, because dribbles leaked into his unruly beard.

"Admit it," Brenda baited him, "you either didn't ask or didn't listen."

"I listened just fine." He slammed the horn cup on the table, sloshing liquid on the plastic tablecloth, then mopping at it with the sleeve of his faded red flannel shirt. "What I heard was a bunch of gobbledygook misinformation."

"So you assumed—as usual—that you understood. Or maybe you thought you knew better."

Doug Whitman faced me and slid a finger across his throat.

I nodded. Not that I needed the sign. Her sniping made it obvious that Brenda's romance with Aston was off again. The big puzzle, at least in my mind, was why and how the relationship switch occasionally slipped into the on position.

"When someone says we'll be setting up an army encampment," Aston ranted, "to me that means the Union. Or the Confederacy. Maybe even the Minutemen. It means history. Way-back-there history. It doesn't mean the Gulf War."

"Only this time it did," Brenda jeered. "I'd give my next paycheck for a picture of you outfitted for a conflict 130 years off the mark."

"Like you never got anything wrong." Aston aimed the rib at Brenda. "Remember Dress Like a Tramp Day?"

Brenda blushed. "That was different."

The microwave dinged and I carried my bowl to the empty seat between Doug and Aston, cheating my chair as far as I could toward Doug. Aston had a tendency to make broad gestures that sent gobbets of gunk flying, and that yellow stuff in the horn looked like it could eat through my clothing. Not to mention my skin.

Gertrude, meanwhile, explained to Ardie how a student teacher hacked Principal Jerome Morrow's e-mail account and sent out a series of memos, one instructing teachers to dress like tramps for a costume day. While others had had taken that to mean we should dress like panhandlers or vagrants, Brenda had tarted herself up as a streetwalker. His gaze drawn to her fishnet stockings, short skirt, and low-cut top, Aston had put the moves on her. That kicked off a relationship about as stable as a building straddling the San Andreas Fault.

"Even if you listen carefully and ask questions," Doug observed in a soothing voice, "it's tough to weed out misinformation. There's so much of it."

"Especially in the stuff that filters down from above." Ardie raised both hands and wiggled her fingers, miming falling rain. "I've about decided there's no point in acting on an edict until it's a week old, until they're finished issuing corrections and amendments."

"Or changing their minds entirely," Gertrude grumbled.

"Or deciding to put it on hold because the person who sent out the memo wasn't listening to the person who ordered it sent," Brenda added. "And they need clarification."

"Or it's the brainchild of someone who doesn't have enough to do," Aston groused. "Or a back-stabbing plan of someone trying to make it to the top by climbing on the bodies of those in the trenches."

"We got a memo this morning saying someone from some curriculum task force would be in school this week to do spot observations." Doug bit a potato chip for punctuation as he leaned my way. "Only, Big Chill says our honchos haven't been informed."

Big Chill, real name Wilhelmina Frost, was the head secretary at Captain Meriwether and the power behind the throne. The honchos were Principal Jerome Morrow and

Assistant Principal Tremaine Scott. Over the years, Jerome Morrow had perfected the art of disappearing from his office and remaining "invisible" for hours at a time. Tremaine Scott, being fairly new at the job, was easy to locate and willing to assume responsibility. It was possible he overlooked a memo from the main office, but it was improbable that both he and Big Chill had missed it.

"Sounds like someone at the top dropped the ball," I observed. "Or didn't include our people in the loop."

"Yeah. And the weird thing about this loop is that it started with a guy who's at a conference in New Jersey this week. Kind of hard to observe from clear across the continent. And the dude isn't picking up his messages. *And* his assistant says she knows nothing about the memo or the observations."

"Or probably anything else," Aston groused. "This school system has too many chiefs. And the chiefs have too many assistants. Someone should stick them in the classroom instead. That's where we could use them."

"Except maybe there's a good reason they aren't in the classroom," Ardie muttered.

Gertrude nodded in support of that statement. "Not everyone is cut out for the front lines of the kid business."

"Or the rear lines," Ardie added.

"The point is," Brenda said, "we don't know if someone else will be doing the observations this week, or if he plans to do them when he gets back from the conference, or what. It's nerve-racking."

"Especially for someone whose hair looks like an explosion in a silo," Aston sniped.

"You should talk! Your beard looks like a rat's nest." Brenda patted her hair. "And this wasn't what I intended. I was completely misinformed about the color and the procedure. All I asked for were highlights. Instead I got three hours of torture with every chemical they had on hand, and I ended up with a color that looks like toxic sludge. The ends were so burned they had to clip them off and now I'm practically bald."

When no one else jumped in to console her, I sacrificed myself. "It's not all that—"

"It's hideous. It's terrible. It's a disaster," Brenda screeched. "You know it. So admit it."

I raised my hands in surrender.

"Sorry. Didn't mean to snap." Brenda tugged at her hair. A few strands broke off and drifted to the table. "When I refused to pay and threatened to go to the paper, they said they'd fix it after school today."

"Fix it?" Gertrude asked. "Or *try* to fix it? What if it turns out worse?"

Brenda paled.

"Sometimes you have to let the mistake grow out. Or you cut it off," Ardie added. "A friend had her hair fried so bad she shaved herself bald."

Brenda gasped and clutched her head with both hands. "Shaved?" Tears glistened in her eyes. "She shaved off *all* her hair?"

"Every strand. Bought a bunch of scarves and hats."

"I have a couple you can borrow," Aston offered.

"Fur hats with tails on them? No way."

"They don't all have tails. Some have faces."

"Ungggsh," Gertrude groaned. "Enough. Somebody change the topic, please."

"Ummm, okay," Doug said. "I caught a little of Rick Rivers this morning. Is he as cold and uncaring as he seems, or is he trying to build a ratings base among people who are?"

I felt my stomach flip and crossed my fingers, hoping the latest spew from Rivers had nothing to do with Mrs. Ballantine, hoping he hadn't claimed she was a porn queen or prostitute.

"He's not exactly brimming with the milk of human kindness," I told him. "One time, when we were collecting school supplies for kids in need, he bragged that he'd never given a penny to charity in his entire life."

"He said that in private? Or on the air?"

"In private. What did he say this morning?"

Doug pushed the remains of his sandwich aside and placed his hands flat on the table. "First, I need to say that I don't usually listen to Rick Rivers. In fact, I make it a point of not listening. But my sister's new boyfriend borrowed my car yesterday and changed all the presets."

"And he set one for Rick Rivers?" I gripped his wrist. "I hope your sister isn't serious about this jerk."

"She's serious about the money he spends on her. And I guess he's an okay guy. But he's not Larry."

Doug and I shared a moment of silence for Larry Tate, owner of Start 'er Up Auto Repair, the man previously in line to be Doug's brother-in-law. Personally, I thought Larry had dodged a bullet. I believed one day he'd look back and see being jilted by his high school sweetheart was a good thing in many ways. But that day was still a long way off, and Larry passed his lonely evenings and weekends fixing cars or cleaning, organizing, and even painting the garage. It was now the spiffiest in town. Business was booming.

"So," Gertrude prompted, "what did Rick Rivers say?"

"Oh, uh, well, first he read the story in the paper about the man they found yesterday in an alley downtown."

I'd scanned that story—if you can call two short paragraphs a story—while I was bolting my coffee. It said little more than foul play was suspected, the man hadn't been identified, and police were investigating. It ended with a plea for anyone with information to call a tip line.

"Then he said it was obvious the man was homeless or a drunk or a drug dealer and probably from somewhere else, like Portland."

So far, none of this seemed especially cold, uncaring, or even surprising. It was possible, even based on the skimpy details provided, that many Reckless River residents might have drawn the same conclusions. Homelessness and substance abuse were issues—rapidly growing issues—in our community. But few of us wanted to admit that some problems on our streets were homegrown—especially not when we could shove the blame onto the huge city across the river.

"That's it?" Gertrude asked.

"Nope. Rivers took a couple of wild leaps and ended up in a land I didn't recognize as the home of the free." Doug put his hand over his heart as if preparing for the Pledge of Allegiance. "He said the man must have come to Reckless River because he thought it would be easier to game the system in a small city. And then he said we should protest spending public money on investigating this case or prosecuting the killer—if he's caught—because the victim was a waste of space. He said the person who killed him did the city a favor by taking out the trash."

Gertrude and Ardie drew in their breaths, straightened in their seats, and curled their fingers into fists as if ready to do battle.

"His words." Doug raised his hands, palms out, and pushed away from the table. "Not mine."

"Harsh words," Aston observed. "Even for a blockhead catering to other blockheads."

"Even if some of what he said is true," Brenda mused, "and the dead man was a drug dealer, we have to have justice for all or we end up with justice for none."

Ardie reached across the table and gave her a fist bump. "If we turn our backs once, it's easy to do it again. And again."

36

"And easy to start saying other groups don't matter as much," Gertrude said. "Like anyone who's a different color or religion, or isn't educated or healthy, or earning a decent income."

We were all silent for a few moments. Visions of burning crosses flashed through my mind.

"Is Dave involved in this case?" Doug asked.

"Yes. And from what he told me before I left for work, it's possible the man *was* homeless."

"Being homeless is a long way from being a drunk or a drug dealer or someone trying to game the system. But I bet even if he was all of that, Dave wouldn't slack off." Doug picked up his sandwich. "And I bet if he hears about what Rick Rivers had to say, he'll work harder."

"Definitely." And not because of my history with the talk show host or the fact that Rivers called Mrs. B a stripper. No, Dave would go the distance because he was a stand-up guy who gave the job all he had, no matter what.

Unless, of course, the job involved cleaning the kitchen.

Chapter 5

When it came to the task of kitchen cleaning, Dave gave the job about half of what he had.

If that.

The dishwasher hadn't been run, but all the plates and glasses that fit were inside. The rest were stacked in leaning heaps, glasses wedged inside others. Swirls of soggy crumbs indicated he'd wiped the counter with a sopping sponge before he abandoned it in a corner of the sink. Telling myself he'd been distracted by his quest for justice, I squeezed out the excess, and sprayed the sponge with bleach water. Then I wiped the counter, started the dishwasher, and took Lola outside and into a sparkling November afternoon. She limped about a hundred yards west along the river path, before she halted and turned around.

"Bet you can't wait to get that cast off, can you?"

She wagged her feathery tail.

"Two more weeks." I bent to stroke her head and scratch her ears, feeling guilty that I intended to leave her at home in a few minutes. I planned to take a brisk walk a mile east upriver. Maybe I'd even jog part of the way.

Nah.

After all, Monday meant my evening water aerobics class, and I needed to conserve energy. So I'd walk, work out the kinks, and enjoy the sunshine. But while I was out, there was something else I could do to raise my heart rate. After I settled Lola beside the sofa with a large dog biscuit, I zipped upstairs to snatch something to justify a stop at the condo manager's office on the way home.

As you probably already know, Bernina Burke and I have a hate-hate relationship that dates to our first encounters. Our conflict is complex. It has layers. It has depth and width. And, before you ask or make an erroneous assumption, she started it.

First, she took a dislike to Cheese Puff. He reciprocated by snarling and barking whenever she appeared, thereby increasing her dislike. When she yelled at him, he barked louder.

Second, she attempted to change condo pet-limit rules to prevent Dave from bringing Lola along when he moved in.

And third, she fell for my ex-husband Jake and became convinced I wanted him back. Acting on that misguided belief, she did all she could to make condo living hell in an attempt to force me to move.

Eventually she saw the light where Jake was concerned. Or at least she saw his intentions to lighten her bank account. She didn't kick him to the curb, but she certainly nudged him into the gutter. Still, she seemed to believe he'd change. And she continued her anti-dog campaign. So we clung to old grievances and demonstrated about as much love for each other as our political parties do.

Recently Bernina became obsessed with taking first place in the condo division of the Reckless River holiday decorating competition. Earlier in the fall Mrs. B, who was under house arrest at the time, agreed to bankroll the project in exchange for permission to create practice space by erecting a huge tent over our joint deck. The tent had come down several weeks ago, but Mrs. B kept writing checks, hoping Bernina's decorating efforts would impress residents of Shoalwater Bend. The manager of that luxury condo complex planned to resign soon, and most of us here at 90 Columbia Lane hoped Bernina would snag the job and put us out of her misery.

Not that we were prepared to write glowing letters of recommendation and pen our names to them. Not one of us intended to twist the truth that much. Even though the truth about Bernina was scary stuff.

If you don't believe me, you could ask any of the maintenance and landscaping companies she'd run off with eagle-eyed supervision and petty complaints and demands. Thanks to crews walking off the job and companies refunding money rather than working for Bernina another five minutes, the shrubbery and lawns were in worse shape than during the weeks Jake had been in charge.

But the objective was to get Bernina out. So, if we were asked, we wouldn't flat-out lie about her, but we'd try to make the truth appear a little less dark and dismal. We had our brushes ready and the whitewash all mixed.

And we had other schemes in various stages of development.

My neighbor Jim was in charge of the oust-Bernina campaign. His checkered background gave him the craftiness necessary for the job, while his white hair and beard provided an innocent Father Christmas appearance. Many women, including a few who resided at Shoalwater Bend, found him attractive, and lately Jim had been encouraging their advances. He claimed he escorted them only to advance our mission, but Jim was on a tight budget. Dinners and movies at their expense probably amounted to more than taking one for the team.

And speaking of team, my job was to discover how Bernina was presenting herself to Shoalwater Bend. Given our relationship history (see above), that assignment wasn't exactly a cakewalk. But substitute teaching taught me that pretending disinterest sometimes rattled the information cage. So, when I returned from my walk, I entered her office holding the single earring I'd plucked from my jewelry box. Casually, I placed it on the file folder atop the heap in the center of Bernina's cluttered desk, the folder marked FIND A BETTER JOB.

Either Bernina was less subtle than I imagined, or this file was a phony. Or a trap.

I glanced around the room, pretending I had no interest in the folder.

She turned from rooting through a file cabinet and studied the earring the same way I might view a scorpion emerging from beneath a napkin at a fancy restaurant. "What's this?"

"An earring," I said without even a trace of sarcasm.

"I know that." She narrowed her mole-like eyes. "Do you think I'm stupid?"

Talk about opening the door.

Six responses—every one of them sarcastic—leaped to mind.

I reminded myself I was here on a mission and clamped my jaws so hard I swear I heard a tooth crack. And me with no dental plan.

I unclamped and settled for giving the provenance—pure fabrication—of the earring. "I found it in the parking lot."

"Hmmm." Bernina slammed the file cabinet drawer and bent over her desk to study the lone piece of jewelry.

Just so you know, I'd chosen the dangling earring from a collection of singles. Some had been with me for a decade while I nurtured faint hope that mates might reappear. This earring

41

appeared more expensive than it was. "I think those are real diamonds."

Bernina bent closer, her voluminous blouse gaping at the neckline and revealing— Well, let's not go there. Bernina continued to peel off the pounds in an ounce-here-ounce-there fashion, but this book could fall into the hands of impressionable young children. Their growth might be stunted should I launch into extensive description of what my eyes beheld. I blinked and shifted my gaze to the wall behind her.

"Diamonds? Pfftt. Any fool can see those stones are fakes."

"Maybe the earring has sentimental value," I suggested.

Bernina snorted.

No surprise there. I doubted she'd had a sentimental moment in her life, unless it involved bidding farewell to a last bite of cheesecake before she swallowed it.

"Well, some people attach meaning to the strangest things." I shrugged. "Anyway, I hoped you could keep it here in case the owner came looking for it. Maybe I could put up a few signs around the complex."

"No signs. You know the rules."

She said it in a way that implied I knew them, but didn't always follow them. Which, when you got right down to it, was pretty much true. Especially since so many of the rules seemed designed simply to give Bernina the pleasure of enforcing them. Like the nitpicky swimsuit cover-up rule for those going to and from the pool. A beach towel wouldn't do. Neither would an extra-long T-shirt. As a consequence, I'd received two warnings in August. By the time the pool closed for the season, Allison had four to her credit. One more and she would have been barred from the pool for a week. If the count didn't start from zero next summer, we'd be swimming in the river to cool off.

(For the record, that would be a last resort. Since my two unintentional dips in the Columbia last winter, I haven't so

42

much as dabbled my little toe in its waters. Allison, who'd gone in only once, and then to rescue me, wasn't likely to be more adventurous. If Bernina banned us from the condo pool, I'd spend more time at the community center. Allison would hang out at the outdoor water park where there seemed to be few rules about how much skin should be covered.)

"Right," I said. "The rules. No signs outside or posted in condo windows facing outward."

She gave me a nod, the jiggling of her double chin making it more comical than curt.

"Could you, um, maybe put a sign up on the bulletin board by the office door so when people come in they'll see it?"

Bernina sighed as if I'd asked her to hike to the top of Mount Hood.

"I'll be glad to make the sign. I don't have any paper with me, but I could write it on the back of that outdated notice about pool fees being due by the first of June."

"It's not outdated. The fees are *always* due then."

"True, but the amount on the notice has been changed four times. There's not enough room to fit in next year's fee."

And I bet that would be higher because I haven't noticed a huge trend toward decreasing costs.

Bernina sighed as if I'd upped the ante on my hike request and asked her to make the trek to the apex of the mountain while wearing clown shoes and a top hat.

I sighed in return.

Honestly, how hard could it be to print out a fresh notice?

"Use it if you must," she said.

"Thanks," I responded in my breeziest voice. "Don't worry about finding tacks for me. There are a couple of spares in the board. And I see a pen on the floor. I'll use that so you can get back to your filing."

Filing? Hah.

More likely she'd been hunting for something she'd misfiled. Or, from the look of her desk, hadn't filed at all.

"I know you're busy. I wouldn't want to make more work for you. I'm sure the owner of the earring will be grateful for your effort."

She grunted, turned her back on me, and opened the file cabinet again.

"It must be so stressful running a condo complex this size without help," I babbled.

Bernina didn't respond.

I reached for the earring, "accidentally" hooking it on the edge of the folder. With a flick of my wrist, I flipped the folder open.

Chapter 6

If the file folder was a trap, Bernina would spin about and catch me snooping.

Heart pounding, I waited, ready to pretend to be freeing the earring.

Bernina went on rooting in the file cabinet.

I bent closer and snooped.

The only thing in the folder was a single thick sheet of bright white paper. A resume. Below her name, address, phone number, and e-mail, Bernina had written her objective. "To use the full range of my experience, education, creativity, organizational abilities, and outstanding people skills in managing a large condominium complex."

People skills?

Who was she kidding?

Bernina had all the people skills of a hungry crocodile loose on a nude beach packed with dozing sunbathers.

But if we wanted her gone, we had to play along. We had to pretend we thought she was as warm and fuzzy as a duckling, and possessed of the motivational skills of Stonewall Jackson holding the line at First Manassas.

I flipped the file closed and zipped to the bulletin board, motoring my mouth as I went. "And it must be especially stressful right now with the decorating competition coming up."

And even more stressful because she'd hired Allison to help string miles of lights. Already Allison had skipped out on a key measuring assignment. She'd also ignored the design plan, and strung white lights where there should have been red. Add in her theater obligations and the upcoming trip to Las Vegas to watch Mrs. B tape *Still Got That Strut*, and no way would she get the job done. And I really couldn't see how she'd work in appearing as a woodland elf and handing out candy to those who came to view the display.

Dave and I were secretly delighted by the possibility she'd bail on the elf thing. The flimsy costume was designed more for July than for December when wind and rain are in the daily forecast and evening temperatures dip to the 30s.

With a screech of metal, Bernina slammed the file drawer and yanked out another. Two paperclips and a rubber band tumbled over the side like jailbirds vaulting the walls in a prison break. Bernina didn't retrieve them.

"The people in charge of the decorating competition should be fired and forced to pay back every cent they've taken home," she complained. "They've messed up everything."

Exactly the way I'd sum up Bernina's performance as condo manager.

But I didn't say that. Instead, I adopted a hesitant delivery. "Um, I, uh, I could be wrong, but I had the impression unpaid volunteers put on the competition."

Bernina snorted. "Well, even if they're paid nothing it's still too much. All they do is sit around and drink coffee and eat doughnuts and dictate to people. They should be forced to get real jobs so they understand the need to be organized and give out accurate information instead of wasting everyone's valuable time."

Said the woman now searching a third file drawer for who knew what. It was a good thing she was on salary instead of an hourly wage, or condo residents would get dinged with additional fees for overtime every month. I concentrated on centering and leveling my little sign about the found earring before I pushed in the first tack.

"First they say this. Then they say that." Bernina abandoned the file cabinet and rooted in a lower desk drawer. "It's one mess of misinformation after another."

I suspected there was more misunderstanding on her part than there was misinformation coming from the committee. Especially since Bernina was convinced she knew it all and didn't need to read the small print or listen to advice.

"Why, just this morning I found out we're not allowed to start decorating until a week before the day after Thanksgiving."

Uh oh.

Allison had already wrapped faux evergreen garland and twinkly lights around the support pillars for the covered-parking canopy. She'd also secured wreaths and ribbons to the fence around the pool area. Having been the victim of blowback after Bernina made Allison correct her original lighting mistake, I wouldn't want to be the person who had to tell her to remove the most recently hung decorations. In fact, I wouldn't want to be in the same area code when she got the news.

"When you see Allison," Bernina said, "tell her the lights and garland and wreaths have to come down."

Eeekk.

That sounded like an order. And a direct refusal of an order from Bernina could result in stepped-up enforcement of petty rules, especially in the vicinity of my condo. If Dave had let his poop-scooping duties slide, and if Bernina spotted piles in the rose garden, we'd all be on double top secret probation.

Time for some fancy footwork of the verbal variety.

"I'd be happy to do that, except, uh, Allison is very proud of having a job and responsibilities. She's made it clear she can handle what's required and she's made it even clearer that I should butt out. She says she's working for you and only you."

Bernina slammed the drawer and yanked out another. "What does that mean?"

"It means if I tell her to take down the decorations, she won't listen. And she certainly won't do it."

"Well, make her listen. Make her do it." Bernina rolled her eyes. "I thought you were supposed to be an expert on dealing with teenagers."

I choked back a laugh. As far as I was concerned—based on my experiences at Captain Meriwether High School—there was no such thing. Oh, there are those who pass themselves off as experts. And maybe they do well up against one or two kids at a time. But if they were tossed into the sub pool and faced with a room stuffed with hormonally charged teens brought together by the mandates of the educational system, I bet most would break out in hives, shriek, and flee the scene. On more than one occasion, as I felt my classroom management skills slipping, repeating "I have a mortgage" was the only thing that kept me from turning tail.

"Oh, never mind," Bernina snarled. "If you think you can manage it without exerting yourself to the brink of exhaustion, tell Allison to come see me. Right away."

Despite the temptation, I refrained from saluting or snapping off a snarky comment. Then, setting a brisk pace, I headed for Jim's condo.

He lived in a one-bedroom unit, much like the one I'd owned before Mrs. B performed some financial sleight of hand

and horse trading that resulted in me acquiring a unit large enough for Dave and Allison to move in. Jim's unit lacked a deck and a view of the river, but possessed a small porch. The view was of the parking lot, but that increased people-watching opportunities. He'd furnished his outdoor living space with a couple of padded lawn chairs and a tiny plastic table. He was in the larger of the chairs, holding a red plastic cup. A hummingbird hovered above it, dipping its bill to sip.

"Come sit," Jim said. "This guy won't be bothered."

I sidled up concrete steps that appeared to have been scrubbed in the past hour, and slipped into the vacant chair. "Hungry little fellow."

"Not much chow around for him. Flowers are dying. Or already dead."

The chrysanthemums in the pots along the edge of Jim's porch might have been on the way out, but all dead blossoms and brown leaves had been plucked and disposed of recently. Jim's porch was spotless. I thought of my kitchen and wondered if there was a word for the exact opposite of spotless. Spotted? Spotty? Spotiferous?

I made a mental note to coin a term at an unspecified date in the future, and turned my attention to here and now. "Shouldn't that hummingbird be on his way south?"

"Not this type of hummer. He's an Anna's Hummingbird. He'll hang around all winter."

Jim said that in a neutral tone. He didn't imply that any idiot should know a few key facts about hummingbirds, especially which ones headed south toward greener, flower-filled pastures in the fall.

"Sorry," I murmured. Albert, my first husband, had been a hard-core birder, but his focus had been on larger birds in general and seabirds in particular. After he fell over a guardrail and plunged to his death attempting to get a closer look at a

49

puffin, I'd shoved his binoculars and bird books in a box and consigned them to the farthest reaches of the top shelf of my bedroom closet.

"Not everybody knows everything." Jim patted my hand. "But don't share that with Bernina or she'll take a vegetable peeler to your tongue."

"If she can find it. The vegetable peeler that is. I got a peek in her kitchen once when she left the door to her living area open."

"Worse than her office?"

"Is the Ebola virus worse than a paper cut?"

The hummingbird circled, clicked, then flew off. Jim set the cup on the tiny plastic table.

"Do you plan to spend a lot of time on the porch this winter running a fly-up fast-food window for your little friends?"

"When the weather's good I will. If I have time. I enjoy their company, but these little guys start feeding before the sun clears the horizon, so it will be mostly self-service." He nodded toward feeders hanging at the outer corners of the porch. "I don't do early unless I have to. And my circulation's not what it used to be." He shook his arm. "Went numb on me waiting on that guy to finish."

"Speaking of numb, I stopped in the office a few minutes ago and got a peek at Bernina's resume. Did you know she has outstanding people skills?"

Jim snorted.

"Not to mention creativity and organizational abilities."

He groaned. "Bernina couldn't organize a collision at a demolition derby."

"I know. If the Shoalwater Bend board members start asking questions—serious probing questions requiring detailed and specific answers—we're doomed. We agreed we'd bend the truth only a little, not break it into small pieces."

50

"Yeah. And not one of us is a world-class liar. That's what it would take to convince them she's got it together."

"Got it together?" I laughed. "We'd be maxing out to make a case for her knowing where it is so she could *attempt* to get it together."

I told him about her futile search for whatever she'd misplaced. He speculated she wouldn't know it if she found it.

The hummingbird returned and Jim raised the cup, using the other hand. This time the tiny bird perched on the rim. He studied me for a few seconds, puffed up his feathers, cocked his head toward Jim, and clicked.

"Barbara's okay," Jim said. "Forget that she thought you were migratory. Not everyone has time to read up on every bird in the world. Stop complaining. Drink your sugar water before my hand falls off."

The hummer seemed to understand because he dipped his bill for a long drink. I'd heard somewhere that hummingbirds burned so much energy moving their wings that they literally had to eat to fly. And, conversely, they had to fly to eat.

Talk about a vicious circle.

At least my eating-working schedule allowed time for hanging with my friends and cuddling with Dave. And at least I had more choices when it came to food. There was, for example, that new kind of cheesy snack stashed right now on the top shelf of the pantry. It claimed to have more genuine cheese taste. Not genuine cheese. Just taste. But, addicted as I was, that was close enough for me.

"Here's a thought," Jim said as the hummer took flight. "How about a few of us make Bernina look good by making ourselves look bad?"

I recalled the stint Jim had done behind bars for drugs and assault years ago. "How bad?"

"Not break-the-law bad."

Phew.

"I'm thinking more like dysfunctional. Demanding. Difficult to manage."

"The difficult and demanding part sounds like a description of Bernina. So does the dysfunctional part."

"I suppose we could use her as a model." Jim grinned. "Although when Verna and Sybil get going they can nail dysfunctional without assistance."

"True." I told him about Sybil's seventh slot machine theory. "I think that qualifies as more ditzy than dysfunctional."

"When it doesn't work, she'll become dysfunctional." He set the cup down and wiggled his fingers. "But I think we can do this without Verna and Sybil. And I think we can provide visual proof of dysfunction. You know what they say about one picture being worth a thousand words."

"I do and I'm all ears. Tell me your plan."

"It involves taking a page from Jake's book."

I rolled my eyes at the mention of my ex-husband. "The book on lying and cheating?"

"No, the book on being a handyman."

I felt my jaw drop. "What? Jake was the worst handyman in the history of handy. Or man."

Jim nodded, his Father Christmas beard rippling. "Precisely."

Chapter 7

I waited, but when Jim didn't elaborate, I was forced to speak. "So?"

He smiled. "So, since Bernina terrorized the latest in a long line of landscaping and maintenance companies, a couple of us have been taking up the slack. We've been raking the area along the trail and trimming the hedges at the far end of the complex, trying to get them even. For decent hourly wages, of course."

I doubted any wage was good enough if Bernina was the boss, but Jim sounded like he was okay with it, so I didn't toss in my two cents. He could, I suspected, use the extra cash. "If you mess up like Jake did, she'll fire you," I warned.

"It's a part-time job, not a career. And I'm doing it only because I'm sadly in need of extra money." He laughed in the way you do when something is more pathetic than amusing. "If it wasn't for that, I would have walked after the first few hours."

"So what's the plan? You're going to start chopping hedges and blowing out circuits like Jake did?"

"Pretty much. But with subtlety and finesse." He fluffed his hair and combed his beard with his fingers. "Say her orders get 'lost in translation.' Say we misunderstand what she wants.

Well, it won't take long for things to get back to the glory days when Jake was in charge."

I smiled as I recalled the brutalized hedge by the trash bins, ragged lawns, broken mower, and fried pressure washer. Then there was the grand finale, the plumbing geyser.

"When she calls us on it, I'll claim the guys who cracked the Enigma Code couldn't make sense of her directions. She'll scream loud enough to rattle windows in downtown Portland. A battle will rage, we'll capture it on our cellphones, and I'll edit it to make us look like the villains and Bernina like a woman driven to the edge by incompetents. Then we'll post it on the Internet. With a few clicks, residents of Shoalwater Bend will believe we're the most defective group of condo owners in the universe."

"Genius," I said. "Pure genius."

He grinned and held the cup aloft for the circling hummer. "Last call," he told the tiny bird. "I have places to go and people to see. And Barbara has to get to water aerobics."

Yikes!

I hadn't noticed how dark it was getting.

"Catch you later."

I leaped from the porch and hustled to my condo, mind churning. Too late to make anything for dinner. Too close to workout time to eat more than a small snack.

Fortunately, I was all about snacks—small and otherwise.

On my way upstairs to retrieve my swimsuit, I tossed a handful of high-fiber cereal down my gullet. Back in the kitchen again, I chomped on a few grapes and scrawled a note for Allison telling her there were heat-and-eat meals in the freezer if she needed more than the burgers she and Josh generally picked up after school. In larger print, I asked her to unload the dishwasher and load in the dirty dishes stacked on the counter. I taped the note to the refrigerator, her usual first stop.

I had, as you've probably figured out by now, few illusions that the job would be done when I returned.

And it wasn't.

Although the tape and a bit of paper remained, the note was missing from the refrigerator. The open microwave door and the frozen meal container beside a trail of dribbles clued me that Allison had nuked chicken fried rice and followed it with ice cream eaten straight from the carton. Music with more beat than tune thumped from her room at the top of the stairs.

Cheese Puff, apparently exhausted from a day of rehearsal, lay on his back in his favorite chair, emitting tiny bursts of gas from both ends. I suspected Mrs. B had, once again, fed him "only a smidgen" of pepperoni pizza or teriyaki beef jerky. Once again I made a mental note to have a talk with her. A firm talk. A talk concluding with an ultimatum—halt the gas-inducing treats or he'd be sleeping in *her* bedroom instead of mine.

Lola, apparently having had enough of Cheese Puff's air biscuits, or signaling the need for a potty break, flopped on her belly with her nose against the sliding glass door to the deck.

Dave, apparently oblivious to any of the above, hunched on the sofa, moving slips of paper on the coffee table as if doing a jigsaw puzzle. A notebook on the edge of the table was open to a pristine page. A pen lay beside it, ready for jotting ideas if they developed. "Was there fresh drama at the pool?" he asked without looking up.

Actually, there hadn't been any drama at all. Since Paulette and I uncovered the scheme to drive down pool attendance and close the facility so the property could be sold to a developer, things were back to normal. The screechy-voiced aerobics instructor was gone and our regular instructor was back. The woman who badgered me about being uncoordinated hadn't turned up. And, thankfully, the music selections hadn't included anything synthesized or from the disco error.

(For the record, I suspect you're thinking the word should be "era." But I'm sticking with "error.")

"It was pretty calm." I draped my swimsuit and towel on the dowels Jim had installed for this purpose in the tiny downstairs washroom. "Except for the great divide of opinion over what Rick Rivers spouted this morning about the homicide you're investigating."

"I'm all for the First Amendment and freedom of speech. But in his case I'd pass on defending to the death his right to mouth off." Dave pushed a slip of paper to the right, then to the left again. "And I'm all for the pursuit of justice, but I might develop a sudden cramp and drag my feet coming to the rescue if someone attempted to cut Rick Rivers' heart out with a dull knife."

"Except he has no heart. How about we stake him out in the hills, slather him with peanut butter, and let him be nibbled to death by squirrels?"

"Bad idea." Dave pushed more paper. "We'd be charged with squirrel abuse."

"Can't have that." I drank a large glass of water and took Lola out into the gloom of night. As usual, she made quick work of the task. In a few minutes I was back inside and scanning the refrigerator shelves. Cheese, pickles, pudding, salad makings.

Nothing rang my chimes. Especially not the white take-out box behind the bowl of grapes. To the best of my knowledge, it had been several weeks since we'd ordered out for Chinese food or brought home leftovers. And, also to the best of my knowledge, leftovers seldom hung around for more than two days. If my recollections were accurate, the contents of the box would be long past their eat-by date. Someone should definitely take action before it became necessary to file an environmental impact statement or call in a hazmat team.

But that someone wasn't me.

At least not tonight.

I left the box in place.

"I get that there are people who agree with what Rick Rivers is saying." Dave picked up the conversation. "Their minds were probably made up before he opened his yap. What worries me is that he could sway people who don't know better and convince them cops think that way. He might hint that we have a secret policy in place already. He might spout that we'll slack off on the investigation because this guy doesn't appear to be upper crust. A rumor like that would spread like wildfire on a windy day."

I closed the refrigerator and turned to face him. "Nobody I know would consider that accurate. Not even for a few seconds. And if they did, I'd make it clear I'd be unknowing them before they could count to five."

"Unknowing? Is that like unfriending?"

"Yes, but with face-to-face attitude."

Dave chuckled. "I don't know which quality I like best—your loyalty or your feistiness."

"Don't limit yourself to those." I stepped aside so he'd have clear line-of-sight to the counter. "There's also my outstanding ability to ignore the mess you and your daughter leave behind."

I waited a few beats for Dave, trained observer that he was, to acknowledge the dirty-dishes situation.

He didn't.

If men are from Mars, apparently they wore blinders on that planet. Or they were followed around by cleaning crews 24/7.

But, hey, I knew how to play chicken. And, starting right now, I would. No matter how disgusting the kitchen got, I wouldn't lift a finger to clean it up. I'd get coffee and a muffin on my way to school, take a frozen meal for lunch, and make a sandwich for dinner using a clean knife I'd store in my purse.

I'd eat the sandwich off a paper towel. When I wanted a drink, I'd wash one glass, or use the water bottle I took to school. And no way would I deal with the box in the refrigerator.

Wondering how long it would take Dave and Allison to notice I was on strike, I opened the freezer compartment and considered the carton of chocolate ice cream swirled with caramel and toasted almonds.

Nah.

Allison had been eating from the carton. Besides, the ice cream contained too much sugar and too many calories to consume so close to bedtime.

My stomach growled its disagreement.

I compromised by reaching for the cheesy snacks mentioned earlier. As they say in those British mysteries I'm so fond of, a few of those would go down a treat. And while I had the box open, I could offload some into a plastic bag to take to school tomorrow. I was finished with sophomores and *Lord of the Flies*, but I'd picked up a general assignment to report to Captain Meriwether for the rest of the week. The lack of specific details meant Big Chill anticipated the need for a body to be thrown into a gap in the front lines of the battle to educate America's youth. Speculating about where that gap might appear made me nervous. And nothing calmed my nerves like comfort food. Especially cheesy snacks.

Plan made and snack provisioning accomplished, I filled my water glass again, turned my back on the dishwasher and the mess on the counter, and sidled over to sit on the arm of the sofa and watch Dave. The slips of paper appeared to be copies of notes scrawled with thick pencil lines on receipts, scraps of food wrappers, and even what appeared to have been a bit of cloth. The scrawls were as legible as anything a toddler might create with a fat crayon on a grooved sidewalk. Squinting, I made out an assortment of words: "skid row, chance, rainbow, hang, soul, powers, five o'clock." There were also three sets of numbers: 1052, 230, and 730.

Dave switched the positions of the numbers. In a moment he moved them back to where they'd been.

"Do I want to know what you're doing?"

He chuckled. "You *always* want to know what *everyone* is doing."

That was pretty much true, but he didn't have to say it like it was a bad thing. I was curious and, occasionally, a shade paranoid. Blame that on my insecure childhood and my days as a radio talk-show producer working for Rick Rivers. Dave might be the same if he had my baggage. "Okay, then," I said, clipping my words, "this is me going upstairs."

"Wait." He grasped my arm as I stood. "Take a look at this and tell me what you think."

"Is that an order, officer?"

"No. Uh, I mean, *please* take a look."

I sat on the sofa arm again and studied the array. "What am I looking at? And what am I looking for?"

He sat back and rubbed his eyes. "These are copies of notes we found in the victim's pockets."

"Does the use of the word 'victim' mean you haven't identified him yet?"

"Yes. We're running his prints, but so far nothing, so we're circulating his picture at shelters and food banks. A couple of people say they've seen him around on the streets, but so far no one knows who he is, uh, was."

Drat.

If they had a name, they could learn where he'd been and what he might have done to hold his life together until someone snuffed it. That might provide context for the scribbles.

But, context or not, I was hooked. "Some of those could have something to do with religion—especially the bits about the soul and powers."

"I considered that. Some of the churches serve meals, and some provide emergency shelter. So we're circulating his picture there, too."

I slid to the sofa beside him. "How are you arranging them?"

"I thought I'd try oldest to newest—based on how dirty and crumpled each one was."

"Isn't that hard to tell with copies?"

He flipped a slip of paper and revealed a number on the back. "I numbered them. Chuck has a set, too."

My competitive spirit fired up. Ever since last year when Detective Charles Atwell considered me a suspect in the murders of Henry Stoddard and Jessica Flint, I'd been out to show him up. A couple of times, thanks to luck, pluck, a few flashes of insight, and friends willing to push the envelope, I had. And this was no time to rest on my laurels. Even now Detective Atwell might be in his lair trying to crack this code. No way would I let him beat me.

Rolling up the sleeves of my sweatshirt, I got to work shoving bits of paper around, trying to build a cohesive narrative. I kept coming back to the religious angle. "Do you know of any churches with services at five o'clock?"

He shook his head. "I could check, but—"

"Wait! Maybe it's not a church service. I bet it's a mealtime."

Dave reached for the notebook and pen.

"If the meal's at a church, or a shelter associated with a church, there might be a prayer or short service before or after. That could explain some of the notes."

"I'll check with shelters and churches in the morning." Dave scribbled a few words that were only slightly more legible than the ones on the scraps of paper. "Any idea what the numbers might mean? Or the reference to chance or a rainbow?"

"I have plenty of ideas, but they don't fit together well. Those words could have appeared in a sermon and stuck with him. The numbers probably aren't the combination to a lock, but they could be addresses where he might get some kind of assistance. The words 'you go' could fit with the numbers as a reminder."

Dave made another note, but in a dawdling way that implied he'd mull over what I tossed out, but probably wouldn't buy much of it. "I hope we get an ID soon. If this drags on, it might interfere with the trip to Las Vegas."

"Interfere?" I sat up straight. "What does that mean?"

"It means I might have to stay here."

Eeekk.

That left me riding herd on Allison and her boyfriend in Glitter Gulch. "But you put in for the time off months ago."

"Yeah, but that was when Lola and I were still on the drug beat."

And that was before he decided to check out a career change, and before they took a tumble into a ravine while training with a search and rescue team. Lola broke her leg and he broke his arm. Shortly after they were sidelined, Detective Atwell recruited him to help out in homicide temporarily.

"But you're due the time off." The thought of dealing with Allison without backup took the stretchiness out of my vocal cords. My voice climbed the scale toward shrill. "You have more than two weeks to draw from."

"You're right." He gestured at the slips of paper. "But I want to get my foot in the door in case there's an opening in homicide. And I'd feel like a rat leaving Chuck alone with this."

Personally, I wouldn't feel like a rat if I left Detective Atwell alone on a small rock in a shark-infested lagoon when the tide was rising, but I kept that to myself. Never mind that I didn't see the attraction, Atwell had been Dave's buddy for years. And the road to a possible new career as a homicide detective appeared to run through him. Drawing in a long breath, I rolled my shoulders to loosen up, cleared my throat, and went back to pushing paper.

An hour later, head pounding and no closer to solving the puzzle, I followed Dave upstairs. I didn't, however, declare myself beaten or declare Detective Atwell the winner of the figure-it-out-first contest. From past experience, perhaps because of my total lack of investigative training or because of my vivid imagination, I knew I was better at thinking outside the box. So I left the slips of paper spread out on the coffee table in case something occurred to me during the night. If I gave my subconscious time—hopefully not too much time because the trip to Las Vegas loomed—I was sure I'd come up with something.

But could I do it before Detective Atwell?

Chapter 8

The next morning I glanced at the scraps of paper for a few moments between taking the dogs out and grabbing a heat-and-eat meal from the freezer. No bells rang in my brain, so I zipped to the door, my objective being to escape before Allison or Dave came downstairs.

I'd decided not to mention that I was on strike because it would open yet another discussion about kitchen clean-up duties. Those discussions were as predictable as they were pointless. Dave would apologize and claim he'd been distracted by his job and vow to try harder. Allison would anchor the other end of the spectrum, claiming she'd cleaned up "lots of times when nobody noticed." She'd back that up with the claim that she was really busy with the play and had tons of homework and couldn't remember everything and had to sleep at least a few hours a night. For a finale, she'd blame me or Dave for not reminding her.

The discussion would end with Allison running upstairs and slamming her bedroom door. Dave would promise to talk with her, claim he appreciated everything I did, and swear he'd make it up to me. While make-it-up meals, candy, flowers, and other activities were nice, I was steadily becoming more practical than romantic. There were times when I'd rather have him sweep the kitchen floor than sweep me off to the bedroom.

Well, okay, let's be honest. I'd rather have him do both. The floor first. That would put me in a more receptive mood.

I reached the door to the parking lot just as I heard Allison's feet thudding on the stairs. In less than five seconds, I slipped out into the November gloom. Visualizing her distress over the absence of clean dishes in the cabinet, I slapped a hand over my mouth to muffle my giggles, and scurried to my car.

Five minutes later I pulled up to the curb beside my favorite local coffee shop. Reckless River baristas, being only a bridge removed from Portland and a few hours from Seattle, were a competitive bunch and on top of the latest coffee-culture trends. But this shop wasn't my favorite because the brew was a higher quality or the design swirled in the froth more ingenious than those created elsewhere. No, I hit this place often because no one sneered at me when I ordered plain coffee with a big splash of milk.

(For the record, I'm not a connoisseur of coffee. I drink it to facilitate the waking-up process in the morning. I steer clear of it in the evening to facilitate the falling-asleep process. I know burnt or weak coffee when I taste it, and I know what I like, but I haven't developed a discriminating palate. Doing so isn't on my bucket list. Neither is learning the difference between a latte, a macchiato, and a cappuccino.)

Today I went all out and asked for a jot of caramel flavoring in my milky coffee. And, without a curl of a lip or flicker of disdain in his eyes, the barista squirted it in.

Then, since I was anxious about where I'd end up today, and since anxiety burns calories, I allowed my gaze to drift from the low-calorie section of the display case. Deciding irritation about household chores would also increase the rate of calorie burn, I ordered a scone with raspberries and white chocolate chunks. Because scones can sometimes be a tad dry, I asked for it to be toasted and buttered.

I promised my conscience I'd walk two circuits of the building during my free period to burn off the calories.

I swear I heard my conscience snicker.

Ignoring it, I arrived, fortified, at Captain Meriwether High School early enough to snag a primo parking spot in the faculty lot. As a sub, I wasn't part of the faculty, but if a position ever opened up, I hoped to be. That's my story and I'm sticking to it if anyone should insinuate I was entitled to park only in the lot at the far end of the building. That's the lot with more craters than the surface of moon.

As I crossed the lobby, I sensed something was amiss. Actually, more than amiss. More like askew, awry, or even amok. And, to be honest, it didn't take a whole lot of sensing. I needed only my ears. Big Chill's raised voice funneled along the short hallway leading to the main office like roaring water from a ruptured dam. Her words were indistinct, but her tone said outrage.

Never mind that she was two inches below the five-foot mark, when Wilhelmina Frost was angry, everyone within range knew it. And everyone ran or took cover until the storm passed.

I hustled to the shelter of the attendance office and, careful not to spill hot coffee or smear butter on anyone, shoved my way into a cluster of teachers and subs, all with heads cocked and ears open. Doug Whitman tugged at my jacket and I inched to his side. "She's all over Tremaine Scott like a bad rash," he whispered.

"Why Tremaine?" I asked as I munched at my scone. Tremaine was that rare breed, the kind who resolved conflict rather than generating it. A former college football star with a ready smile and a lot of smarts, he'd arrived in the middle of

65

the previous school year, replacing Jessica Flint who had made the mistake of falling for my smarmy ex-husband Jake. That, in turn, had made her prey for Jake's girlfriend of the month, a steroid pusher who'd shoved Jessica into the Columbia River—and later did the same to me. Unlike Jessica, I managed to survive. "What did Tremaine do?"

"Nothing to equal what he's getting from the Chillster." Doug tapped his chin and pointed at my face. "Butter."

"Thanks." I scrubbed with a napkin.

"She's irked about the new retirement policy. Tremaine got in the line of fire when he reminded her she had to return a document to HR by the end of the week."

"Poor guy. He should have done that in an e-mail. At the end of the day. After she'd left."

"You know Tremaine. He's all about the personal approach."

True. And that was part of the reason he was standing still for a double-barreled verbal barrage from a woman he outranked. Anyone else in his position would have cut her off. Or cut her down to size.

I sipped coffee, considering the other reason he hadn't run or launched a barrage of his own. Tremaine, like the rest of us, had a healthy fear of Big Chill. She cast a long shadow. She'd been at Captain Meriwether long enough to know where all the bodies were buried. She may even have buried a few of them herself.

Doug toed the briefcase I'd set on the floor in order to free my hands and stuff my face. "Who are you in for today?"

"I don't know." Anxiety hit me like a bucket of cold water. Would I be sent to chemistry? Biology? My fingers went numb and I tightened my grip on the cardboard cup of coffee. I didn't do well with things that could blow up or had to be dissected.

"The job line message said to report to Captain Meriwether for the rest of the week. That's it."

"Too bad. You'll have to check in with the Chillster and catch a dose of residual wrath."

"Lucky me." I glanced at the clock high on the wall. Twenty minutes until the first bell. That gave me darn little time to pick up my assignment, read through the instructions, get the attendance sheets, race to a classroom, and—

"Prepare to meet your doom," Doug said. "Tremaine's taking off like a scalded cat."

I stuffed the remains of my scone in its little white bag and shoved it in my briefcase. Then I raised the briefcase to my chest, and held it like a shield.

"Wish I could come with you," Doug said in a totally-full-of-crap tone that implied exactly the opposite, "but I've got to, um, run by the library and, uh, check on some supplemental reading for my freshmen."

I'd subbed for Doug's freshman class. They were as likely to tackle supplemental reading as I was to win an award for advances in quantum physics.

"Liar," I hissed.

Doug didn't stick around to defend himself. He and the others stampeded into the hall and, with eyes focused on the opposite wall, passed Big Chill's office in a tangle of elbows and textbooks. The sweet-faced attendance clerk shot me a sympathetic smile, but didn't volunteer to walk a mile in my shoes, let alone the three yards to Big Chill's door.

I swallowed hard—glad I'd eaten only half of the scone and taken only a few sips of coffee—and considered my options. Unfortunately, there were none. My quest for more money in my end-of-the-month paycheck led to Big Chill's office.

I considered my approaches—sympathy, shared outrage, indignation, or feigned ignorance. I went with ignorance, adopted the jaunty step of someone who had just now arrived, and entered her office with a perky "Good morning."

She countered with a scowl that could have stopped a clock. A large clock. A clock the size of, say, Big Ben.

I continued my act. "Are you okay? You look a little . . . feverish."

Actually, she looked a lot more than feverish. She appeared to have run through a forest fire before taking a bath in boiling oil. Her face flushed the color of fresh lava and her eyes burned like twin propane torches. "Sit," she commanded, pointing the sharp end of a pencil.

"Uh, okay." I made a show of checking my watch. "But I don't have much time."

"You have plenty. You're working with me today. And the rest of the week."

Yikes.

Every nerve cell in my body screamed "RUN!" But, pathetic as I knew it was, I went on with my ignorance act and sank into the chair in front of her desk. "Doing what?"

"Cleaning up a mess." She snapped the pencil in half. "A mess I didn't make."

That told me something—although not much—about the task. But it told me a lot about her attitude toward it. And, given the mess made by others in my kitchen, I understood her feelings about the job I'd be helping with. The flare-up at Tremaine Scott, however, was something else, something to ask about only if I was tired of living.

With a double clang, Big Chill tossed the pencil pieces in a trash can. "I'll retire when I'm good and ready."

I nodded.

"If they think they're going to con me into going to a seminar to prepare for retirement, or force me out with a blizzard of BS and a mountain of misinformation, they can think again."

Since she was clearly venting, and since her venom was aimed at others, I felt brave enough to sip coffee before I nodded again.

"The day I'll leave this office for good will be the same day they get their act together. And from what I've seen so far, that will be the day after never."

I sipped and nodded, nodded and sipped. She plowed on, blasting the HR department, their relatives, neighbors, and even their pets. When the bell for the first class rang she cocked her head, leaned forward, and turned her steely gaze on me. "Do I look old to you?"

Fortunately, I had finished a sip and started a nod, so when I choked, I didn't spew coffee.

More fortunately, she went on before I came up with a way of saying "No" that sounded sincere and not like I actually meant "Maybe a little."

"Don't answer that. Forget I asked."

She snatched a folder from the corner of her desk and flipped through the contents. "Finish your coffee and I'll tell you what you'll be doing."

Relieved to have dodged a bullet the size of one of those big blue mailboxes found on street corners, I did as I was told.

No one knew how old Big Chill might be, and no one was bold enough to ask. But there was plenty of evidence—including gray hair, wrinkles, an occasional cracking creakiness in her voice, age spots on her hands, swelling in her knuckles, and comments about the way things used to be—to indicate that she was no spring chicken. And then there was the blood pressure scare during the last school year that resulted in her buying a motorcycle in an effort to reduce stress.

Not that she didn't look terrific. Her hair, sometimes rinsed blue and sometimes green or even pink, was perfect. Her nails were manicured and painted. Her wardrobe was stylish and well-coordinated. She owned several pairs of designer eyeglasses. And I'd never seen a wobble in her walk, not even when she wore heels two inches higher than any I'm brave enough to wear.

Sitting across from her in my subbing attire of black jeans and a blue T-shirt under a blue-and-black striped shirt, I felt like Cinderella before she got tapped with the magic wand. In fact, I felt more like I'd been whacked with an ugly stick. Several times. If there was such a thing as a grooming confessional, I'd be in there right now reciting my transgressions. I hadn't had my hair trimmed for eight weeks, my eyebrows needed plucking, my nails were ragged, and my cuticles were overgrown and splitting.

Maybe, I thought, I was lucky Dave didn't overwork his observational skills at home. And I was definitely lucky that he preferred what he called "the natural look." But perhaps I'd let nature take its course a little too far. I vowed to get a trim on the way home, then spend some quality time with my manicure kit and tweezers.

Big Chill stood and stuffed the folder in the file cabinet behind her desk. "Remember when that student teacher hacked the system and dumped all those grade reports?"

"It would be hard to forget." I'd spent hours entering numbers to help reconstruct grades. "Especially the part where you rounded him up on your motorcycle like a stray steer." I glanced out the window. "I haven't seen your bike in the parking lot lately."

"Sold it." She moved closer and lowered her voice. "No one else needs to know, but I took a spill last month. Scuffed my leathers and gave myself a good scare." She gave my shoulder a squeeze. "That's when I decided taking a cruise now and then would do as much to knock my blood pressure down. I'll be off to the Caribbean over the winter break, and I'll check out Scandinavia next summer."

"I'm green with envy." I tossed my coffee cup in the trash can. "I'm also ready to earn my pay, so point me at the project."

"It nice to see you're starting with a good attitude." She led me to the small conference room down the hall from her office. "Because I can almost guarantee you'll be singing a different tune an hour from now."

She was right.

Jeremy Connor, the student teacher who'd schemed to land a job at Captain Meriwether by dumping grades to discredit teachers and create an opening he might fill, had dumped other stuff as well. But this time he'd dumped information in the files instead of out.

"No one noticed until a few days ago when a bunch of grade reports came back because the addresses were wrong. Really wrong." Big Chill fanned a stack of envelopes—one of many stacks on the industrial gray table. "Looks like he made up street names based on cartoons and superheroes."

She dropped the heap in front of me and I spotted Batman Drive, Yogi Bear Lane, and Captain America Avenue.

"You'll have to correct these. And that means phone calls. Families break up. They move. They forget to let us know. We can't assume that the paper files from last year are still valid."

I surveyed the heaps of envelopes. About 150 of them. Bad, but not too bad.

"And we can't assume that's all he did." She scooped a giant printout from a chair and plopped it on the table, then pointed to a laptop. "So you'll have to read through each student's file, compare the computer and paper versions, and look for problems—missing stuff, extra stuff, weird stuff. When you find a problem, fix it."

Great. There were about 1600 students enrolled at Captain Meriwether. This task made spinning chaff into gold look easy. This task would be like spinning chaff into platinum. Or plutonium.

"Why you?" Big Chill asked my unspoken question. "First, Tremaine recommended you. And I seconded his recommendation. You're tenacious. And you're meticulous. I know you'll check the last file as carefully as the first one."

I love praise as much as the next person. But I'm not wild about praise that sounds more like manipulation thinly disguised as sucking up. "When's the deadline? How long do I have to do this?"

"Take as much time as you need." She headed for the door, pausing only to toss an evil laugh over her shoulder. "Just be finished by the end of the week."

Chapter 9

By the time I left school, my vision was blurry, my head ached, and my shoulder muscles had knots everywhere—except where they had kinks. Sadly, I'd barely made a dent in the stack of envelopes. Even reminding myself that Big Chill had rewarded my efforts in the past didn't make me feel better. All I wanted to do was to go home and flop on the sofa. Then I remembered the view from my usual flopping position included the kitchen.

I decided I wasn't ready for that, so I stopped off at a hair salon for a trim.

The interlude was so relaxing—except for the part where they waxed my eyebrows—that I went next door for a manicure. From there, I hit the post office for stamps in case I wrote that letter to my parents. Walking up the steps, I experienced that skin-crawly feeling you get when you're being watched. I lifted my gaze from my buffed and shining nails and glanced around.

No one wearing a hockey mask. No one firing up a chainsaw. Nothing out of the ordinary.

The only vehicle on the street was an aging baby-poop brown van cruising past. It had tinted windows, and a bent rear license plate. The driver, half turned in the seat, seemed to be checking addresses. A hat covered his or her hair.

The van turned a corner and was gone.

The skin-crawly feeling faded.

Half an hour later, when I emerged from the grocery store chomping on a dark chocolate covered caramel swirl ice cream bar, the crawly feeling hit me again. I paused by a trash bin, licking dribbles and settling my purse on my shoulder while I scoped out the terrain.

I spotted a brown van, parked a few spaces away from my car. One corner of the rear license plate was dog-eared like a page in a book—exactly like the plate on the van cruising by the post office.

Coincidence?

Possibly.

Reckless River isn't a major city. What were the odds there would be two older vans the same color, and both with bent license plates?

Slim.

And what were the odds I'd see the van twice in one day?

Not so slim.

Because this is a small city, there are only a few supermarkets. The van's owner might also prefer this one. This *could* be pure coincidence.

Still, I couldn't talk myself out of the skin-crawly feeling.

So, instead of going home, I pulled out of the lot at a speed barely this side of unsafe and headed for a gas station not far from the post office. As I filled my tank, the van passed. Twice. Both times the driver was facing away from me. Both times the driver's short-brimmed black hat was crammed low. I couldn't make out hair color or facial features.

I tossed the concept of coincidence out the window.

Someone was following me.

But why?

A dozen answers ping-ponged around my brain. The scary, heavy-duty reasons for being followed included robbery, carjacking, kidnapping for ransom, murder, white slavery, or revenge. Lighter answers included mistaken identity and pranking by high school students. Not one answer involved someone tracking me down to inform me I was a long-lost heir to a shipping fortune, or to deliver a hefty check from some lottery I didn't remember purchasing a ticket for.

My hands shook as I screwed on the gas cap, and it took me two tries to slide the key in the ignition. Some of the more frightening scenarios seemed a little far-fetched. But not extremely far-fetched. Mrs. B loved me and might pay a considerable sum in ransom. Jake's incarcerated former steroid-using girlfriend could hire a thug to exact revenge. White slavers could be operating in Reckless River and looking for mature—

The van drove by a third time.

Curiosity overpowered fear.

In pursuit of the van, I gunned my car across the gas station lot and onto the street. We both caught the light and shot through the intersection. Spewing a cloud of exhaust, the van picked up speed. After locking my doors and digging my cellphone from my purse, I pasted my front bumper to the van's rear as we roared six blocks to a red light.

The van's rear windows were filthy, but I caught a glimpse of the driver in the side mirror. Beneath the shadow cast by that noir-movie hat, I made out a heavy chin and the upturned collar of a beige coat.

The light changed and the van took off with a squeal of tires and a cloud of noxious black smoke. Coughing, I stayed with it, memorizing the license plate letters and numbers as I drove. My plan, such as it was, involved following the van a little longer, then peeling off. If the van followed me, I'd call Dave while driving to the downtown police station.

We hit another red light. This time I left a few feet between us to avoid as much exhaust as possible. I also accelerated at a more leisurely pace when the light changed.

The van sped up.

I hit the gas.

The van slowed down.

I followed suit.

The van sped up once more and turned left, squeaking in front of an oncoming city bus. I considered abandoning the pursuit. But when the bus passed, I saw the van had pulled to the curb a few blocks along a residential street.

Again, curiosity trumped fear. I turned left, then right at the first intersection, then left, down two blocks, and left again. A left at the next intersection put me on the same street as the van, facing it, but half a block farther along. Before I gave myself time to consider how things might go south if the driver had a gun, I nosed up to the van and blasted my horn.

The windshield was almost as dirty as the rear windows. And the driver shielded her face with her arms.

But not before I got a glimpse.

I knew that face.

I knew it well.

It was one of the first faces I'd seen when my vision cleared after a harrowing trip through the birth canal. It was there every day of my childhood. And many of the days since. And on a good percentage of those days I've wished I could go a year or so without seeing it except in photographs.

I killed the engine, flung the door wide, and stalked to the van. Up close, the color bore even a closer resemblance to a deposit in a diaper. I gagged, swallowed, and, using the best-defense-is-a-good-offense technique, hammered on the window.

"What the heck are you doing?" I shrieked at my sister.

Iz uncovered her face and scowled.

"I got your license number. I was about to call the police."

She rolled down the window. "You weren't supposed to see me." She spoke in her usual tone, the tone that implied she was right and I was wrong.

"I wasn't supposed to notice a vehicle that has 'disgustingly ominous' written all over it?" I kicked the door, dislodging a flake of paint the size of my ear. "A vehicle driven by someone acting about as casual as a first-time bank robber with his ski mask on backwards?"

Iz pulled the brim of her hat lower.

"Why were you following me?"

Iz tucked her chins. "I was practicing so I can tail that cheating husband without being spotted," she mumbled.

"Another few months at the rate you're going and you might hone the skill necessary to achieve that. *If* he loses his eyesight between now and then."

Iz opened her mouth to counter my insult with one of her own, then huffed out a sigh. "It looks easier on TV."

This from someone who bashed television programming almost as often as she bashed men. Or me.

"Jumping from a speeding car looks easier on TV. Breaking down a door looks easier. Even cooking looks easier," I raged. "Which one of those activities do you intend to try next?"

"Okay, so I messed up," Iz mumbled.

"Wait! Say that again." I held up my cellphone. "Let me record it for posterity."

Iz batted my hand aside and reversed a couple of feet. "Out of the way. I have places to be."

"Like a paint shop?" I kicked the fender, releasing a whole shower of flakes. "I'd trade this in on something less disgusting. People remember things that make them want to puke."

"Move." Iz crimped the wheels and gunned the motor.

"And, speaking of indigestion, is that barbecue sauce on your chin?" I bounced up on my toes to get a look inside the van. "And is that a sack of tortilla chips on the passenger seat? What happened to the diet?"

"I'm taking a day off."

"To take a day off, you have to have something to take a day off from. Not counting the time you've been asleep, I bet you haven't followed the diet for more than two consecutive hours."

"Out of my way or I'll run you down."

I wasn't entirely sure she wouldn't make good on that threat so, after a few seconds I stepped aside. But I remained in rant overdrive. "I hope you didn't buy this heap. If you did, get your money back. Or trade it in on something less noticeable. Maybe you can get that psychedelic bus Ken Kesey took on that cross-country tour with the Merry Pranksters in the 60s."

Iz roared off, enveloping me in a putrid cloud of exhaust.

I coughed and choked for a full five minutes.

The story I could tell and retell was worth the nausea.

When I got home, the dishwasher had been emptied, but the heap of dirty plates and glasses remained, filling most of the counter. A note tucked under a mug informed me that Dave would be late. He'd penciled a series of hearts after that statement, then added that he hoped I could take Allison to rehearsal and bring her home if she couldn't find another ride.

"Sure thing," I snarled. "Love to. I live to serve."

Lola whined and I knelt to stroke her head and assure her none of my vitriol had been intended for her. Since Cheese Puff

78

wasn't in residence, I assumed he was next door with Mrs. B and getting all the exercise he needed—and possibly more than he wanted. Left to his own devices, he was all about lounging around. "It's you and me, Lola. Want to go for a walk?"

Always game, Lola struggled to her feet and, cast thumping, followed me out the door and across the deck. Fog lay thick on the river, sending tendrils across the trail. Clouds sagged low overhead, and the setting sun seemed to have given up on efforts to penetrate the gloom. And why not? It was, after all, November.

I zipped my windbreaker and reminded myself that a week from tomorrow we'd take off in a chartered plane for Las Vegas. The whole gang. Me, Dave, Allison, Josh, Mrs. B, Jim, Verna, Sybil, Iz, Penelope, Cheese Puff, and Lola. Even if Las Vegas turned out not to be quite as warm and dry as I hoped, it would be a change of scenery and a change of pace. In her usual spare-no-expense manner, Mrs. B had rented a huge house away from the bright lights, and reserved several rooms at the casino hotel where *Still Got That Strut* was taped. She'd also arranged for a Thanksgiving feast, and hired cars and drivers.

Have I mentioned that I couldn't wait to leave my mundane life—especially the kitchen issues—behind?

Lola clomped down the steps and took a few paces along the trail to the left. Then she halted, growling, the hair on her back standing up.

I fingered the cellphone in my pocket and peered into the gloom. The trail was deserted. Not a single runner, dog walker, or baby-stroller-pushing mother. "What is it, girl?"

She growled again, punctuating with a single sharp bark. She aimed her muzzle at the area beneath Mrs. B's portion of the deck.

Telling myself it was still broad daylight—or what passes for broad daylight in the middle of November in Washington—I called to Lola again. "What do you see, girl? Is that renegade duck back? Is there a raccoon under the deck?"

Lola's response was a deeper growl and a trio of barks like exclamation marks.

Drawing my cellphone from my pocket, I eased up the steps, intending to lock the gate and make a run for the condo, yelling for help with all the breath I had.

Then I remembered my sister.

"Iz," I shouted. "If you're lurking around practicing surveillance, you're doing a crummy job. Pack it in and go home."

Iz didn't utter a sound. Neither did anyone else.

Except Lola. She growled again.

Back in the summer, a young man practicing urban survival techniques had camped under the deck for several days, scavenging food from around the condo complex. He'd gone off to college in September, but I didn't doubt the cave-like area behind the rose bushes might be attractive to others. True, water dripped through the spaces between the deck planks, but with thick plastic sheeting and a way to fasten it to the supports, an enterprising person could construct a shelter. That same person might decide to check for unlocked doors around the complex and discover mine or Mrs. B's. We often left the sliding glass doors unlatched to make visiting back and forth easier.

I shivered and fingered the phone again. Should I call Jim?

He'd certainly come. But he'd also certainly laugh if I'd called for no good reason.

I peered into the gloom again but still saw no one. "Let's go in, girl," I called in what I hoped was a casual voice. "When Dave gets home he'll take you out." With a flashlight. And his gun. "Let's go."

Lola barked once more, but didn't obey.

Odd behavior for a dog so well trained.
"Come, Lola," I called. "Come."
Lola didn't move.

Chapter 10

I reached for Lola's collar.

"Pssssttt."

The sound came from beyond the steps that led to the rose garden from Mrs. B's portion of the deck.

I gripped Lola's collar. "Good girl. Good warning." I spoke with as much force as I could muster. "Don't attack until I tell you. Then go for the throat."

"No," a voice in the darkness croaked. "Don't let her attack. It's me, Barbie. It's me."

Crap.

Much as I didn't want to find a squatter lurking beneath the deck, and much as I didn't want to find my sister, I wanted to come across my ex-husband even less. I skipped over any form of greeting or questions about what Jake Stranahan might be doing here. And I skipped over telling him, for the millionth time, that I hated to be called Barbie. "Go away."

"I need your help."

"Go away."

"You're my last resort."

"Go away. Now. Or I'll call the Committee."

"No. Don't do that," he whined. "Please don't tell them I'm here."

When Jake was released from jail under a plea bargain that mandated hundreds of hours of community service, the Committee made it clear to Bernina Burke that her holiday decorating budget would evaporate like spilled water in the Sahara Desert if Jake was spotted on the property. Members didn't take that stand because they considered Jake dangerous or because they thought it would bother me to see him around. No, they declared their position because Jake was chaos on two legs. Like a tornado in a trailer park, he left a trail of wreckage in his wake.

"I won't say a word to anyone if you go away right now."

He stood and edged around the steps. "Please, just listen to me, Barbie."

"Call me that again and I'll order Lola to rip your face off and eat it."

Lola had been trained to sniff out drugs, not attack. She was generally mellow and sweet-tempered, but she'd never warmed to my ex. She backed up my threat with a vicious snarl.

Jake crouched behind the steps again. "Don't let her loose. I'll never use that nickname again. Honest."

If I had a dollar for every time I heard that last part, I'd have enough portraits of George Washington to wallpaper the living room. Jake's character wasn't built on honesty. Or on other positive traits beginning with H, traits like humility, humanitarianism, or helpfulness.

"Say what you need to say," I ordered. "Then get out of here."

"Okay, okay. Well, first of all, it wasn't my fault."

"Amazingly, it never is. I bet even those times you cheated on me weren't your fault."

83

"They weren't." Jake stood and came at me, arms stretched in beseech mode. "Those women threw—"

"Not listening." I slipped the phone in my pocket and stuck my fingers in my ears. "Grow up. Take responsibility."

Jake hung his head and toed the bark mulch spread around the rose bushes. He brought his hands together as if in prayer.

I shook my head.

He knelt and gave me puppy-dog eyes. Stupidly, he kept a smarmy smile pasted to his lips.

I shook my head again.

Lola limped over beside him and sniffed at his jacket. Then, displaying her own form of body language, she hunched and dropped a steaming heap.

Jake leaped to his feet and stumbled to the trail, waving one hand in front of his contorted face.

Lola, meanwhile, clomped up the steps to the deck with a job-well-done expression.

"Good girl," I praised as I fell in behind her. "You deserve two biscuits for that."

Tail wagging, Lola headed for the condo.

"Wait," Jake called. "Please. Seriously, I need your help. I was misinformed about how the judge defined community service."

I stepped through the gate, closed it behind me, turned, and hit him with a mega-dose of sarcasm. "That surprises me no end. Knowing you, I'm certain you read the agreement document carefully. Probably several times. And I'm certain you listened to every word the judge and prosecutor had to say, and asked incisive questions to clarify your situation. So I can only assume that somehow the rules changed between the time you read the document and the time you signed it. I can only assume this is a travesty of justice unprecedented in the annals of the Reckless River judicial system."

Jake nodded like one of those toy dogs you sometimes see in the rear windows of cars. "A travesty, yeah, that's what it is." He climbed the steps, pulled a folded paper from his pocket, and thrust it toward me. "See, I didn't know I wasn't supposed to be paid for community service, and I didn't know I was supposed to stay away from all of the guys I did business with before."

"Really?" I batted the paper aside. "Because that sounds like no-brainer stuff to me."

"Sure. To you. Because you went to school more years than I did."

In the interest of getting this conversation over with, I passed on pointing out that during those years of education I paid attention.

"So, I was helping a few guys out with a few real estate deals and they slipped me some walking-around money. And it was all good until someone ratted me out. And now I have to find even more community service projects real fast and apologize to the court in writing. And my lawyer says the apology better be good or else—"

"I get it." I leaned over the gate, snatched the paper from his hand, and tore it in half. "You want me to help you lie."

Jake put his hand over his heart. "No. That's not it at all. I want—"

"You want me to turn fact into fiction."

"Well, maybe, kind of, but only a little. And if you help me, this is the last time I'll ever ask you for anything. Honest. I promise."

By now you've figured out that Jake's definition of the word "honest" is as far from mine as Indiana is from India. And I bet you've also figured out that his promises have a shelf life of two or three days. Or less.

"I'm desperate," he moaned. "I'm practically homeless."

Meaning the latest woman he'd sweet-talked into taking him in was approaching the end of her rope. And meaning he didn't have a replacement lined up yet.

The child in me wanted to tear his letter to confetti and release it to the wind.

The adult in me waffled.

Jake incarcerated was a drain on society. Jake out of jail was, well, a boil on the backside of society, but at least a boil that was making restitution and kind of paying its own way. Or at least bilking only one or two members of society at a time. "Okay. I'll see what I can do."

"Tonight?"

I skewered him with "the look" every substitute teacher masters if he or she wants to cut through the chatter and get the attention of a classroom full of teenagers.

Jake winced. "Tomorrow?"

I held the look.

"The day after tomorrow?" Despite the nip in the air, sweat glistened on Jake's upper lip. "I'm really in a bind."

"I'll see what I can do," I repeated, putting extra space between each word.

"Okay, uh, great. Thanks. I'll call you."

"Don't even think about it."

"Right. I won't think about it. So, you'll call me?"

"No."

"Then how, um—?"

"I'll leave it in a plastic bag tied to the railing. The bottom of the railing."

Without another look at the man who had wooed me, won me, and wounded me, I headed for my door.

I was almost there when I was startled by another voice from the gloom. "That was very adult of you, dear."

Mrs. B, cradling Cheese Puff in her arms, stepped from her unit. "Helping Jake get on with his life will benefit us all."

"Especially if he goes off to live that life in another state or country."

"That would be ideal. But I'm afraid Jake is very fond of Reckless River."

"And the thousands of Reckless River residents he has yet to bilk."

Mrs. B patted my shoulder. "Now, dear, I want you to know I wasn't being nosy. I was bringing the little prince home when I heard you talking with someone. I couldn't help but hear it was Jake, and I thought I'd stand by."

"In case he needed help?" I asked in a teasing voice.

"Exactly. I have no worries about whether you can handle yourself where he's concerned."

"Especially when I have Lola to back me up by leaving a token of her lack of esteem inches from his bended knees."

Cheese Puff yipped as if to say he could have done the same—although with less mass and weight. He also had no love for Jake. My ex had never harmed my little mutt, but dogs are intuitive creatures. Cheese Puff must have picked up on Jake's belief that pets were a waste of time and money.

I opened the door to my unit. Mrs. B took a single step across the threshold and halted. "Would you like some help cleaning up the mess in your kitchen?"

"No." I laughed. "Because I don't intend to clean it. I'm on strike."

"I see. Have you posted notice?"

"No."

"So you're waiting for Dave and Allison to realize that you've walked off the job?"

"Right."

She chuckled.

"It will be a long wait," we said in unison.

"Don't get me wrong," she said. "I have profound respect for Dave. He's a wonderful man and he's good for you. And Allison, well, she's got a good heart, and I think she'll grow up to be a fine young woman. But she's still a work in progress."

"Very *slow* progress. But even on her pouty days she's far less self-centered than Jake."

We shared another laugh and Mrs. B snuggled Cheese Puff against her extra-long royal blue sweatshirt, kissed his scruffy orange head, and handed him to me. "He's worn out, but he has his moves down perfectly. We're going to beat Glorree Morning by a mile. He was born to be on the stage."

"He was certainly born to hog every scene he's in," I agreed. "Tell me you didn't reward him with pastrami or pepperoni."

"Only a little." She turned on the heels of her tap shoes and made a fast retreat to her unit. "See you tomorrow, dear."

Before I could suggest Cheese Puff spend the night with her, I heard her door slide closed and the lock click. For a few fleeting seconds, I thought about pounding on the glass, or retrieving my key to her front door and dumping my dog inside. Then I remembered all she'd done for me in the past year or so and decided I could suffer through. I also decided that if Cheese Puff fell asleep in his favorite chair, I would "forget" to carry him upstairs when I went to bed.

With that in mind, I fluffed the cushion with my free hand and deposited him upon it.

He grunted his thanks—or at least that's how I interpreted the sound—flopped, rolled into the crack between the cushion and the side of the chair, sighed, and closed his beady little eyes.

The copies of the slips of paper found in the pockets of the murder victim were still on the coffee table. Since I had nothing better to do, I made myself comfortable on the sofa and pushed the scraps around while hoping to see a pattern. I'd decided the numbers stood for letters of the alphabet and was going for a pen and pad to decipher the code when the landline rang.

"No thanks to you I got to rehearsal," Allison carped.

"You were supposed to call if you needed a ride," I countered.

"I did. I called a bunch of times from the mall and the pizza place. Your phone is off."

And, I saw when I retrieved it from my pocket, it was. Not only off, but out of juice. The whole time I'd been chasing the stalker who turned out to be Iz, and confronting the lurker who turned out to be Jake, the phone was dead. I would have been better off with a grapefruit or a cocktail fork in my grip. "Sorry," I mumbled. "Gotta charge it. Call me on the landline if you need me."

"I won't! I got a ride here. And I'll get a ride home. So don't worry." Her tone got even snarkier. "Not that you will."

That, of course, was a lie. I worried about Allison pretty much 24/7, but my concerns were far different from hers. While she stressed out about hairstyles and nail polish and whether her outfits were cute enough, I agonized about her diet, her self-esteem and entitlement issues, and whether some boy would take advantage of her. Some boy other than Josh. Make no mistake, he had plenty of hormones, but he was far more of an adult and far more aware of consequences than Allison. He was also far more focused on avoiding those consequences and not facing Dave's wrath.

Crossing my fingers, I made a wish that Dave would be able to identify the homicide victim in the alley and solve the case so he'd be free to go with us to Las Vegas next week. Without him along to deflect Allison's slings and arrows, I was likely to lose control and launch a few volleys of my own.

"Why does Dad have all those words from lines from the show?"

"Lines?"

"In the living room. On the table." She ascended to new levels of snippiness by drawing out the word "table" into about five syllables.

I glanced at the slips of paper. "Those are about a show?"

"Yeah."

"What show?"

"*My* show," she said, implying that I was functioning on only a single brain cell and it was on life-support.

"*Little Shop of Horrors*? That show?"

Those were stupid questions. In fact, they were so stupid Allison didn't bother to take a shot. She simply sighed, then blurted, "Gotta go. The stage manager's yelling 'cause the plant voice guy was late and the number one wino isn't here. Again. And there's no understudy and no way am I taking that part and putting dirt on my face even if Frankie begs me. I'll quit!"

She disconnected, leaving me staring at the slips of paper and wondering what they had to do with *Little Shop of Horrors*.

Thanks to my office computer, the Internet, and a speedy search engine, I didn't wonder for long. The words and phrases were bits of several songs.

But why would a homeless man have—?

I smacked my forehead.

A few minutes ago Allison told me one of the winos hadn't turned up. Again.

What if the murder victim wasn't homeless? What if he was dressed that way for his part in the performance?

Chapter 11

Trotting back to the living room, I shoved aside the words from the show. That left only numbers scrawled on bits of paper. I decided 230 and 730 were probably performance times. The four-digit number could be the address of the theater.

I dashed to the office, confirmed that theory with a little Internet sleuthing, and called Dave. "He's an actor," I blurted.

"Who's an actor?"

"Your murder victim. He had a part in the show Allison is in."

"Slow down. Start again. What are you talking about?"

"The guy you found in the alley. He was in *Little Shop of Horrors*."

Perhaps because he'd come to respect my ability to see connections, but more likely because he was frustrated and fresh out of better ideas, Dave didn't hang up. He did, however, express a few hundred degrees of skepticism. "And you know this because . . . ?"

"Because the words on those pieces of paper are from songs in the show."

Dave was silent for a few seconds.

"You can look it up if you don't believe me. Hey, the alley he was found in, was that, by any chance, the one behind the theater?"

Another silence.

Then, "I guess you could say it's an *extension* of the alley that runs behind the theater."

"The theater that's located on Main Street? At 1052 Main Street? The theater that schedules performances at 2:30 and 7:30?"

"There's only one theater downtown I know of," he said in a curt voice. "And it's on Main Street. I don't know about the performance schedule. But—hold the phone. You could be right. Those were the numbers he had in his pocket."

I decided to disregard the "could be" part and congratulate myself on handing him a break in the case. "Everyone connected with the show is in rehearsal right now," I informed him. "Except one of the winos. Allison says he's missing. Again."

"Yeah?"

"Yeah. So I bet he's your victim. And don't worry about thanking me, you can do that later, when we're alone and—"

"Right. Sure. Great."

He hung up before I got more specific about the nature of those thanks. Not that I'd intended to get *too* specific. After all, this isn't that kind of book.

Anyway, feeling smug about moving the investigation along, I taped the pieces of Jake's letter together and sat at the dining room table to read it.

Smug turned sour in an instant. In the first place, Jake's handwriting gave new meaning to the word "illegible." In the second place, his spelling was beyond the valley of atrocious. And in the third place, he started off like this: "Dear Judge, this wasn't my fault."

By now you probably realize that none of this surprised me in the least. Jake, after all, was Jake. The odds of him changing were right up there with the former planet known as Pluto demanding a recount and getting reinstated as number nine in the solar system lineup.

Deciding to take a rip-off-the-bandage approach and get this project over with, I carried his scribbling to my office, looked up a few words meaning "sorry" and a few more meaning "misunderstanding." Then I did a little research and came up with the name of the judge, the address of the courthouse, and the correct form of salutation. Using phrases like "accept full responsibility" and "beg the forgiveness of the court," I crafted a two-page letter. It didn't sound a bit like Jake had written it. But that was the point, right?

Going above and beyond, I provided an addressed envelope and a stamp. As I stuck letter and envelope in a plastic bag, I had a thought. Jake needed community service opportunities. The community theater needed, among many other things, a replacement actor to play the part of the wino. I zipped back to my office, brought up the theater company site, and wrote a note for Jake suggesting he call Frankie DeMille and offer to help out.

Under cover of darkness, I taped the bag to the railing. Then, in the interest of getting things settled as soon as possible, I called Jake at the number he'd noted on his rough draft and, without a greeting or farewell, told him the letter was ready.

As a reward for my efforts, I ate a few cheesy snacks, plugged my phone in to charge, and went upstairs to relax. It was only 8:30, an hour shy of my usual lights-out time, but I was working my way through a stack of mysteries set in Scotland, and they were darn good. Besides, propped up on a pile of pillows, I was farther away from those dirty dishes.

93

A slamming door and stomping footsteps jerked me from a dream about broad-shouldered men in kilts. As I rubbed my eyes, Allison stormed in. "I hate Dad. He ruined everything. Everything!"

She belly-flopped across the foot of the bed, wailing and tearing at her hair. Chewing the scenery, as they say in the theater.

I adjusted my glasses and slipped a bookmark in the novel, but said nothing.

"He made us stop rehearsing—just when I was going to sing my first song all the way through."

She rolled onto her back and drummed her heels on the bed. "And then he said we all had to be questioned—except me because he knew where I was when the guy was killed. And then, in front of everybody, he told me to call you to come and get me. Like I'm a little kid or something."

The gnashing teeth and pounding fists did little to convince me that sentence was inaccurate. I glanced at the landline phone on the nightstand and took a wild guess. "You didn't call."

"I'm not a baby. I can get home on my own. It's not that far."

Less than a mile. But distance wasn't the issue. Dark of night and scary people who roamed the shadows—those were the issues.

Downtown Reckless River wasn't large—maybe ten blocks by four if you're feeling generous—and its nightlife was, well, anemic at best, especially on a weeknight. But if she'd called for help, someone might have heard.

Once she got out of the core area though, Allison had to walk along a narrow road that paralleled the Columbia River. That road didn't show up in the dictionary under "well-lit." And this time of night it wasn't well-traveled.

"And there's probably not gonna be any rehearsal tomorrow," Allison lamented. "Dad says they have to search the theater for evidence. And Frankie's really angry because we're already way behind. And it's not fair that Dad and Detective Atwell can barge in and mess everything up."

Never mind that it hadn't been fair when a member of the cast was murdered.

Allison stopped thrashing and glared at me. "Well? Say something."

Wouldn't I just love to. Wouldn't I love to say, "Grow up." Or, "What were you thinking walking home from downtown?" Or maybe, "Could you just once think about someone other than yourself?"

But it was up to me to be the adult in the room. And, sometimes, silence is the most powerful weapon in the adult arsenal.

I used it like a cudgel.

After a moment, Allison winced. "Why are you giving me the substitute teacher look?"

I wasn't. Or at least I hadn't intended to. Probably, sometime during the past year, it had become an automatic response to being in close proximity to a teenager.

"I'm not doing anything wrong," she sniveled. "Don't I have a right to be mad after what Dad did?"

I held my expression. Staring past her and letting my eyes slide slightly out of focus helped. And thinking about that stack of dishes downstairs kept me from exhibiting the least sign of sympathy.

Allison leaped from the bed, plucked a tissue from a box on the bureau, blew her nose, and paced in a tight circle. "Walking home in the dark was kinda dumb, huh?"

"Kinda."

"And Dad's not trying to mess up the show. He's trying to find out who killed the guy who played the wino." She tossed the tissue in the wastebasket and sat at the foot of the bed. "I didn't even know his name. He was sort of stinky but at least he didn't try to cover that up with a bunch of cologne. And when someone brought cookies or chips he ate way more than his share. And he was kinda sarcastic—even more than you."

I wasn't sure whether to take that as a compliment or an insult, so I said nothing.

"But he had good ideas and he really got into the part. He wore a costume for every rehearsal right from the start, even though we don't have to do that until after Thanksgiving."

Considering the body odor and the "costume," it occurred to me that Dave's first instinct might have been on the money. The man in the alley might have been homeless. What he'd had on was perhaps less of a costume than it was the sum of his wardrobe.

"And he had lots of good ideas about what the winos could do in the background and before the show. And ideas about blocking and gestures and stuff. He wasn't pushy, though. He really cared about the show."

For a long moment Allison frowned and picked at a loose thread in the quilt, then she faced me. "If Frankie really needs me to play that part, I should do it, huh? Even if I don't want to. And I should do the best I can."

"That would be extremely professional."

Also, based on what I'd seen in the past year, it would be extremely out of character.

And perhaps also unnecessary—*if* Jake acted on my suggestion and if Frankie DeMille saw him as wino material.

How Allison would react to having Jake in the show was another can of worms.

"The show should come first." She raised her chin. "The whole performance should be more important than the parts of individual actors."

"So I've heard. It's one of those teamwork things."

She sighed, her shoulders slumped, and tears glistened in her eyes. "I shouldn't be all about me all the time. I shouldn't blame everyone else. Especially you and Dad. And Josh."

Breakthrough!

Part of me wanted to leap from the bed and do a happy dance. But I held that in check and shrugged in the most casual way I could manage. "I'd certainly like it if you made an effort to take more responsibility. And I know your father would, too."

"Yeah." She picked at the quilt again. "It's just . . . it's hard."

I nodded. "It's a habit. Habits are hard to break. Even when you really want to. Even when you know things will be better if you do."

"Did you ever try to break a bad habit?"

"You bet." I displayed my freshly buffed fingernails. "I used to bite my nails and chew the skin around the edges. I tried everything—painting icky-tasting stuff on them, wearing gloves, getting my friends to mock me."

"My friends are good at mocking. They'd like that."

"I expect they would, but it might not work. It didn't for me. I toughened up and did my best to ignore them."

Allison studied my hands. "But you stopped."

"Not until I figured out why I was doing it."

"Why?" Allison flopped on her side and wiggled up beside me. "Why were you biting your nails?"

"Because I was anxious." I stroked her hair. "I've told you about my brother dying and my parents checking out emotionally and Iz raising me."

Allison snorted. "When I think of Iz raising you I remember those stories where kids are dumped in the wild and raised by wolves." She raised her hands. "Sorry."

I laughed. "No apology necessary. It was primitive nurturing for sure, but at least Iz has opposable thumbs so she could braid my hair."

"Did she do a good job?"

"No. She yanked it so tight my eyes looked like this." I placed my fingers at the corners of my lids and pulled so I peered out through narrow slits. "And my vision was so blurry I couldn't read aloud when the teacher called on me."

"Dad used to do that to my hair when I was really little." Allison copied my facial expression for a few seconds. "So, how did you stop biting? How long did it take?"

"Months. And I backslid a lot. But every morning I told myself things would be okay. I told myself I had a warm place to live, new clothes when I really needed them, and plenty of food so I never went hungry. And I told myself Iz wouldn't abandon me."

"Even if sometimes now you wish she would?"

We shared a fist bump and a laugh, then Allison rolled from the bed and headed for her room. "I'm gonna go think about how to be better."

Words I'd longed to hear for many months.

She halted and looked back, her face pinched. "Don't tell Dad I walked home. Okay?"

"I won't bring it up. But if he asks . . ."

"I know. If he asks you won't lie to him." She said that with regret and what sounded like pride. "G'night."

I brushed my teeth and slipped on a long-sleeve T-shirt and flannels, my mind on what I didn't tell Allison. Sure, I'd stopped biting my nails. But I'd exchanged that habit for another—snacking. And, as long as new kinds of cheesy snacks kept appearing on grocery store shelves, I doubted I had the willpower to kick that habit.

When the alarm went off, Dave groaned and pulled the pillow over his head. "Wake me up before you leave. *Right* before you leave."

I attempted that an hour later, tossing aside the pillow, shaking him, and finally calling Lola to lick his feet. "Actors," he grumbled as he sat up. "Kindergarten kids might have paid better attention to us. And given us more coherent answers. But don't get me started."

"I won't." At least not at the moment. But all bets were off on later, because it sounded like he could work up an entertaining rant. "Gotta get to school." I rubbed my lips across the stubble on his cheek, kissed him, and made for the door.

"See you— Hey, what's with the pile of dishes? Are you on strike or something?"

"Or something," I called over my shoulder.

"Huh?"

"You're a detective. You figure it out."

Chapter 12

Despite the usual cacophony emanating from the cafeteria, and the caustic comments made by teachers congregating around the copy machine, Captain Meriwether High School seemed quieter and calmer than yesterday. I assumed that meant Tremaine Scott hadn't pressed the pesky retirement-form-request issue with Big Chill. When I spotted the smug smile on her face, I knew that assumption was correct and leaped to a new one—she'd cowed the HR department as well.

Good thing she was in my corner.

At least most of the time.

I made faster progress with the student records than I had the day before and rewarded myself by joining my posse in the teachers' room for lunch. Today's topic had a familiar theme—misinformation. Previous concerns about classroom observations had been laid to rest when it turned out the guy from the central office hadn't been at a conference, but instead at a job interview. It had gone so well he'd been offered the job and accepted, effective immediately. So the dangling sword had been sheathed—if indeed it had ever dangled in the first place.

"Turns out," Doug confided, "the e-mail sent out was a draft saved about a year ago that somehow got resurrected and distributed."

"Wow. And no one noticed the original date on it?"

"Apparently not."

"Shoddy work. Sloppy." Aston stuck a two-pronged barbecue fork into something vaguely resembling, to my untrained eye, a chunk of fresh cow pie scooped from a wet pasture. Brownish red juice squirted in Ardie's direction. She raised a paper plate like a shield, deflecting the squirt to the plastic tablecloth.

"With those reflexes," Gertrude observed, "you should be coaching the volleyball team."

Ardie flashed a smile, lowered the plate, and placed it on top of the spatter.

"I'm sure you'd be a great coach. But the point is," Brenda sniffed, "no one in this room should need reflexes like a cat in order to survive the lunch period." She fingered her hair, spiky and a bright magenta. "No one should have to be on constant alert to defend against an assault by . . . by whatever that noxious substance might be."

"Elk heart," Aston said. "Rare."

"Too much information." Doug folded foil around his sandwich, grasped his cola, and made an exit at a brisk pace.

"I like that boy, but he has a weak stomach. Never would have survived a winter on the frontier. Would have starved to death by spring." Aston raised the fork and tore at the impaled heart with his teeth.

My stomach knotted in a way that made it clear anything I sent down would be sent back up.

"Elk heart. Disgusting." Brenda shook her head and popped the lid off a plastic container. A chunk of something gelatinous quivered on a bed of lettuce leaves, releasing the scent of wet dog, mint, and overripe bananas seasoned with a liberal dash of sage and oregano.

"Ewwww. Talk about disgusting." Gertrude waved a hand in front of her face. "I think it's time we laid down some rules about what's acceptable fare for lunch and what isn't."

Brenda frowned.

Aston glared. "Sounds like you're about to trample on the Constitution. What I eat comes under freedom of expression. And what's wrong with elk heart? People have been eating it for years. Centuries."

Gertrude glared back. "That doesn't mean you should eat it in here where you subject us to a second-hand experience."

"There are exceptions to the First Amendment," I reminded him. "You're a history teacher. You know that."

Aston's expression indicated that maybe he didn't know— or at least didn't remember.

"Anyway, if you're going to eat it in here, it shouldn't be served up like that," Brenda said.

"Like what? It's not raw. It's on a plate. I'm using a fork."

"A barbecue fork," she jeered. "And you don't have a knife. And the presentation is primitive."

"Presentation?" Aston poked a grubby index finger in her direction. "Now you're making rules about how food looks. And about the utensils I have to use. Why do I need a knife if I have teeth?"

"Because your teeth need to be brushed."

"Enough!" Ardie slapped the table. "We're heading back where we were when I joined the group. Aston, if you want elk heart or anything else gamy, fishy, or outside of what the rest of us—Brenda excepted—consider the mainstream, slice and dice it at home. Better yet, slide it between a couple of slices of bread so the contents are halfway hidden. And from now on, spare Doug the details. In fact, spare us all."

Aston glowered and dropped the chunk of meat to his plate. Ardie deflected the resulting splash of juice, then turned to Brenda. "That mainstream thing goes for you, too. Just because you call it cutting-edge cuisine doesn't mean everything you bring is a delight to our senses. And if you and Aston want to trade insults, please do it outside of this room."

Brenda's eyes bulged and her cheeks puffed out. "But he—"

"He baits you," Gertrude said.

"And you bait him back," Ardie added. "It's exactly the kind of behavior we try to discourage in the classroom. It's what we come in here at lunch to get away from."

"And we don't feel there's humor in it," Gertrude finished. "It's getting on our nerves."

"Well." Brenda seized her bowl and stood. "I won't stay where I'm preached at and insulted."

"Neither will I." Aston raised his fork and, the elk heart dripping juice, headed for the door.

Their collision sent them both sprawling.

It also left a stain on the carpet and a stench in the air that challenged custodians for months to come.

When I cruised toward my parking spot at the condo complex that afternoon, I saw Jim had put his misunderstanding plan into action. A series of holes and accompanying mounds of dirt graced several patches of lawn.

Bernina Burke, clipboard in hand, was steaming toward his door.

Naturally, I parked and trailed along behind. Angry as she appeared, I doubted she'd look back and see me, but I took the precaution of using a row of parked cars as cover.

She pounded on Jim's door with the force of a wrecking ball, and screeched his name for good measure.

Sidling closer and making myself as one with the shadow cast by the porch a unit down from Jim's, I counted seconds. I hit 108 before Jim opened the door, yawning, combing his beard with his fingers, and doing his impression of a man awakened from a nap. I say "impression" because even from my hiding place I spotted the trace of a smile on his lips and the twinkle in his eyes.

"What are all these holes?" Bernina yelled.

"Um." Jim blinked. "They're, um, holes. Depressions in the ground. Hollowed out areas."

"I know what a hole is, you idiot. Why did you dig them?"

Jim gave her a gape of surprise. "Why? Because you told me to."

"I did not. I told you to look for moles. Look for their mounds."

"Right." He nodded. "Dig holes. In the ground."

"No. I said to level the molehills."

"Chills?" Jim scratched his head. "Nope, I was plenty warm. I never get chills when I'm shoveling. Of course, I do tend to work up a sweat, so if it was a really cold day with a brisk wind—"

"Not chills. Molehills." Bernina screamed like she was auditioning for a role in a slasher movie. "Do you need a hearing aid?"

"No." Jim tapped his ears. "I already have two."

"Then why don't you use them?" Bernina bellowed.

Jim frowned. "Huh? A fuse in unit 10? What about it?"

"There is no fuse. We have breakers in every unit. Breakers. Not fuses." Bernina tore at her hair. "Pay attention. Turn on your hearing aids."

Jim shook his head. "If I check the fuse, of course I expect to be paid."

"No. Forget the fuse." Bernina pointed at his ears with both hands. "I'm talking about the things in your ears, man. You need to be tested."

"Somebody tossed beer cans?" Jim peered toward the trash bins. "And you want them arrested?"

Bernina hauled in breath for another barrage, but Jim gripped her shoulders and turned her toward her office. "Hey, you seem pretty upset. Why don't you go to your office and wind down before you have a stroke? I'll stop by later and we can talk about what you want me to do after I check that fuse and take care of the beer cans."

With eyes as glazed as doughnuts, Bernina stumbled off, muttering under her breath.

"Genius," I called when she was out of earshot. "Incredible acting. Pure genius."

Jim cupped one ear. "Who are you calling a sour, mean cuss?"

He held the pose for a few seconds, then collapsed in one of the porch chairs, slapping his knee. "That was the most fun I ever had with my clothes on. Can't wait for tomorrow. We're supposed to repaint the stripes in the parking lot."

"And instead . . . ?"

"We'll check the drainpipes for rot." He crowed with delight. "With any luck we can get a bunch of them taken down and disassembled in the parking area while she's out to lunch."

I applauded.

Remaining in the chair, he took a bow. "She usually takes a two-hour lunch. But there are a lot of drainpipes and getting them all down won't be a snap, especially since we'll need extension ladders."

"Be careful," I urged. "Take your time. And try not to laugh too hard while you're on a ladder. It could be hazardous to your health."

When I got to my unit, I found Dave and Detective Atwell on opposite sides of the dining room table hammering away on their laptops. Giant-sized fast-food to-go drinks stood close at hand. Dave shot me a grin. Atwell favored me by raising his right index finger from the keyboard.

Such an expansive gesture made me feel all warm and fuzzy.

Not.

"Desks in the cop shop collapse?" I asked as I stowed my school bag in the hall closet.

"Came here for lunch."

"Hope you brought it with you."

"We did." Dave surveyed the stacks of dishes on the counter. "Good thing we didn't need plates or glasses. Stuff seems to be piling up."

Atwell sucked at his straw, making a bubbling slurp I took for condemnation of my homemaking skills.

"Piling up? Really?" I feigned surprise and turned to assess the heap on the counter. "Golly gee, I guess things *are* stacking up. I hadn't noticed. I've been keeping busy, you know, subbing, taking care of Lola, chauffeuring your daughter, helping you make a breakthrough in the case."

Atwell raised the next finger in line.

I smirked. He was *such* a sore loser.

"Yeah," Dave muttered. "Thanks for the tip."

"Did you make any progress?"

"Well, that depends on how—"

"Yammer. Yammer. Yammer." Atwell slammed his laptop closed and stood. "I can't work under these conditions. I'll see you at the office." He checked his watch. "In half an hour."

The second the door slammed, I mimicked his voice and actions.

Dave didn't crack a smile. "I know you got off on the wrong foot with him—"

"Wrong *feet*," I corrected.

Dave rolled his eyes. "Right. But believe it or not, I'm learning a lot from him."

"Like what? How to get hacked off when someone else finds a clue? How to treat people like dog po—?"

"I get it." Dave raised his hands in surrender. "He's not a people person."

"I'm not sure he's a people."

This time, after a struggle, Dave smiled.

Vindicated, I raised my hands. "Sorry I needled him. My defense is that I couldn't help myself. He's a big target, and it's so darned easy to make him see red."

"He saw a lot of it last night. Those theater people are a different breed. If something didn't affect them specifically, they didn't pay any attention." Dave shut down his laptop. "Do you realize how hard it is to conduct a serious interview with a guy dressed as a plant?"

I tried to suppress a smile. I couldn't.

"One woman thought I 'wouldn't mind' if she practiced a few dance steps while I interviewed her because she had a leading role and this was her big break." He closed his laptop. "And then there was the director."

"Frankie DeMille."

"Right. She didn't know the dead guy's last name or address. Called him 'Mr. First Wino.' Told me it was no big deal because it's amateur theater and no one gets paid so she doesn't have to keep tax records for the actors. Made it sound like details were beneath her and the dead guy was a pain in her patootie because he didn't own a cellphone."

Given what I knew, that sounded about par for Frankie's course. "Did anyone else know his name?"

107

"Only his first name. Max. Or Mat. Or maybe Mack. Or Mitch." Dave shrugged. "Like I said, if it didn't affect them, they weren't interested. And they say he mumbled."

"And not one person asked him to repeat his name? Or spell it?"

"No. Thing is, the guy had some major-league body odor, so no one prolonged a conversation or got closer than they had to. But—get this—no one complained to the director because they figured he was a method actor and learning the part from the inside out."

I remembered Allison sounding off to me about the odor. She hadn't mentioned the concept of method acting but, as I recalled, she'd said at least he hadn't tried to cover up his body odor with cologne.

"The assistant director said he admired the guy's commitment to the role and to the show. A few days ago she even changed things around and made him the understudy for Seymour. Said he had a great voice and lots of ideas about blocking and 'bits of business.'" Dave shuffled a batch of papers into what passed for order and stuffed them in the bag with the laptop. "Whatever that expression means."

"It means you haven't been listening to your daughter."

"Huh?"

"She explained that last week. It's something an actor does, some kind of action. It's intended to get the attention of the audience."

"And steal the scene?"

I shrugged. "If the person doing the bit of business is Allison, then it's safe to assume that's the purpose."

"A star is borne." Dave slung the strap over his shoulder and lifted the bag. "That's borne with an E."

We shared a laugh and he headed for the door. "Anyway, we're going forward on the assumption that he was living on the streets. We pried a publicity shot out of the director and we're circulating it around the missions and churches and homeless camps. With any luck, we'll get a name soon."

"Well, if you get tired of spinning your wheels, you can put Iz on the case."

"Not funny."

Neither was that pile of dishes. But I took the high road, and didn't go there.

Chapter 13

Where I did go, after taking Lola to the rose garden, was to Mrs. B's condo. After a long day bent over printouts and a close encounter with the ever-charming Detective Atwell, I needed something frothy in a tall, frosted glass. Lola, perhaps because she knew Mrs. B bought biscuits of superior quality, tagged along.

We found Mrs. B in her favorite chair, Cheese Puff asleep in her lap, sacks of frozen corn on her ankles, phone to her ear. She motioned to the cabinet containing various kinds of alcohol—also superior to the brands I stock. Have I mentioned that Mrs. B is rolling in dough?

"You'll do nothing of the kind," she told the person on the other end. "If you drop out of the show, I'll drop out as well."

Uh oh.

Assuming she was talking about *Still Got That Strut*, and talking to her competitor, Glorree Morning, I hastened to the cabinet and mixed myself a rum and grapefruit soda—light on the rum because I'd be driving to water aerobics soon. But not too light because if Mrs. B dropped out of the reality show, the trip to Las Vegas dropped off the calendar. And that would lead to much wailing and gnashing of teeth—most of it done by Allison, and not at low intensity or volume.

And Allison's reaction would be nothing compared to the way Dario O'Brien would take the news.

I tossed Lola a couple of biscuits from a decorative jar that was probably worth more than my car, swallowed a third of my drink, fanned myself with a napkin, and sat in a padded rocker.

"But let's not cross that bridge today," Mrs. B went on. "You get that foot up, medicate with something poured over ice, and call me in the morning."

She signed off with a couple of air kisses.

I raised my eyebrows, but said nothing. Mrs. B didn't like to be rushed. She scratched Cheese Puff's head, shifted the sacks of corn to her knees, and turned the full force of her sapphire gaze on me. "You won't repeat any of that to Dario, will you, dear?"

There may have been a question mark on the end of that sentence, but I recognized it for the order it was. "Not a single syllable," I promised.

She nodded and we sat in silence again, me sipping, Mrs. B stroking Cheese Puff's ears while he snuffled and snored. "Glorree took a fall this morning," she said.

"Practicing her routine?"

"Getting out of bed. She stood up too fast and had a dizzy spell. Fell over and twisted her ankle." Mrs. B shook her head. "She was probably faint from hunger—Dario says she's trying to shed a few pounds. But you have to be careful with your diet when you get to our age . . ."

What that age was, no one knew for sure. And no one with the least bit of common sense or instinct for self-preservation was about to ask. My guess, based on my usual sketchy math, was right around 70.

"Glorree never had strong ankles. Not like I had." She moved the sack of frozen corn from her right knee back to her ankle. "But time catches up with all of us. Now and then I'm a little wobbly first thing in the morning. It could have happened to me."

"Do you think *she* would offer to drop out if you were injured?"

Mrs. B thought that over, sipping from a martini glass as she did. "The Glorree from back in the day certainly wouldn't. She'd have seen it as an opportunity to advance her career. But now—"

"Now her career is in the rearview mirror," I said with more than a hint of snarkiness. "Except for this competition. It's her last chance to grab the brass ring. She'd never drop out—except to get you to do the same so she could drop right back in."

"You make a good point, dear. Although you make it in a very suspicious and uncharitable tone." Mrs. B took a long sip. "I suppose I want to think the best of her. She's one of the few links to my past."

"But if one of your other links heard you offering to drop out, he'd—"

"Blow a gasket."

That was the understatement of the year. Dario O'Brien's reaction would make the 1980 eruption of Mt. St. Helens look like a small bowl of instant oatmeal boiling over in a low-powered microwave.

And then there was Peabody Fontaine. The blogger enamored of all things showgirl would be devastated. He'd featured Mrs. B on his blog several times in recent months and e-mailed her nearly every day to update her on plans for a gala fund-raising event following the competition. He'd turn on her in a heartbeat and share scathing comments with his followers.

112

"Is there a backup plan? In case one of you is injured and you can't compete against each other?"

"I don't know." Mrs. B twirled a tuft of hair on Cheese Puff's head. "I suppose Dario would have to bring back one of the previous competitors. Or bring in someone from a production at one of the big casinos."

"Someone younger? That wouldn't be fair."

"I'm sure the judges would make allowances."

I didn't buy that. I thought they'd see the unbalanced competition as an opportunity for catty remarks comparing Mrs. B to someone carrying far fewer years. "How long does a twisted ankle take to heal?"

"It all depends on how much damage you did." Mrs. B moved the sack of corn from her left knee to the ankle. "And your age and physical condition. And how bad the swelling is. And how you treat it. And whether you can stay off it for a few days."

I counted days on my fingers. "Glorree's got a week and a half before the competition. Do you think that's enough?"

"If the injury isn't too bad." Mrs. B plucked a fat olive from the bottom of her glass. "And if she doesn't try to practice."

Given Glorree's desire to see her old rival go down in ostrich-feathered flames, the not-practicing part didn't seem likely.

"I'll call her on Monday and see how she's doing," Mrs. B said.

"And after that you'll run the situation by Dario before there's more crazy talk about dropping out?"

"Yes, dear." She popped the olive in her mouth.

"Promise?"

She nodded, but I had a suspicion the fingers covered by Cheese Puff's hair were crossed. Mrs. B was a determined woman. A stubborn, determined woman. Most of the time that tended to work in her favor. And mine. Which is why I don't view those traits only as character flaws.

The sound of breaking glass welcomed me home.

"It's not my fault," Allison insisted in a voice nearing screech level. "Dad stuck those glasses inside each other and I couldn't get them apart so I kind of tapped them on the edge of the counter and the next thing I knew . . ."

She waved her hands, directing my attention to shards of glass scattered across the floor. "I was loading the dishwasher. I was trying to take responsibility and help." Her tone implied this was the kind of thing that happened when she charted such a course. It further implied that I should order her to steer clear of such actions in the future.

I refused to buy in.

"Next time put cold water in the top glass and let it sit for a minute. Meanwhile, the broom is in the pantry. I'll get newspaper to wrap the pieces in so they don't cut through the trash bag and hurt someone."

"It's all Dad's fault the glasses broke, so we should leave the mess for him." Allison's lower lip poked out. "Besides, I don't have time to clean it up."

I glanced at the clock. Rehearsal was hours away. "Why don't you have time?"

"Because I have to take down every single one of the stupid decorations so I can put them back up again starting on Friday. Then Josh and I have to go out for dinner, and I have to be at rehearsal early tonight, and—"

(For the record, I noticed several uses of the words "have to" in that lengthy sentence. I made no effort, however, to point out that these activities weren't mandated by law. Nor did I mention that "have to" and "want to" were different animals.)

"I appreciate that you have a lot to do," I said with about as much sympathy as I might muster for a billionaire whining about his tax bill. "But going off and leaving broken glass on the floor isn't responsible behavior. Cheese Puff or Lola could step on it."

The lip protruded farther. I pushed mine to the limit and held it until I felt the tendons—or ligaments, or possibly muscles—in my jaw screaming in protest. That took about five seconds. When it came to pouting, I wasn't in Allison's league. But then, I didn't put in the hours of practice she did.

Losing patience as fast as the Arctic is losing ice, I gave up on any pretense of empathy. "Broom," I ordered in my most severe substitute-teacher voice. "Sweep."

Allison slouched to the pantry, got the broom and dustpan, and attacked the mess as if it might attack back. Not to cast aspersions, but it seemed as if she intended to work so slowly and to such minimal standards that I'd become frustrated and take over. In the interest of being able to use the kitchen some time before I collected Social Security, I almost did.

But then I took another look at the clock.

Water aerobics class began in twenty minutes.

No time for dinner. And no way to reach the refrigerator without climbing over Allison. But after that drink next door, I needed something in my stomach. Fortunately, there was always an emergency granola bar in my school bag.

I gobbled it as I stuffed my suit and a towel in my swim bag.

Allison was still sweeping when I headed for the door. "Call me when rehearsal is over and I'll pick you up."

When I got back from water aerobics, the glass shards were gone, but the broom leaned against the counter, the handle of the dustpan stuck out from beneath the stove, and stacks of dishes still cluttered the counter. Lest I be tempted to suspend my strike long enough to make a dent in the mess, I took Lola outside, retrieved Cheese Puff from Mrs. B, and went upstairs to read and relax.

Allison didn't call until after 9:30, thus doing nothing to help me reach my goal of following up relaxation with a full eight hours of sleep. And, wound up as she was when she tumbled into the car outside the theater, I doubted she'd be able to sleep before midnight at the earliest.

"It's all messed up," she wailed. "It's a disaster. The guy who comes on at the end and wants to pot a whole bunch of little plants dropped out. Frankie wants me to wear a suit and put on a mustache and wig and play his part."

This sounded more like an opportunity than a disaster. But what did I know? Well, I knew that Allison was vain about her appearance, so the mustache thing wasn't likely to fly, even if it guaranteed a few moments on the stage.

Knowing better than to point that out, I went with a non-committal "Oh."

"No. No way," Allison responded as she snapped her seatbelt. "Don't even think of trying to talk me into doing it. I'd look dorky in a suit. And the mustache glue smells like wet shoes."

"Ah," I said, expanding my side of the conversation by 100%.

I pulled away from the theater and beat a hasty retreat through downtown Reckless River as Allison chattered on.

"She told me to think it over, but I don't need to. I won't do it. I'm the understudy for Audrey, I can't go messing up my voice and timing and stuff by learning a whole bunch of new lines."

116

I doubted the role was huge, so the learning process wouldn't involve "a whole bunch of new lines." I upped my conversational input another 50%. "Okay."

"Not even if she begs me. Not even if everybody in the cast begs me."

Having made her position abundantly clear, Allison folded her arms across her chest, stuck out her lower lip, and drummed her heels on the rubber mat.

Instead of going for, say, a three-syllable response, I concentrated on driving—until I spotted a familiar baby-poop brown van parked outside an antique store. I slowed and eyeballed it as we approached, but saw no sign of my sister. Either she was slumped behind the wheel, out of the vehicle and in pursuit of her quarry, or lurking in the shadows.

"What are you looking for?" Allison asked.

"Iz."

"Here?" Starting with a cross, Allison made a complicated series of signs with her fingers as if that would ward off my sister. It hadn't worked yet, but possibly the charm required a cumulative effect.

"That's the van she rented." Curiosity trumped my desire to hit the hay. I wheeled my car to the curb a few spaces behind the van.

"She couldn't find anything uglier?" Allison performed another complicated series of finger movements and rolled down her window to peer at the van. "What's she doing here?"

"I don't—"

"I'm on a job," Iz said.

"Yow! You practically blew out my eardrums." Allison clapped her hands over her ears and leaned away from my sister's face framed by the open window. That face was pastier than usual. Blue-black bags sagged beneath eyes shot through with red lines. Her trench coat had picked up several new

117

wrinkles and a smear of what appeared to be strawberry jam on the collar. The smear resembled the outline of the state of Idaho. Only upside down.

"Ssshhhh," Iz hissed, emitting a blast of air substantial enough to inflate the average tire. "He's in there." She pointed at an ice cream shop across the street and halfway up the next block. "He might hear you."

"Or you," I noted. "And I thought that shop closed at 8:00."

"It does." Iz opened the rear door and flung herself across the back seat. The car rocked and bounced, making me wonder about the integrity of the shock absorbers. "The guy's working on a sink clog. Hey, how about you watch him while I catch some Zs?"

"How about we don't," Allison said. "I have school tomorrow."

"Ten minutes." Iz folded her arms across her chest and closed her eyes. "That's all I want. Maybe 20."

"No," I said. "It's almost 10:00, and I have to work tomorrow."

"Take a sick day."

"Substitutes don't get paid if they take sick days."

"Then you should find a real job."

Talk about the pot calling out the kettle. "Get out of the car."

"Come on. I'm fried." She flung her arm over her eyes. "This guy's a plumber. He gets called at all hours of the night to take care of leaks and clogs and overflows. Then his wife calls me and I have to get out of bed and follow him."

The child in me wanted to ask if she still thought being an investigator was easy. And then maybe suggest that *she* get a real job. But I settled for simply enjoying her exhaustion.

"Why?" Allison asked. "Why do you have to follow him?"

"Because his wife thinks he's cheating on her," I explained.

118

"Is he?"

"Not that I've seen so far. But he's a man. He will."

Allison rolled her eyes. "I hope you get paid even if he doesn't, 'cause if he's like my dad, he won't cheat. He won't even think about it."

I felt a swelling of pride. Allison felt Dave was the loyal and faithful type. That reinforced my belief that I'd made a good choice. And maybe the plumber's wife had made a sound choice, too. Maybe she was insecure.

"If these plumbing emergencies are wearing you out," I told Iz, "imagine what they're doing to him. I doubt he has enough energy to cheat."

Iz sat up and pointed a finger at me, but just then the door of the ice cream shop opened and a burly man emerged carrying a tool box. A smudge of grease ran along the side of his face from hairline to jaw. His red T-shirt was stained, the knees of his jeans filthy.

"It's afoot," I said.

"What?" Iz asked.

"The game."

"Huh?" Iz scowled.

Allison giggled.

"What are you talking about?" Iz asked.

"I'm talking about you getting out of the car, Watson. And into your mobile pile of poop. You've got a plumber to tail."

Chapter 14

As I left for school the next morning, my headlights passed across the trash bins at the far end of the parking lot. Jim and three older male residents were hard at work with metal bars and bricks. I had no idea what their objectives were, but I expected that elevating Bernina's blood pressure to the danger zone was high on the list.

As for Big Chill, as I found when I got to school, her blood pressure was already far inside the scary range. I doubted a tranquilizer dart designed to bring down a charging rhino would take the edge off.

"I hope you finish that project this afternoon," she said through tight lips. Her tone implied that only the final five words of that sentence counted. The way her gaze slid toward her phone told me she'd had a call from above—and I don't mean a call in a spiritual kind of way. The frost in her gaze as it swept over me made it clear there was no point in mentioning I'd been led to understand I had the rest of the week.

I swallowed hard and, lips straining, tried for a confident smile. "I should be able to."

She glowered.

I deleted the "should" and answered again, crossing my fingers as I did.

The glower cooled a few degrees.

"I'll eat lunch while I work. I'll stay late."

The glower cooled further and I scurried to the conference room and got to work. By waving off everyone who stuck their heads in to chat, and by trimming my lunch break to the time it took to nuke my pasta and carry it back to my workspace, I finished up at 12:53. Skipping the Olympic dismount, I carried the stack of envelopes, the printout, and the laptop to the Chillster's office.

"Thank you." She wrenched the heap of envelopes from my hands. "Take the rest of the day off."

Those were words I didn't need to hear twice. And, being relieved to get away from the glacial atmosphere of her office, I didn't linger to ask whether I should still plan on being assigned to her tomorrow, or whether she would free up my Friday so I could take another job. I figured I'd play dumb, show up at the usual time, hope the storm had passed, and keep my fingers crossed that she felt guilty enough to round up a plum assignment for me.

(For the record, a plum assignment meant lesson plans that called for me to do more than show a movie, students who were at least mildly interested in the subject, and a room with functioning heat. If that room happened to be located fewer than 100 yards from the nearest faculty restroom, I awarded bonus points.)

Because I sometimes found it amusing, I hit the radio's scan button on the way home and listened to snippets of music, talk, and ads. That's how I found myself hearing the voice of Mrs. B's nemesis, Rick Rivers. To my total lack of surprise, today's topic was one he harped on at least three days a week—

excessive government regulation. And he was harping live, even though his shift would have ended a few hours ago and this time slot should have been filled with satellite programming. I suspected Rick was filling in because of a technical glitch or, possibly, further budget slicing.

"You know what?" he asked in a voice with an edge like a dull knife. "These storm troopers who inspect restaurant kitchens have crossed the line. They've gone too far. A little dirt never killed anyone. All the experts I checked with say being exposed to germs is beneficial. That's how you build up resistance."

I grinned, recalling the health department restaurant score report in yesterday's paper. Zero was a perfect score, and at least half the restaurants listed had hit the mark. Most others scored somewhere below 20, but the place run by Rick's buddy—a place I won't name because said buddy has anger management issues—pulled a whopping 215 and had been shut down. We weren't talking about greasy smears and a few unfriendly germs. A score at that level told me the restaurant was a breeding ground for a massive outbreak of food-borne illness.

So, as you might guess, I had no quarrel with the standards, the single-mindedness of inspectors, or the closure. If, faced with regular inspections, the place couldn't meet safety standards, imagine how lax things would be if there were no inspections. Can you say salmonella? Can you say E. coli?

Since Rick ate there several times a week, you might think he'd be more concerned about food-safety issues and his own health than about possible government overreach. But I happened to know that Rick, because he frequently mentioned the name of the restaurant—in a casual way he insisted didn't qualify as advertising, but rather a fact about his life listeners longed to know—never paid for a single meal. And, because I knew Rick to be a stingy, miserly, penny-pinching tightwad, I was willing to bet he never left so much as a dime on the table for a tip. Considering the loss of his free slot at the feeding trough, his outrage about what he perceived to be excessive rules rang hollow and insincere.

But the average listener didn't know what I knew.

The average listener was probably nodding and thinking of the regulations and red tape he was subject to—everything from speed limits to construction permits, from vehicle emissions tests to tax returns.

And if that average listener was starting a business or building a home, the number of hurdles to jump multiplied. In fact, hurdles—and misinformation about them—explained why the Reckless River Sandwich shop wasn't open yet. Not health department regulations, because Lana Dylan, who'd been a waitress most of her life, saw that no food-handling corners were cut or even shaved. No, the doors were still closed because of signage and parking lot issues. And don't ask me what those issues are because the last time Verna tried to explain it to the Krammee's Reconstruction Committee, eyes rolled back, heads swiveled, and at least two members went home gibbering like baboons.

"Something ought to be done," Rick Rivers yammered. "We need to take back this city, this county, this country."

"This radio station," I said, twirling the knob and silencing him.

How much would it cost to buy the station? Couldn't be much. The signal wasn't powerful. It pretty much fell off the tower and faded away at the edge of town. Perhaps the next time Rick referred to Mrs. B as a stripper, I'd suggest she wave her checkbook, buy the place, and fire his scrawny butt. We could put Verna and Sybil on the air and do better in the way of entertainment. And we'd cut the flow of misinformation.

Although, given Sybil's flights of airheadedness, we probably wouldn't cut it by much.

As I cruised toward my parking spot, I noticed Jim on his front porch enjoying a sunbreak. A friendly hummingbird hovered above the rim of a red cup in his left hand. I parked, noting that the holes in the lawn had been filled in, but the trash bins were leaning at about a 20-degree angle. Giggling, I made my way across the lot to his abode.

"Leaning trash cans?"

Jim cupped his right hand around his ear. "Huh? What?"

I planted my rump in the chair beside his. "Another instance of auditory malfunction?"

He raised the hand as it taking an oath. "I swear I didn't realize she wanted us to clean the trash bins. What I heard was 'lean' the trash bins. So that's what we did. I'm not accepting a bit of the blame for this. She needs to enunciate more clearly."

He folded his hand so only his index finger stuck out as a perch for his feathered friend. "Of course, when I told the story to the folks at Shoalwater Bend, I left off the last bit and made out like Bernina is a perfectionist who wants things done right. That explains why she ran off all those landscaping and yard maintenance companies."

"That might work. If nobody asks the companies for their side of it."

"True." Jim grimaced. "But, anyway, I said all the residents here like and respect Bernina so much that several of us pitched in to gussy up the grounds. Unfortunately, we're a bunch of fools who can't be bothered to ask questions if something seems weird, and we generally spend our days running amok."

The hummer clicked agreement, zipped a couple of circles around Jim's head, and landed on his finger.

"How much more amok are you planning to run?"

124

"Well, I had plans to paint new stripes on the parking lot—using washable paint, of course—but Bernina fired me. I'm done effective at the end of the day or as soon as I get the trash bins level again, whichever comes first."

"Congratulations?"

Jim grimaced again. "I'd been counting on making a little more money before the waste hit the whizzer. Especially with winter coming on."

And utility bills going up. If Dave wasn't sharing costs with me, I'd be in the same boat.

He sighed and the hummer departed. "Guess I better dust off the old resume."

A resume with a big gap where he'd done time as a young man. "I hear they're looking for part-time help at the library."

"Thanks, but these old joints couldn't handle all that getting up and down to put books back where they belong. And I don't suppose they'd let me refuse to work in the kids' section."

We both sighed.

"Can't blame you," I said. "All those sticky fingers and high-pitched voices. I'll take high school where the voices are deeper and the fingers are more likely to be covered with greasy potato chip crumbs."

"Or orange dust from those cheesy snacks you love," Jim teased.

"Point for you." I stood. "Thanks for taking a hit for all of us with the Bernina project. I'll be on the lookout for potential jobs."

"Not as a department-store Santa." He tugged at his beard. "And no cracks about how the store that hired me to listen to rug rats' demands could save a fortune on makeup and stomach padding."

"Never crossed my mind," I lied.

To my surprise and delight, I discovered Dave had loaded the dishwasher, scrubbed the pots, and was in the process of wiping the counter. To my greater delight, he was doing that not with a soggy sponge, but with a vinegar solution and paper towels.

"My hero," I enthused without a trace of sarcasm.

"The mess wore me down." Dave raised his fists and punched air. "So, even though I have only one fully functioning arm, I assumed my secret identity as Cleaning Man. Doing battle with grease, grime, and grubbiness."

"And winning his way into the hearts of women everywhere."

"Hearts are fine." He gave the counter a final swipe. "But this job was on a par with assembling a bookcase with my toes, so I'd really like to win my way into—"

I cut him off with a kiss.

After all, this isn't an X-rated story.

"Ummppph," he grunted when we broke. "Wish I could stick around for a little more of that, but lunch hour is about up and Chuck and I have places to go, people to see, murders to solve."

"Are you making progress?"

"We have a name. Max Quiring. The vast systems that keep track of every aspect of our lives are even now being winnowed in search of more information."

He hooked his messenger bag on his shoulder and glanced at the gleaming countertop. "I wiped Lola's nose prints off the door to the deck and drew the curtain so she wouldn't make more until you saw what clean glass looks like. You know, maybe we should seriously consider hiring someone to come in and take over a few of the chores."

126

"What?" I slapped my hands over my heart and took a step back. "And abandon budgetary restraint?"

"Financial caution is overrated. Besides, I never had a budget until I met you. And somehow I made it to the end of every month."

"Without resorting to peanut butter sandwiches devoid of jelly?"

"Only occasionally," he said with a touch of pride.

"What about doing it all ourselves? What about rugged individualism?"

"We're not living in a log cabin a hundred miles from the outskirts of nowhere." He headed down the hallway. "It's tough to be a rugged individual with indoor plumbing, electricity, and a laptop."

"Good point. What about character-building lessons, and setting an example for Allison?"

"I'm all for those. In theory. And I think we're seeing some progress on the character building, but most days I'm too fried to make an all-out effort on the good example stuff."

"Same here. But if we hired someone to clean up our messes, I'm afraid we'd let things slide even more than they're sliding now. And I'm really afraid of what we'd have to pay to have Allison's bedroom and bath cleaned."

Dave paled and gripped the doorknob. "I hadn't thought of that. The cleaning person might need toxic waste gear."

We laughed in the way you do when you're trying to make light of something that makes your stomach contents curdle. Allison's personal space looked—and sometimes smelled—like something from a dystopian novel or perhaps the aftermath of an explosion at a low-rent fashion and makeup shop.

I sighed. "Honestly, this place isn't that big. If we got organized, and we all pitched in an hour a day, and if we kept on top of things, we—"

"Could have a clean condo. And by the time we did the shopping and cooking and laundry, and handled all the many crises and distractions that pop up, we'd have no energy for the things we'd rather be doing. And I'm talking about more than reading and swimming and watching TV." He nuzzled my neck. "If you get my drift."

"I get it." I stood on tiptoe and rubbed my cheek against his, feeling his stubble. "Maybe we could hire someone to clean the common area downstairs. And maybe sweep the deck."

"And vacuum the stairs," Dave said. "You hate that chore."

I did. It was a balancing act that involved securing the vacuum cleaner with one hand while pushing the wand with the other. What made it even more difficult was Cheese Puff's habit of attacking the rug attachment.

"We'd still have to do some cleaning up ourselves," I said as he opened the door. "You'd have to pick up the shoes and socks you leave by the sofa."

"And you'd have to gather up the newspaper and the dog leashes and popcorn bowl."

"And Allison would have to collect her jacket and hair clips."

It was Dave's turn to sigh. "This might be more trouble than it's worth." He kissed my forehead. "Let's talk about it later when neither of us has to rush off."

"When might that be?"

"When we're on the plane to Las Vegas?"

"It's a date." I pushed him through the doorway. "But you won't be on that plane if you don't get back to work and solve this murder."

Chapter 15

As I watched him drive off, I spotted Jim and a couple of his pals heading toward the trash bins. A light clicked on in my mind. Jim was as neat as they came. Jim needed money. Jim wasn't afraid of hard work. Jim already had a key to my condo and, as a member of the Cheese Puff Care and Comfort Committee, was in and out at least once a week checking on the dogs. Jim seemed to enjoy organizing and straightening. And, most important, Jim was already familiar with our failings and family dynamics.

While I was taste-testing a fresh bag of cheesy snacks and pondering what we could afford to pay for his services, there came a knocking at the door. Okay, to be honest, there came a hammering—the kind of hammering that usually comes right before a voice calls, "Police. Open up!"

But when the voice called out, it didn't belong to an officer of the law. No, it belonged to the woman voted least-likely to be my BFF, Bernina Burke. "I know you're in there, so don't try to pretend you're not."

I held my breath and willed myself anywhere but here. Well, almost anywhere. The Gobi Desert wasn't high on my want-to-visit list, and neither were war zones, drought-and-famine-stricken nations, and countries run by heavy-handed dictators who didn't care much for women—especially women with persistence and attitude.

Bernina hammered again. Louder. Longer.

In the interest of saving the hinges, I went to the door. Using it as a shield, I opened it a few inches and peered around the edge. My eyes beheld a spectacle I assumed was Bernina's attempt to pay homage to Thanksgiving—brown slacks, an orange serape, and huge earrings in the shape of turkeys. "Something I can do for you?"

Besides call in a wardrobe intervention team?

"I need to talk to Allison. Where is she?"

I checked my watch. "Still at school."

And, hopefully, being exposed to knowledge in her sixth period class instead of roaming the halls or hanging out in the girls' room.

"How long before she gets home?"

A question without an exact answer. Allison's ETA depended on whether she rode the bus, got a ride with Josh, or squeezed in a car with other friends. The ETAs for options two and three further depended on where they stopped along the way and for how long. Bernina's glower, however, told me she wanted a down-to-the-minute answer. So I gave her one. "An hour and 47 minutes."

Bernina raised her pudgy arm and turned it so she could study her watch. Lips moving, she added, frowned, and added again. "So, 3:17?"

I nodded, making a mental note to get in my car no later than 3:05 and take off. Returning library books or grocery shopping would be a pleasure compared to a second encounter with Bernina if Allison didn't show.

"She made a real mess of taking down the decorations and putting them in the storeroom."

I kept my face still and refrained from displaying even the least sign of what I was thinking. Of course Allison had made a mess. She was angry and in a hurry.

"There are holly leaves and spruce needles everywhere. The ribbons are creased. The light strings are in a total tangle," Bernina fumed, her turkey earrings swaying. "The displays go up again tomorrow. And everything has to be in place by midnight on Saturday."

She impaled me with her gaze, a gaze that demanded a serious response.

Dang, it's difficult to take a woman seriously when she has turkeys in her ears.

I cleared my throat. "Ah."

Bernina waited a beat, and then apparently decided that was all she'd get out of me. "She's a terrible worker. I'd like to fire her."

Like to? That sounded like a pink slip wasn't imminent. "Oh."

"But I already fired Jim and his pals."

"Hmmm. I didn't realize there's a limit on how many people you can fire in a 24-hour period."

"There isn't," she snapped.

I waited.

Bernina's glower lost power and disintegrated to a sulk. "I refuse to hire them back."

I waited again.

"I have my principles."

News to me.

"They're worse mess-ups than Allison." She clenched her fists. "I won't ask them to help, no matter how long it takes us to put up the displays."

"But, um, didn't you just say there was a deadline for having the decorations in place? Saturday at midnight. Couldn't this place be, uh, disqualified from the contest if everything isn't up on time?"

And, more importantly, couldn't our plans to secure another job for Bernina be derailed?

"Of *course* there's a deadline." Her tone implied that I needed directions in order to breathe. "Of *course* we could be disqualified. But you know what? I'm about to the point where I don't care. All I get from the organizers of this chicken-salad decorating contest is misinformation. And a long list of things we're not allowed to do."

Uh oh.

Bernina was no longer gung ho for the contest. This was bad. Very bad. Our scheme to get Shoalwater Bend to hire her depended on a decent showing in the competition. "But there are other people on your decorating team, right? Other people besides Allison?"

"Not anymore."

Meaning she'd driven them all off.

I clutched at straws. "Can you get some temporary help? Like maybe from an employment agency?"

"No budget."

"I could talk with Mrs. Ballantine." She'd already sunk enough in this project to match my salary for the next year, but in the interest of getting Bernina gone, I bet she'd lay out more.

"No time. We have to start in the morning. As soon as we have enough light."

This time of year in Reckless River the sun didn't manage to scale the horizon until close to 7:30. And if the cloud cover was as thick as usual, there wouldn't be much in the way of light until noon—if then. But that wasn't the only problem with Bernina's plan. "Allison has school in the morning."

"I'm aware of that. She said she'd skip."

132

It probably won't surprise you to know Allison hadn't bothered to share that little factoid with me. And smart money said she hadn't mentioned her plans to Dave, either. If she had, there was no way I could have missed the fallout. After he'd seen the row of Ds on her first-quarter grade report he'd decreed that the only excuses for skipping were coming down with bubonic plague or breaking a major appendage.

Being realists, neither of us expected Allison to make the honor roll. Heck, we didn't even expect to see anything higher than a C. What we did expect was a bit more effort and focus.

"I wouldn't count on her skipping school," I told Bernina. "Her father will confine her to her room if she does, and you'll find yourself decking the halls on your own."

Bernina's glower returned. "She promised."

I refrained from saying that Allison's promises were worth as much as counterfeit money. "How about asking for volunteers?"

Bernina snorted. "No one in this sorry excuse for a condo complex has ever volunteered for any of the projects I suggest."

True.

"Sure, they turned out to make bird feeders and plant that ridiculous butterfly garden. But where are they when the decks needed to be stained or the pool area pressure washed?"

The short answer was they were out of town. Or at least out of their condos and hunkered down with friends or in hotels. The longer answer was that before Bernina's reign, these tasks had been hired out to professionals and, consequently, done well. But her sparkling personality had driven off every self-respecting professional around.

I accentuated what little positive there was. "Mrs. Ballantine got behind the decorating project. She donated a lot of money."

"Hah. Only because she wanted to break condo rules and put a canopy on the deck so she'd have rehearsal space while she was under house arrest."

True.

"Tell Allison I want to see her ASAP." She narrowed her eyes. "You know what ASAP means, don't you?"

Armed squirrels aren't pushovers?

I opened my mouth to say that. Then I had second thoughts, snapped my lips shut, and nodded.

She tapped her watch. "I'll expect her no later than 3:22."

And I'll expect substitute teachers to get a gigantic raise next week. The odds against either happening were in the same astronomical range.

"Got it. 3:22."

Orange serape flapping, Bernina steamed off toward her lair. I grabbed a piece of paper from the recycling tub in the office, scrawled a note for Allison, and set it on the stairs. Then I started the dishwasher and got the mop from the pantry. Since Dave and Allison had pitched in, my strike was over. Well, over except for doing something about that box of noxious leftovers in the refrigerator. I had my limits.

I'd cleaned half the floor when there came a knocking at the sliding glass door to the deck. This knocking was far less violent but every bit as insistent as Bernina's. And, since it was at the back door, it was probably a friend or neighbor. And that almost certainly meant one of those little crises and distractions Dave mentioned earlier. Don't get me wrong, I love our friends and neighbors, but there are days when I feel that love more than others.

"Come in," I called.

"Can't," Mrs. B's muffled voice called back. "The door is locked."

Leaning the mop against the counter, I trotted to the door, yanked the curtain aside, and flicked open the lock.

Mrs. B hurried inside, her tap shoes clicking on the linoleum. Cheese Puff followed in a moment, his stubby muzzle held high, a haughty look in his beady eyes. He stalked to his favorite chair, leaped up, and burrowed between the cushion and the arm, his back to me.

Meanwhile, Mrs. B pulled out a chair at the end of the dining room table farthest from Cheese Puff's chair and sat. The expression on her face could have been used to illustrate the word "exasperated" in the dictionary.

"Your dog," she sputtered, "your dog is lazy, spoiled, entitled, and obstinate."

I failed to smother a laugh. "That's hardly a news flash. And you—"

I caught myself before I accused her of contributing to and often being amused by those very qualities.

"And I what?"

"And, uh, you should know. You've been with him every day, working on your routine."

"That's the problem." Diamond rings flashing, she pointed at Cheese Puff. "He's *not* working. Not for the past few days. He did his bit two or three times. That's all. Now he won't even do that. No matter what I say. No matter what kinds of treats I offer. He sits his little bottom down and doesn't budge."

Her voice caught and I thought she would cry, but she seemed to tap a fresh well of anger. "I threatened to find the rogue duck that attacked him and adopt it. I even brought in little Apricot, that adorable kitty from next door, and told him he was out of the act and the cat was in."

Major threats. The duck was capable of doing physical damage. But the kitten represented a different kind of danger.

From the moment they'd met, Cheese Puff recognized Apricot as a rival for Mrs. B's affection. "And?"

"And nothing. He didn't even look up when I danced with Apricot in my arms. He won't obey a single command. He won't even look at me. Every time I ask him to do something he . . . he passes gas."

"Poot." Cheese Puff punctuated her accusation with a demonstration.

"See." She waved her hand. "See what he does!"

This was no time to bring up the fact that the meaty treats she fed him created a substantial amount of that gas.

She covered her face with her hands. "What was I thinking? My performance will be a disaster. I'll be booed off the stage."

Chapter 16

"No one will boo. The performance will be awesome." I knelt by the side of her chair and patted her shoulder. "Cheese Puff adores you. And he adores an audience. I think he's just tired—and maybe bored with the repetition of practice. When the moment comes, he won't let you down."

Mrs. B swiped at tears with her knuckles, leaving smears of mascara on her cheeks. "Are you sure?"

"I'm positive." I crossed my fingers behind my back. Like many small dogs, Cheese Puff was all about himself and he had clear ideas about how things should go. If he'd made up his tiny mind that he was done with show business, then Mrs. B's performance was toast. "Let him have a few days off—from the routine *and* from the treats."

Cheese Puff raised his head and turned to stare at me, curling his upper lip in a snarl as if to say I shouldn't attempt to derail the treat train. Careful to lean so Mrs. B couldn't see me, I stuck out my tongue in response.

She pulled a tissue from the pocket of her oversized sweater and blotted her face. Then fresh tears welled. "Am I fooling myself, dear? Am I a senile old woman trying to prove she's not over the hill? Should I call Dario and tell him I simply can't do this?"

"No. No. And no." I stood and paced around the table. "You can't quit."

Eyes flashing, she wadded the tissue and threw it on the floor.

I halted and thrust my hands toward her. "Bad choice of words. No one tells you what you can't do. So let me rephrase. I think you shouldn't quit."

"And why not?" she asked in a voice so cold it would make camping on an Arctic ice floe seem like a cozy experience. The tone told me not to play the disappointment card and describe the reactions of everyone who'd been looking forward to the Las Vegas trip. Not that I'd intended to. I'd had enough manipulative guilt laid on me over the years. No way did I want to lay it on anyone else. With the exception of my sister. And maybe Allison. Or a few select others in the case of extreme emergency—emergency being a flexible term in my personal lexicon.

"You know why not," I told her, buying time to get my thoughts—a paltry few—together. "Because you never quit on anything in the past."

"I could start quitting. Right now. How hard could it be?"
Crap.

There went my best argument. I paced another lap around the table, ideas churning.

"Think of Peabody Fontaine and that fund-raising event."

"Peabody thrives on conflict. He'll have more to blog about if I don't show up." She kicked the wadded tissue. "I'll send him a check to cover what's he's out for the event plus what he might have raised."

Shot down by her knowledge of human nature and her checkbook. I paced another lap.

138

"Think of all the viewers who will be disappointed. Thanks to you, the show got a whole bunch of free publicity."

"I think most of the thanks should go to Jackie DeWill, dear."

Technically that was probably true. Glorree Morning's "secret" daughter had taken it upon herself to frame Mrs. B for murder to try to insure her mother would win. The tabloids loved the story. "But your style and class and determination more than balanced the salacious stuff."

Mrs. B smiled in a way that was part encouraging and part challenging. "What else do you have in your arsenal, dear?"

The short answer to that was "not much," but I forged on. "You can't quit because you owe this to the hungry teenager inside you. She made it to Las Vegas with almost nothing and she became a headliner and never lost her moral compass along the way."

Mrs. B said nothing, but her eyes no longer flashed.

This debt-to-the-past angle might be the ticket. Sure, there was some guilt-tripping involved, but I'd force myself to overlook it.

"Think of Dario. Think of all he went through to find you and persuade you to do the show. Think of how much he loves you and how proud he is of you. Think of how much he's looking forward to seeing you on stage again."

A tiny smile lifted Mrs. B's lips. Her affection for Dario was definitely her Achilles heel. But, unlike that Greek hero of the Trojan War, she had not one, but two soft spots. I stepped to the door, looked out, aimed my gaze toward a tiny patch of blue sky, and spoke in a trailing-away whisper. "But, of course, Marco . . ."

I heard Mrs. B shift in her chair. "What about Marco?"

I feigned discomfort and confusion and kept my eyes on that patch of blue, a patch steadily shrinking as more rain-laden clouds rolled up its western edge. "I, uh, I don't know. I guess I thought that since it would have been too dangerous for him to go back to Vegas, he wouldn't have wanted you to go. But I bet he would have been thrilled to see you in feathers and sequins and glitter again."

Mrs. B sighed and I guessed she was reliving the days when Marco sat in the front row at every show, when he sent dozens of roses to her dressing room, and when he spirited her away to midnight champagne suppers.

Clouds swallowed the patch of blue and I fired my last shot. "On the other hand, maybe Marco would have told Dario to take a hike and insisted you forget about the show. Or maybe, when Dario showed up, Marco might have packed you off for another trip around the world to stay ahead of mobsters and hitmen."

"They're all gone now," Mrs. B said in a far-away voice. "All Marco's enemies are dead and buried."

If they ever existed.

Rain spattered the glass door. "What about their grudges?" I turned to face her. "Are they buried, too?"

She flipped the fingers of her right hand as if whisking away the thought. "Yes."

"You're sure?"

She tilted her head and studied me. Was she wondering whether I knew Marco's on-the-run-from-the-mob story had been just that? Or was it possible she'd believed his tale back in the day? And possible she still believed it now?

I didn't get the answers to those questions because she stood, tugged her sweater to straighten the hem, clicked her heels together, and went to Cheese Puff's chair.

"Forgive me, my little prince," she cooed. "Barbara is right. You need a break."

140

Cheese Puff raised his scruffy orange head, blinked, and made a snuffling sound.

"Of course we're going to win," she told him. "We're going to turn in a flawless performance and get a standing ovation."

Cheese Puff grunted, wiggled from the crevice, and presented his belly for a rub. Mrs. B obliged. "You're going to be a star, the most famous dog in the country."

I held back sarcastic comments like "He already thinks he is." Grabbing the mop, I left them to their lovefest, hoping Cheese Puff was back on track, but fearing this was only a short truce in the war of wills.

As I rubbed at a sticky brown spot near the stove, I glanced at the clock. 2:13. Seemed like a mere two minutes ago I was bonding with Bernina at the front door.

That reminded me of the latest potential crisis.

I leaned the mop against the counter and unloaded on Mrs. B.

"Those decorations have to go up!" She knotted her fingers in the long hair of Cheese Puff's tail, drawing a yip of protest. "We have to at least come in second in the competition. Bernina has to look like less of a loser to the hiring committee at Shoalwater Bend."

She was preaching to the choir.

"If Bernina's so far over her head, it's time for the Committee to pitch in and get the decorating done."

I visualized members of the Cheese Puff Care and Comfort Committee—most well into their golden years and not all that steady on their feet—climbing ladders and lugging boxes. "Remember to put the ambulance service and emergency care facilities on alert."

Mrs. B winced.

"And prepare to open your wallet. Without incentive, no one will jump at the chance to work for Bernina."

She winced again. "This project is out of control. It's going to cost me more than our trip to Vegas."

For a moment I thought I'd have to fire up my powers of persuasion once more, but then she raised her chin in a way that signaled she planned to see things through. "Perhaps, I could hire a few of Allison's friends."

"Probably. But there's school tomorrow. They couldn't get started until late in the day."

"If everything was organized and ready for them . . ." she mused. "The decorating has to be completed by Saturday at midnight?"

"So Bernina says."

"Do you suppose someone will come around and check?"

I shrugged. "If Bernina is to be believed, the coordinators of the event probably have no clue that they've set a deadline, let alone that they should enforce it."

Mrs. B snorted. "Then let's assume the poop is about to smack the spinning propeller." She leaped to her feet. "Time to do some organizing. Find Jim, tell him the situation, and tell him not to disband his crew of merry men. I'll round up Verna and Sybil and have them find the others. We'll rendezvous at my place at 4:00 and confer over cocktails."

Cocktails. Of course. Where members of the Committee were concerned, there was darn little alcohol-free conferring.

"I'm so glad you brought this up, dear. It will give me something to focus on while I'm taking a break from my routine."

And, with a flurry of tapping, she was out the door.

I finished mopping, then grabbed a coat and set out for the trash bins at a foot-dragging pace. I felt as if I'd emerged from the grip of an undertow and been deposited in a heap of broken shells barely above the tideline.

Jim and his motley crew were knocking loose the final bricks and leveling the bins once more. Their raucous laughter probably had more to do with the empty beer bottles lined up on the sidewalk than with the fact that this was the last of their goad-Bernina projects.

"Good news," I said. "You've got another few days of work around the complex."

My announcement was greeted by both groans and cheers. "Working for Bernina?" Jim asked.

"Sort of."

One man kicked the trash bin. Another mimed shooting himself in the head. Two others muttered profanities almost as bad as the ones I heard in the halls at the high school.

"Define that," Jim ordered. "Tell me what you mean by 'sort of' before I have a full-blown mutiny on my hands."

To gasps of dismay, I explained that Bernina was no longer fully committed to the decorating project. "The good news is that Mrs. Ballantine is stepping up. She'll pay you and some kids from the high school to get it done."

Grumbles morphed into mumbles of approval.

"She's having an organizational meeting at her place at 4:00," I added. "With cocktails."

"And little sausages?" two men asked in unison. "In puffy pastry?"

"With that spicy sweet mustard sauce?" a third man said in the wistful voice of a child on the day before Christmas.

"I'll see to it." Jim rested a shovel on his shoulder. "She usually has the makings in her freezer. Let's put the tools away and get cleaned up. Can't be tracking mud on Muriel's carpets."

I tagged along as he led the way to the toolshed on the other end of the parking lot. "Would you be interested in a part-time job that involved some cleaning and organizing?"

"Maybe. If it didn't involve working for Bernina."

143

"How about working for me? And Dave?"

"And Allison?" He quickened his pace.

I jogged to keep up. "Well, uh, you wouldn't be working 'for' her. But, yeah, she's part of the equation."

"From what I've seen at your place, she's a big part. And it's more like a random string of numbers than an equation."

I wasn't offended. And I didn't attempt to downplay the situation. Nor did I attempt to continue with the math image. "Except on the days it's more like a shipwreck on the reef at Chaos Island."

He grinned. "You said it. Not me."

"We're slobs, I admit it."

"You're not a slob. When you lived alone, your place was neater. And cleaner."

I noticed he didn't say "neat and clean," but decided not to point that out. A percentage of a compliment was better than none at all.

Jim halted at the toolshed door, pulled a ring of keys from his pocket, and fitted one in the heavy padlock on the door. Then he patted my shoulder with his free hand. "You took on a lot with Dave and Allison. You're overwhelmed. Under water. Anyone can see that."

Could they? It wasn't like I'd gnawed my nails to the quick or torn out my hair or had a tattoo of a high-water mark on my forehead. "How? How can anyone see that?"

Jim held the shovel crosswise in front of his chest like a very narrow shield. "Well, your eyes are sometimes a little wild and bloodshot. And some days you sigh at the end of every other sentence."

Bloodshot I'd admit to. Some nights, occasionally for pleasurable reasons, I didn't log eight hours of sleep. But wild? And what was with this sighing. I'd know if I was doing that, wouldn't I?

"You may not realize you're sighing," Jim said. "And maybe 'wild' wasn't the right word. But sometimes you look like you're watching an avalanche rumbling down the mountain toward you."

I sighed, caught myself, and nodded. "Sometimes I feel like I'm running from an avalanche. I love Allison, but the drama makes me nuts. And nothing we do seems to have a lasting effect. We've tried encouragement, bribery, and loss of privileges. We've run out of ammunition. And she's winning the war."

Jim patted my shoulder again, opened the toolshed door, stowed the shovel, and stepped aside so the others could find places for their pry bars and wedges. "What would you like me to do?"

Everything!

I took a long breath to keep from blurting that. "Don't you want to know what we can afford to pay before I answer?"

"Sure. But I figure it won't be much. And I figure we can negotiate."

Not my strong suit. Based on past experience, I tended to view negotiating as a process designed to wear me down until I was exhausted enough to give in. But then, most of my negotiating had been with Allison. And Jake. Both master manipulators. Jim seemed fair and direct, but . . . "Okay. We'll negotiate."

He closed the toolshed door and snapped the padlock. As members of his crew hustled off to wash up, he gazed down at me.

I tucked my hair behind my ears, tugged my coat tighter around my chest, straightened my glasses, and gazed back, waiting.

Jim slid the ring of keys into his pocket, but said nothing.

145

I tugged my coat tighter. "Um, who goes first in the negotiating?"

"Well, I thought you would." Jim laughed. "But I'm flexible. How about we go to your place and talk while I scope out the job?"

Worked for me. For the first time in days, the downstairs area was fairly clean.

Or so I thought.

Chapter 17

When I opened the door, I left my fool's paradise behind. The discarded backpack, rumpled sweater, ballet flats, and scarf were evidence that Allison had returned from school.

Groaning out an apology, I bent to retrieve the backpack.

"Leave it," Jim ordered.

"But someone might trip over—"

"Leave it," he repeated.

"I've asked her a hundred times not—"

"I know you have."

I toed the backpack, pushing it toward the wall. "I could shove—"

"Leave it." His voice was as cold as a metal flagpole in the heart of a Montana winter.

I left it.

We proceeded to the living area where we found more signs that Typhoon Allison had passed through. A crumpled burger wrapper lay on the table beside several dribbles of catsup, pieces of a cone-shaped cardboard container littered the kitchen floor I'd just mopped, and both dogs licked at patches of grease where I suspected French fries had fallen when Cheese Puff (the logical suspect as long as Lola was stuck in a cast) nudged the container from the table. The note I'd left for Allison was on the sofa. The throb of music and the slamming of dresser drawers upstairs told me she was in residence.

Was it only two days ago she'd vowed to try to grow up and do better?

"Looks like the avalanche caught you again." Jim grasped my shoulders and steered me toward the sofa. "Why don't you sit down and let me handle this?"

Music to my ears. Music so soothing I moved the note about seeing Bernina to the coffee table and sank among the cushions as he climbed the stairs. I didn't ask *how* he intended to handle things. I'd reached a stage in my relationship with Allison where I felt there was more backsliding than progress. Nothing in the way of bribes from Mrs. B made a permanent difference. Nothing Dave and I did or said seemed to have a lasting impact. So I wouldn't be squeamish if Jim used a little intimidation or maybe tossed out a few threats more potent than anything I'd employed.

Having licked the last bit of grease and salt from the floor, Cheese Puff and Lola abandoned the kitchen. The Puffster didn't so much as glance my way while he resumed his place in the chair, but Lola nudged my knee before flopping at my feet. I stroked her silky ears while I listened to the debate raging above.

The words weren't clear, but the rumbling tones of Jim's voice made it apparent he was laying down a law of some kind. The phrases I made out from Allison's responses made it clear she was using time-honored excuses, falling back on being busy and in a hurry. She'd likely follow that with claims of being saddled with adults who set ridiculous goals, had unrealistic expectations, and didn't care how much she had to sacrifice to do a thousand picky little chores every day.

148

The tone of Jim's rebuttals was strong, firm, and without a trace of poor-baby sympathy. In a few minutes Allison halted her protests. After a brief silence, Jim spoke again. His delivery got faster, his tone warm and persuasive.

"If he's trying bribery it won't work," I told Lola. "At least not for long. Allison builds up immunity fast."

Lola grunted her agreement and tipped her head to indicate it was time to scratch the ears I'd been stroking. I complied.

My fingers were tiring when Allison hustled down the stairs with Jim at her heels. When they reached the bottom, he checked his watch. "Three. Two. One. Go."

Allison scurried along the hall collecting her possessions. She raced to her room, returned on the run, wiped the table with a damp sponge, swept the floor, and returned the broom and dustpan to the pantry.

"Five minutes and 37 seconds," Jim announced. "But I'm adding on a minute because you missed a chunk of cardboard the dogs dragged under the dining room table."

Allison dove for it and stashed it in the trash, then beamed a self-satisfied smile my way. "Jim's doing a time management study. He and I are going to find faster ways to do chores and stuff. He's going to write an article about me for a magazine."

Jim shot me a wink as if to say *writing* an article wasn't the same as *publishing* an article. "Of course, these scientific studies take time. Sometimes it's necessary to observe a subject for several months, even a year."

"Sometimes more," I said. "Or so I've heard."

"It all depends on the hypothesis," he agreed. "And whether the experiments bear it out."

"And the scope of the study?" I suggested.

"This will be a *big* study," Allison said proudly. "With a big article. And lots of pictures of me, right?"

"Well, I'll be writing for a scientific journal," Jim told her. "So there will be mostly charts and graphs."

Allison's lower lip protruded.

"But I'll make sure there's at least one picture."

The lip protruded farther.

"Two pictures," Jim amended.

"And one will be a portrait, right?" Allison framed her face with her hands. "And it will fill a whole page."

"Well," Jim said. "I'm not sure that—"

"He'll negotiate that when the article is accepted," I insisted.

Jim frowned.

"Fiction," I mouthed.

Jim nodded. "Right. I'll tell them the article must include a portrait. And several shots of you at work cleaning your room, helping Barbara in the kitchen, maybe sweeping the deck."

"Faster and faster," Allison agreed.

"*Better* and faster," Jim corrected. "Remember, we're looking for more efficient ways to do things. And to find those ways you'll have to do things the usual way first, maybe many, many times before you hit on a way to increase productivity. After we all get back from Las Vegas I'll make up a spreadsheet for chores. You'll enter your times and I'll check to see if you get seconds or minutes added for poor performance."

"I won't," Allison said in a smug voice. "I'll do so good I bet you subtract time."

That will be the day.

I concentrated on Lola's ears so my expression of disbelief wouldn't show.

Allison scooped up the note that said she should see Bernina. "The decorations don't count, do they? Because I only have to do them once, not every day. And because Bernina's a pain and keeps wasting my time making me do things over and

150

hardly doing anything herself. Somebody should do a study on her!"

Jim blanched, but before he was sucked into a conversational swamp, Allison closed the topic. "Nobody would want to do that, though, because they'd have to spend time with her." Her lower lip pushed out. "Like I do."

Silence reigned for long moment. Then I pointed to the kitchen clock. "She's expecting you in two minutes."

With a reverberating wail, Allison raced for the door. "Josh is taking me to rehearsal," she yelled. "I'll call you when I'm done."

After a wall-shaking door slam, silence reigned again.

"You're a genius," I told Jim. "How did you come up with the productivity study idea?"

"Bolt from the blue." He paced around the kitchen, opening cabinets and peering at the contents. "Almost discarded it before I remembered how starstruck Allison is and how much she wants to be famous."

I chuckled. "The thrill might be gone when she realizes a scientific magazine isn't the same as the ones she devours. But in the meantime she might develop a few good habits."

"Or at least better habits. I was amazed at how many arguments she came up with for why she had to make a mess and why she didn't have time to clean it up." He smoothed his beard. "I bet if I wrote an article on how much time some teenagers spend avoiding and explaining and excusing I could actually sell it."

"And I bet your computer couldn't make a spreadsheet big enough."

"True. And I can't afford a new one. Not even with what you'll be paying me."

My stomach flipped. I hadn't discussed this plan with Dave yet and it seemed I'd committed us to another drain on our extremely shallow resource pool. "How, uh, how much will that be?"

"Ten dollars a day." He ran a finger along the kitchen windowsill and examined it for dust. "Maybe a few bucks more. But I'll come in only on weekdays and only on the days you sub."

My stomach settled. We could handle $50 a week and a little more, especially if the results were less stress and a neater and cleaner condo.

"I'll wipe the counters and table, sweep a little, dust some, and run the vacuum over the rug and his majesty's chair." He shot Cheese Puff a look that implied he felt my entitled mutt was a long way from royalty—no matter what Mrs. Ballantine thought. Cheese Puff raised his head and lifted one side of his upper lip as if to say he thought Jim should take a long walk off a short pier while wearing ankle weights and carrying a refrigerator.

"You coming next door?" Jim hitched at his pants.

"Yes." But not with any degree of excitement.

I was opposed to the decorating project for several reasons. 1) It was Bernina's idea. 2) It was expensive—not that I'd had to pony up any of the cash, but I thought the money could have been better spent making the holidays brighter in other ways. 3) So far, what I'd seen and heard led me to believe the process of getting the display up would be as well organized as the rush to get off campus when the lunch period bell rang at Captain Meriwether High School. 4) Because of the first reason, the display was bound to tip the tasteless meter into the red zone. 5) I wasn't fully convinced a holiday display, especially one that was bound to be gaudy, garish, or gross, would do anything to help Bernina land the position at Shoalwater Bend.

Bernina, as you know, comes with a lot of baggage. She had never been one to try to win friends and influence people—at least not influence them in a positive way. I suspected there was so much accurate—and by that I mean negative—information circulating about her, that no amount of sugarcoating could alter the outcome. Even an amount of misinformation equal to that doled out by recent political campaigns wouldn't be enough to convince the Shoalwater Bend hiring committee that she was the best candidate.

But, as you well know, I've been wrong before. On a semi-regular basis.

And, since Mrs. B was like family, and since I owed her the kind of emotional debt I owed my sister—and, in Mrs. B's case, was happy to make efforts to repay—I'd be there.

And I was.

Frothy drinks, bowls of snacks, nuts, and olives, plates of tiny sandwiches, and those popular pastry-wrapped sausages with spicy mustard dulled the sharp edges of complaints about working for Bernina. Within an hour the group was in agreement—a last-gasp effort to whitewash Bernina's skills would be made, rain or shine, beginning at first light. Mrs. B agreed to take it upon herself to carry the news to Bernina.

"And bring back a drawing of her plans," Jim instructed.

"Definitely," Verna agreed. "All we've heard so far has been rumor and speculation."

"What has Allison told you?" Sybil asked me.

"Many things. All different. And conflicting."

"For example?" Verna prompted.

I ticked the reports off on my fingers. "Only white lights. Blue and white lights. Giant wreaths. Only red lights. Small wreaths. Plastic garland. Real garland. Only green lights. Huge ornaments. Not-so-huge ornaments. Inflatable cartoon characters. Inflatable religious characters." I halted and drew in a breath. "Live reindeer and a sled for them to pull up and down the street. Red and white lights. Inflatable deer on the roof of the parking canopy. Elves giving out candy to anyone who comes by to gawk. Inflatable camels. Drifts of plastic snow. Real candles. Fake candles. And plastic flamingos with red and green scarves."

I glanced around at the open-mouthed expressions and finished up. "I don't know what she decided on—except for the bits Allison put up and had to take down when Bernina finally read the contest rules and requirements."

"Bernina told me she was misinformed about the rules," Sybil said.

"If you believe that," Verna sniped, "I can get you a great deal on renting the Taj Mahal for your next birthday party."

Sybil's expression changed from hopeful to confused and then to hurt.

Mrs. B leaned across Verna and patted Sybil's hand. "Don't ever change, dear. The world needs people like you to balance the cynics."

"And fill the cynics' wallets," Verna whispered to me.

I pretended I hadn't heard. It was, as I've confided before, safer to avoid even the least appearance of taking sides when Verna and Sybil disagreed.

"Well." Mrs. B stood and dusted her hands. "I believe Jim hasn't turned in his keys to Bernina yet, so he and I will survey the contents of the storeroom this evening. We'll also make a run to a sporting goods store and pick up some wet-weather gear." She pointed to a yellow pad on the counter. "So if you'll note your clothing and shoe sizes before you leave, we'll be all set for tomorrow, and the meeting will be adjourned."

She paused for a second, her eyes twinkling as she surveyed the group and noted the rush to seize the last of the sausages. "Unless I hear a motion that we have dessert before we depart."

"I move we have dessert," Sybil crowed. "Lots of dessert."

"Second," Verna said. "Double desserts all around. Who's in favor?"

A groan of pleasure rippled through the crowd.

"Seems the groans have it and the motion is carried." Mrs. B opened a series of bakery boxes, revealing a tall chocolate cake, rows of cookies, a pecan pie, and an apple tart. The groans gave way to the clatter and scrape of forks on dessert plates.

Chapter 18

Having scrapped all intentions of sticking to a diet—or at least a diet designed to result in losing weight instead of gaining it—I was undoing the button on my jeans when Allison called for a ride home from rehearsal. Stuffing myself behind the wheel, I headed for the theater, hoping she'd still be in the positive frame of mind generated by Jim's ruse.

She wasn't.

"How could you do that?" she wailed as she tumbled into the car and slammed the door. "He'll ruin the show."

"Do what?" I pulled away from the curb. "Who will ruin the show?"

"You know who!" Allison crossed her arms and shoved her lower lip to full extension. "Jake."

"Jake?" I echoed. "As in . . . Jake? The Jake we know and loathe?"

"If there's another one like him, I want to stop the planet and get off."

"Same here. But what has he done now?"

"You know what he did." She aimed a finger at my head. "It was *your* idea. He said so."

156

A tiny bell rang in some far recess of my brain. It brought with it a vague memory of working on Jake's letter to the court and— OMG, it *was* my fault. I suggested he help out at the theater to help fulfill his community service requirements.

I started to blurt an apology, then decided to save it for a time when I'd A) done something a lot more reprehensible and B) I was truly sorry. In this case I wasn't. After all, I'd intended no malice. In fact, my intention had been to do a good deed for Jake. And for the theater.

Knowing a defense was pointless while Allison was in a full-blown snit, I said nothing for several blocks. Then, realizing the question might also result in explosions, I asked, "What did Bernina want?"

"What does Bernina always want?" Keeping her lip thrust out, she mimed tearing at her hair.

Fortunately, I'd had a lot of experience translating pout-speak. "To boss someone around?"

"Right." Allison crossed her arms again with a sigh so powerful it made the school parking permit dangling from the rearview mirror sway. "So why did you bother to ask?"

It appeared that another change of topic might also result in my conversational legs being cut out from under me, so I went on the offensive. "You didn't promise to cut school tomorrow to put up decorations, did you?"

"No," she said in a defiant voice.

"You're sure?"

"I think I'd know if I did." Defiance morphed into defensiveness. "Are you accusing me of lying?"

I tap danced around the answer to that question. If Bernina was to be believed, Allison had vowed to skip school. "Bernina sometimes makes assumptions," I said.

"She can make an ass-umption of herself all she wants. I'm not cutting school to help her. In fact, I might quit on her."

Not good. Following through was something Allison needed to do more of. It was important to honor her commitments—even those she made to people like Bernina. But bringing that up wouldn't fly right now. "Mrs. Ballantine is getting the Committee to turn out first thing in the morning to pitch in. I bet by the time you get home from school a lot of the work will be done. And if you have friends who want to come and help, Mrs. B will pay them."

"Probably not enough to have to work with Bernina."

True. But the money would help fill a gas tank or buy a few burgers.

"Josh might help. If he gets done doing interviews with Lana."

I'd forgotten he and Lana were in the final stages of hiring staff for the Reckless River Sandwich Shop.

"But he probably won't get done. He always thinks of one more question to ask." Allison emitted a sound that was half moan, half sigh, and all drama. "It won't be any fun doing the decorating without him. It will be just a job."

"Well, not every job is fun." Take mine, for example. "I thought you were counting on the money you'd make to buy outfits to wear in Las Vegas?"

"I was. But maybe I'll borrow from Mrs. Ballantine. And you."

Also not good. The last time she borrowed from my closet she ruined my favorite pair of heels and a darn nice dressy blouse. On the other hand, she'd ruined them while running from a woman who was trying to kill us, so I'd overlooked the loss—especially since Mrs. B shelled out for stunning replacements.

This was not, however, a good time to bring any of that up and create more drama-laden conflict. I tap danced once more. "Maybe you should plan to shop when we get there. I don't

158

think I have much that's Vegas-worthy. And when Mrs. B cleaned out her spare room to create her dance studio, she gave most of her dresses and shoes to the theater."

"And I still don't get why she didn't ask me if I wanted some."

Because you would have wanted them all. And there's no room in your closet now.

What I said was, "Maybe you'll get a role in a production where you'll wear something that was hers."

"And maybe Cheese Puff will sprout wings and fly. Frankie DeMille doesn't like me."

I didn't mention that Frankie had taken her on after auditions had closed, and after Allison had demonstrated her lack of singing ability. And I didn't suggest that meant she saw something in Allison. Instead I made a non-committal grunt. After that we rode in silence, me on the lookout for Iz's disreputable surveillance van so I could avoid contact with her, Allison pouting and issuing the occasional lung-emptying sigh.

"She likes the guy actors more than the women. And she really likes Jake."

Most women did. At first.

"She likes him a lot. She's all flirty when he's around. She says he has a face made for the stage."

There was no denying Jake was handsome. There was also no denying that, like beauty, handsome was only skin deep.

"She says he'll need a lot of makeup to look sorry enough to be a wino and she'll help him with it every night. And she wants him to understudy Seymour, like the wino guy who got killed was doing. Even though one of the other guys wanted to do that. And even though Jake never acted before."

While it was true that Jake had no experience on the stage, in real life he was always acting—acting like he cared about

159

anyone other than himself, acting like he was sorry for what he'd done, acting like he intended to do better next time.

"And Audrey's all 'Jake is so hot.' And if he makes a suggestion she's all 'Thank you for your insight.' And Seymour's all jealous. So no way will he pretend he's sick and take a night off like he was going to before when she would have had to kiss the wino guy who got killed. Because now Audrey might get to kiss Jake so she won't pretend to be sick too. And I'll never get a chance to go on and be the star now that I won't have to kiss the dead guy wino, either."

I didn't grasp most of that—and maybe you didn't, either—but I got enough of the gist to ask, "Audrey and Seymour—I mean, the actors who play Audrey and Seymour—are involved? With each other?" Not that I cared, but since I wasn't being snarled at or accused of something, I figured I'd contribute to the conversation.

"He wishes they were. He wishes they were *real* involved. But he'd be sorry. She acts all sweet and innocent like her character. She's even got the same name as her character, so she thinks that makes her really special. But underneath she's not like the Audrey in the play. Underneath she's a scheming bit—" Allison clapped her hands over her mouth for a second. "I didn't say it. Not all the way."

I eased over the speed bump at the entrance to the condo parking lot thinking about habits and how hard they were to break. The word Allison almost said was, unfortunately, part of her at-school vocabulary, but Dave insisted she clean up her act at home in preparation for the day she'd get a job and interact with the public. My opinion was that her attitude toward both work and authority would be a bigger issue than her language. But I hadn't shared that for several reasons—one being I was pretty sure Dave already was aware.

Speaking of Dave, I found him sprawled on the sofa sipping a beer while Lola licked his bare feet.

(For the record, there are a lot of things I don't get about dogs. For example, I don't get their interest in roadkill, cat poop, and other things that turn my stomach, including feet that have been too long inside a pair of aging running shoes.)

Allison gave him a hug and, at high speed, filled him in on her day. Dave nodded periodically, raised an eyebrow occasionally, and finished the beer. When she trotted upstairs he pointed the bottle at me. "Translation and commentary?"

"In a minute." I nuked a mug of water and plopped in a tea bag. I honestly didn't care much for tea, but this brand claimed it would calm and relax me. Dunking the bag, I filled in the details of Jim's fictitious productivity study, the status of the decorating project, Jake's role replacing the dead man in the production of *Little Shop of Horrors*, and Allison's reactions to all of the above.

"I'm surprised Jake hasn't connected with the theater before," Dave mused.

"Actually, so am I." I tossed the bag in the trash and sipped at my tea. It was a vicious yellowy orange and tasted like a freshly mowed lawn smelled—including the scent of lingering fumes from a gas-powered mower. "Except I guess he got all the attention he craved when he worked in real estate and at the gym with the steroid-selling woman who almost killed me."

"It must have been hard for him in jail with no women to admire him."

I glared at Dave over the rim of my mug. "You're not feeling sorry for Jake, are you?"

"Never." Dave raised his hands in protest. "Just wondering how a narcissistic personality copes when he's deprived of an audience. Would the mental punishment be more potent than being deprived of physical freedom?"

"Maybe you should do a study."

"A study of Jake? Not on your life. My goal is to spend less time in his vicinity, not more." Dave drained his beer, sat up, and sniffed the air. "What's that you're drinking?"

"Tea."

"It smells like a hay barn in the heat of summer."

"Well, it tastes like the aging manure caked on the floor of that barn."

"I don't want to ask how you know that." Dave squinted at the mug. "And if that's true, why are you drinking it?"

"The blurb on the box claims it will help me relax and get to sleep." I rubbed the back of my neck. "And before you ask why I need to relax, I have a long list of reasons. I've been up later than usual this week ferrying Allison, Big Chill had me working on a tedious project that tied my shoulder muscles in knots, I'm worried about what she'll stick me with tomorrow, and I'm really worried about the holiday decorating competition. This place could end up making Las Vegas look like the poster city for subtle lighting and energy conservation."

"All valid reasons for being tense." Dave stood, pried the mug from my fingers, and dumped the contents down the drain. "But I know something that will relax you way better than a mug of tea. And, coincidentally, what I have in mind will work for me, too."

With a wolfish grin, he headed for the staircase.

I lingered behind only long enough to switch off the lights and give the dogs each a rawhide chew to keep them occupied.

Chapter 19

To my surprise and delight, when I arrived at school the next morning Big Chill assigned me to help out in the room set aside for students doing catch-up work. Some of my "clients" were woefully behind on assigned reading and projects for science and history, but most were motivated and glad to have some help. Consequently, when the final bell rang, I was feeling pretty darn positive about the future of America's youth and the world in general. Even thick drops of rain pounding the parking lot didn't dampen my glow.

And then Allison popped into the car and asked, "Where can we buy barf bags?"

An off-the-wall question. Even for Allison.

"Why?"

"Because when people come to see the displays Bernina planned, they'll probably need them." She crammed her backpack in the footwell and snapped her seatbelt.

My positive glow evaporated like my childhood dreams of finding a pony standing beside the tree on Christmas morning.

"If I'm still supposed to be an elf, I could fill my basket with barf bags and hand them out instead of candy." She folded up her knees and parked her feet on the dashboard. "And if it rains really hard, I could wear them on my feet instead of those stupid shoes Bernina ordered to go with my costume. I think they're made of toilet paper."

I slipped the key in the ignition, but didn't turn it. If Allison, who firmly believed the "less is more" theory was a crock, thought Bernina's concept for the holiday display would be gag-inducing, then how would it strike me?

Allison tapped her toes on the dash, moving her feet together and apart, leaving smears of mud in twin arcs. "Are we going home or what?"

"Or what" seemed like a better choice, even if "or what" was, say, bathing feral cats without protective gear or taste-testing a dozen dishes featuring fennel, beets, and liver. "We'll go when you put your feet where they belong."

Allison groaned.

"And wipe the mud off the dash."

She groaned again, plucked a tissue from the console, and rubbed at the mud, grinding it into the pattern of tiny indentations in the faux leather. For a moment I entertained the idea of suggesting she clean it with a damp sponge when we got home, but then pictured her using the dish sponge or the loofah from my shower. I felt the beginning twinges of a headache and decided to let the mud issue slide. After all, it wasn't like my car was in pristine condition. And it wasn't like there wouldn't be more mud before summer came again.

I turned the key, checked for skateboarders zooming through the parking lot, and backed out of my space, the headache blooming behind my eyes. Would the condo roof be lit up with so many red bulbs the place appeared to be on fire? Would jostling crowds of inflatable figures pack the lawns and sidewalks like tailgating football fans? Would a cartoon dog or bird nestle in a manger? Would paramedics have been called so often to tend to ladder-related falls that they parked at the gate to save travel time?

"I don't even know when I'm supposed to dress up like the woodland elf," Allison complained. "I told Bernina I couldn't do it every night because of rehearsal and she was like we had a deal and I was like the deal was off and she was like I'd have to do it when the judges come only she doesn't know when that is and every time she asks they give her a bunch of bul— baloney. But I think she doesn't listen."

Said the pot about the kettle.

I smothered a smile.

"And the costume she got me is lame. It's like up to my chin and almost down to my knees. And the tights are really thick and baggy."

News Dave would be glad to hear.

"And it's raining like every night." Allison gestured at the windshield and the wipers trying in vain to keep the glass clear. "Really hard. And even if Bernina lets me wear a raincoat— which she won't because she says it would mess up the look and elves can run between the raindrops—the hood would make my hair look as bad as hers. And Josh thinks that's no big deal but if anyone from school sees me I'll have to drop out and change my name and take a bus to somewhere far away and get a job in a coal mine."

I tuned out and, rubbing a spot between my eyes with my fingertips, drove home at a pace slow enough to make a Galapagos tortoise so impatient he'd try to pass on a double yellow line.

A truck with a lift bucket blocked the drive and also our view of any decorating that had been done. Leaving her backpack behind, Allison leaped out and, braving the remnants of the rain shower, raced around the obstruction. That left me to wedge my car in a spot on the street.

(For the record, parallel parking is something I try to avoid. No matter how many times I remind myself how to line up my car, how far to crimp the wheel, and when to turn it in the opposite direction, I have never been able to slide into a space in one smooth and sinuous move. Maybe it's the word "parallel" that makes it so difficult. Geometry was never my thing.)

With two start-overs and a series of herky-jerky movements, I got within a foot of the curb. Close enough. The only time I'd ever seen a traffic cop on Columbia Lane he'd been dropping Dave off after a case-closing celebration. And that was back in the summer.

Lugging Allison's backpack and my briefcase, I made my way around the truck, noting that one of Jim's buddies was up in the bucket and draping a string of lights around the tall evergreen beside the condo sign. Given the distance and the gloom of the afternoon, I couldn't tell what color those lights were. Guess I'd find out when the plug met the socket.

As I rounded the front of the truck, it was apparent sparks were already flying. And they were not, despite what appeared to be miles of extension cord snaking here and there, sparks of the electrical variety.

Bernina Burke, resplendent in a puffy brown full-length hooded raincoat that made her look about as slim as the average walrus, shook a finger at Dave. Members of the Committee, all clad in yellow waterproof jumpsuits and black rubber boots, watched. "I demand you file a report," she screeched. "I demand you conduct an investigation into this robbery."

"As I explained before," Dave said in the slow and patient voice he used when he felt his audience was more than a few slices shy of a loaf, "I'm assigned to homicide now. I don't investigate theft."

166

"Robbery," Bernina screamed. "It was robbery."

"Technically it wasn't rob—"

"Technically I don't care. Technically I want the robber caught. I want him thrown in jail. And I want my decorations back. All of them."

Dave nodded and resumed speaking in that soothing voice that, when I didn't want to be soothed, makes me want to throttle him. "Well, like I already told you, you'll need to do an inventory and make a list of what was stolen."

Head down so I wouldn't meet Dave's eyes and somehow shatter his calm, I sidled around, and tucked myself in between Jim and Mrs. B. Once I set the backpack and my briefcase on the ground, she removed a rubber glove and slid her hand into mine. "Someone broke into the storeroom last night and made off with half the decorations," she whispered.

"The tacky and tasteless half?" I asked.

Her sapphire eyes widened in surprised innocence. "Amazingly, yes."

Not amazing at all if you remembered, as I did, that Jim had a key to the storeroom. Not amazing if you recalled that Mrs. B had accompanied him there yesterday evening to survey Bernina's stash of trashy decorations.

"Bernina got us started putting up the clips for the lights and then she went to lunch earlier than usual, so she just now noticed." Mrs. B's eyes twinkled. "And I'm afraid that if she can't keep better control of her inventory, I simply can't hand over another dime for this project."

The volume of Dave's voice increased a shade. "As far as I can see, there's no evidence of a break-in. The padlock wasn't cut, the hasp is intact, and the hinges aren't damaged."

"Maybe the robber picked the lock," Bernina raged. "Or snuck in my unit and stole the key."

"Key? There's only one?" Dave asked.

"Yes. On a ring with the ones for the toolshed and cabinet out by the pool. Everything was locked up tight when I went to bed last night and the keys were in my desk drawer. They were still there this morning. All of them. So if someone stole the storeroom key, they put it back after they robbed me."

Points to Dave for not attempting to define robbery or suggesting that someone made a copy of the storeroom key. Which was exactly what I suspected had happened. In fact, the person probably had the duplicate key in his possession right now.

As if he knew what I was thinking, Jim rubbed the top of his right thigh through his plastic rain suit. He rubbed with two fingers the way you might if you were checking that a key hadn't fallen out of your pocket. I refrained from yelling, "Gotcha!"

Dave's gaze followed mine and his eyes narrowed. Then he cleared his throat and deepened his voice to an "official" tone. "As I've been telling you, I'm assigned to homicide right now and I'm working a case that's getting colder by the minute. You'll need to talk with someone in property crimes. But first, as I've said, you'll want to make a list of the stolen items and determine the value."

"You're no help at all. Not that I ever thought you would be." Bernina's icy glare shifted to me. "Considering the person you consort with."

She made it sound as if consorting involved public sex, illegal drugs, virgin sacrifice, manipulation of the stock market, watering down alcoholic beverages, and stealing change from a Salvation Army kettle.

"Again, I'm sorry I couldn't help." Dave made it sound as if not being able to help was a good thing, right up there with reversing global warming.

"I'll bet you are," Bernina snarked.

168

Dave tipped an invisible hat, shot me a quick wink, and headed for his car at the pace you might set if you were fleeing a tsunami.

"I'll get the bucket truck moved so you can get out," Jim called.

I suspected he was relieved to have an excuse to get away from Bernina and perhaps to hand off the storeroom key to one of his cronies. Sooner or later she was bound to figure out he'd made a copy. To make sure that was later, a distraction was in order.

"Got a rain suit for me?" I asked Mrs. B in a loud voice. "And a pair of boots? I'm ready to get to work."

Bernina shot me a look that said I'd never done a lick of real work in my life. I squeezed Mrs. B's hand and responded with a plucky smile aimed at my nemesis.

"Oh, what's the point?" Bernina surveyed the boxes stacked beneath a tarp. "All the good stuff is gone. The inflatable camels, the manger and the gnomes that were supposed to go around it, the dancing reindeer for the roof, the Santa tanning on a beach towel, and every single string of red and yellow lights. Every one!"

Mrs. B released my hand, stepped forward, and patted the padded shoulder of Bernina's coat. "I know you're discouraged, but I also know you'll soldier on and complete the project. That's how you keep this place running so smoothly." She turned to the others. "Am I right?"

After a longish pause, she received a mumbled affirmation.

"It doesn't matter if we win or lose the competition," Mrs. B said in a cheerleading voice. "The important thing is that this condo complex participates, and that we share the spirit of the season. Right?"

"Right," the others echoed in a half-hearted way.

"So we'll do what we can with what the thief didn't take. And perhaps we'll find some residents have decorations they're willing to donate to our effort. Decorations that will mesh with what wasn't stolen."

I interpreted that to mean that Mrs. B had "just happened" to stock a supply of tasteful lawn art and lighting while she and Jim were out last night buying rain suits. Further, I imagined she'd distributed her finds among other residents.

And she had.

So, as some returned to stringing blue and white lights from the eaves, others scattered to their units and returned with large silvery snowflakes, a row of metal trees designed to hide the trash bins, garlands made from holly and hemlock, wreaths, and ornaments the size of basketballs.

I got suited up and went to work with Allison—who finally emerged from our condo once Bernina migrated toward her office. We joined the garland crew, wrapping porch supports with greenery and strings of white light. It was slow going, and when darkness fell we'd completed only about a quarter of the project.

Jim and his posse, meanwhile, finished stringing blue and white lights on the tree at the top of the driveway, festooned it with silver garland, and hung a single crystal icicle at the tip of each branch. When that was done, they hauled out huge blocks of foam. Each block had been painted to look like a gift and wrapped with metallic ribbon. When those were stashed beneath the tree, Jim held up a plug. "Shall we see how it turned out?"

No one refused his offer and in a few seconds the lights twinkled on.

"It's beautiful," Mrs. B sighed.

"Nordic," I said. "Tasteful. Understated."

"Gnomes would have been better than packages," Bernina groused.

Allison tugged on my sleeve. "Where do you think the gnomes and all the other stuff went?"

"I don't know for sure," I whispered, "but I suspect they were relocated to the holiday display section at the animal shelter thrift store."

Shortly after dawn the next day, despite wind and rain, we were back at it, taking breaks only for coffee and hot chocolate. As the morning wound down, we gathered at Mrs. B's to chomp on a selection of sandwiches and soups she'd had catered in, and to listen to the interview she'd taped with Rick Rivers.

Rick didn't work on weekends but, in addition to setting aside interviews with newsmakers, he put together a best-of program for Saturday and Sunday. Since Rick considered everything he uttered to be his best, he pretty much slapped a bunch of stuff together, providing no transitions, and paying absolutely no attention to audio levels. As his former producer, it hurt my ears to listen, so I was trying to shut it out while I waited for the clock to tick around to 11:30 and Mrs. B's moments of fame. But when Rick launched into a diatribe against non-profit organizations and the community theater in particular, I abandoned my cream cheese and veggies on rye and gathered near the radio with the others.

"A business—a real business—could use that space," the Rickster railed. "But we provide a tax break to a bunch of primping and prancing actors. And then allow them to charge ridiculous prices for tickets to performances no one wants to see."

"That's why they sell out every show," Jim told the radio.

"It's time we overhauled our tax laws," Rick continued. "No more breaks. No more breaks for anyone. I don't care who you are or what kind of good deeds or community service you *claim* you do. You pay to play and you pay your way, like everyone else."

"I bet there are for-profit businesses in this town that get more tax breaks than the theater," Verna speculated.

"And while I'm on the subject," Rick Rivers' voice rose to an insulted howl, "let's talk about some of the other so-called arts. Do we really need ballet? Does anyone give a fig about chamber music? Does anyone even know what it is? And what about pottery classes and music in schools? Talk about wasting—"

Jim twirled the volume knob to the left.

Mrs. B, white around the lips, said, "I can't believe I did an interview with that . . . that troglodyte."

"Careful," I warned. "You're insulting cave dwellers everywhere."

"All right then, I can't believe I sat in the same room and spoke with a man who has a brain the size of a sesame seed and a heart to match. Does he ever listen to himself?"

"All the time. But what he hears is filtered through what he believes and what his friends believe."

Mrs. B poured a tot of brandy in her mug of coffee, took a long swallow, and added another tot.

(For the record, I'm not certain of the exact amount of liquid in a tot, and I'm not a reliable judge of pourage amounts, but if you forced me to guess I'd say each of those tots was the equivalent of a shot. Depending on whether you define a shot as an ounce or as an ounce and a half, Mrs. B had just added two or three ounces of potent, aged, and expensive brandy to her java.)

"Reckless River is a one-radio-station town," Jim said.

"And Rick Rivers is a prime example of what you get when there's no competition," Verna added.

172

"Maybe," Sybil said as she pointed a potato chip at Mrs. B, "you should start a radio station."

Chapter 20

Mrs. B frowned and shook her head. "I don't know anything about running a radio station."

"Barbara does," Allison crowed. "She knows a lot."

"I don't know a *lot*," I clarified. "But even if I did, I'm done with radio. I'm pursuing a teaching career. Remember?"

"You might be in pursuit, but you haven't caught the career yet," Sybil observed in a voice without the least degree of snarkiness. "So you have time to help Muriel."

"Starting up a station could take years," Verna said. "And cost a fortune in licensing and programming and engineers and on-air talent."

"Rick Rivers doesn't have any talent," Allison pointed out.

"Except for annoying people," Jim said.

Sybil licked salt from the potato chip. "Maybe you could buy that station and make him shut up."

"I can't buy a radio station because I don't agree with the programming," Mrs. B said.

"Why not?" Sybil crunched the chip as she talked. "You bought a restaurant. And you practically bought the auto repair shop."

174

"The restaurant is an investment. And I *loaned* Larry the money for the shop," Mrs. B said in a clipped voice.

Sybil shrugged as if to say that was a mere technicality. "It's not a very big station. How much could it cost? How hard could it be to run it?"

We had only a few seconds to ponder that before Jim twirled the volume knob again. "Interview time."

"And now," Rick Rivers said, "we'll chat with Muriel Ballantine, the aging Reckless River woman about to compete on the nationally televised program, *Still Got That Strut*. She claims she wasn't a stripper when she performed in Las Vegas many years ago. She claims she didn't sleep her way to the top of her 'profession.' She claims—"

Mrs. B whimpered like a trapped animal.

Jim uttered a few choice words I won't repeat and clicked the radio off.

Verna fanned Mrs. B with a napkin and led her to her favorite chair.

I poured fresh coffee in a mug and added a generous tot of brandy. Mrs. B gripped the mug like a lifeline and brought it to her lips with trembling hands.

"I've a good mind to drive over there and pummel him to a pulp," Jim growled.

Three of his crew raised their fists in support. A fourth went for the knife block. Another picked up a hassock.

"Except you'd be wasting time and gasoline. He's not at the station," Verna told them. "All that was pre-recorded."

"Barbara might know where he is," Sybil suggested.

I shook my head. I didn't know. But I could speculate. Last year Rick and a few of his like-minded buddies always gobbled a huge Saturday lunch at an all-you-can-eat buffet. Lingering for hours, they'd dissect the latest local, regional, and national issues, and rehash their plans for how things would improve

175

when "their kind of people" came to power. I'd met some of Rick's buddies when they stopped by the station during my tenure as his producer. Although they were mostly pot-bellied and out of shape, they bought their clothing from the XXL section. While Jim and his pals were in good condition for their age, they weren't in the same weight class. They weren't even close. They'd have to rely on preemptive first strikes and fancy footwork.

It didn't sound like my idea of a fair fight, so I feigned ignorance and shook my head again. "The last thing I want to think about is where Rick Rivers might be. The less that man pops into my brain, the better."

"And the less he talks, the better for all of us," Sybil insisted. "That's why Muriel should buy the radio station."

Mrs. B waved a hand, dismissing the notion, but there was something about the set of her jaw and a tightening around her eyes that made me wonder if Rick Rivers' days on the air in Reckless River might be numbered. With the way media outlets had been shrinking and folding, I doubted buying the station would qualify as a sound investment. But recently I'd gotten a look at Mrs. B's finances. I knew she could afford to make such a large purchase and chalk it up to revenge instead of reason.

By dusk, all that remained was to hang wreaths and ribbon on the fence around the pool. Since Allison had tossed all that in the storeroom when Bernina realized decorating couldn't officially begin until yesterday, everything was slightly the worse for wear. While Verna and Sybil bemoaned the state of the red faux velvet ribbon, fluffed greenery, and attached hooks, Mrs. B commandeered Jim and headed out for "one more quick shopping trip to pick up a few little things."

Those few things included fresh ribbon—wider and a shimmering gold—and a small herd of mechanical deer crafted

176

from grapevine sprayed with gold paint. When Jim and his posse positioned them on the pool deck and plugged them in, it appeared they were bending to sip.

"With the fence and stuff it's like they're in a zoo," Allison exclaimed.

"The sunbathing Santa would have been better," Bernina muttered.

"Perhaps," Mrs. B said in a mild voice. "Unfortunately we weren't able to find another. Or much of anything else at this late date."

"Did you check in Portland?" Bernina asked.

"She hasn't had time to check," Verna snapped. "She's been working her fingers to the bone on your stupid dec—"

"We checked yesterday," Jim said. "Every place was sold out. The only store in the region that has one left is in Boise. Even with expedited shipping, it wouldn't be here before the decorating deadline at midnight."

"Is he lying?" Allison asked me in a whisper.

"Probably. Do you want to call him on it?"

She thought for a moment. "I guess not. A fat plastic Santa in a thong bathing suit is just wrong on so many levels."

Words to live by.

"Maybe we could leave a space for it," Bernina suggested. "We could put out a beach chair and make a sign saying Santa is coming back in a few minutes."

"How about we draw a chalk outline on the parking lot?" Allison crowed. "Like at a crime scene. An outline with a big belly. And a beard."

Sybil giggled.

Verna smiled.

Bernina scowled at them, then smiled. "The rules say we're allowed to tweak displays after midnight."

Jim coughed. "I read the rules last night, and I interpret that to mean we can replace bulbs that blow out and restring lights the wind dislodges. We can also switch out and/or move extension cords. I didn't see anything about adding a fresh element, even if there's a placeholder. And there's a specific clause that says we can't swap out displays unless they're identical."

"None of this is what I had in mind," Bernina said in a mournful voice as she paced to the end of the pool fence. "My vision was far more artistic. And we had everything we needed to carry it out. Until that thief robbed the storeroom."

We all hung our heads in a moment of silence. Bernina didn't realize it was also a moment of trying to contain our joy.

Finally, she shrugged. "I guess we did all we could with what we had."

"I can't believe she has the nerve to say 'we' did it," Allison whispered. "She just walked around and criticized."

"Some bosses are like that," I told her.

"Well, I'm not going to work for bosses like her ever again."

"Good luck with that," Verna said. "Sometimes you need the job so badly you have to suck it up and work for an idiot."

"Yes, dear," Mrs. B chimed in. "And sometimes you have to work for bosses who are far worse than merely ignorant. So take this experience as a life lesson."

"Okay." Allison pouted. "But how come life lessons always suck?"

"No pain, no gain," Jim said.

"Unless you're talking about weight gain," Sybil mused. "It never hurts me to put *on* a few pounds, but dieting is torture."

It wouldn't be if you dieted like Iz, I thought.

Then I shivered. Sometimes it seemed that simply thinking her name summoned her like a rogue genie popping out of a lava lamp.

"Shall we light it up?" Jim asked.

"Is it after 6:00?" Bernina pawed at the cuff of her coat and squinted at her watch. "We can only test separate sections before 6:00."

"I've got 6:02," Verna said.

"6:03 on my watch," one of Jim's bunch called. "I say we plug 'em in."

"Cross your fingers," Mrs. B ordered as the men headed for the sockets with Bernina on their heels barking orders.

"Why?" Verna asked. "We don't have enough here to take out the power grid. Not if it's all hooked up right."

"I did my part right," Allison insisted. "No way can you blame me if something blows up."

"I'm more worried about how it will look," Mrs. B said. "It's one thing to imagine it, and quite another to experience the reality."

The same could be said of war.

Or marriage.

"I'm closing my eyes." She gripped my arm. "Tell me when to look."

Section by section, lights blinked on until the entire complex was lit, including the metal trees set up to screen the trash bins, and the tall evergreen at the head of the drive.

"It's beautiful," Allison exclaimed.

"And nothing blew up?" Mrs. B asked.

"Not yet," I assured her.

Mrs. B opened her eyes and clasped her hands together. "Exactly as I imagined," she whispered. "All blue and silver and green and gold."

And not an inflatable gnome in sight.

Maybe we had a shot at winning this competition. And a shot at getting Bernina off our backs.

We adjourned to Mrs. B's once again for pizza and mulled wine and assorted dessert goodies. Dave, who turned up late, made do with what remained—the Hawaiian ham and pineapple pizza.

"I'm not saying there's anything wrong with the concept," he told me as he picked pieces of fruit from his slice. "I'm just saying pineapple on pizza is not my thing."

Since more than half of the giant pie was left, I guessed most of the others felt the same way. "If you'd let me know you'd be here, I would have saved some of the carnivore conglomerations."

"It's okay." He rolled up his slice. "I didn't know we were done for the day until Chuck threw his stapler and put a crack in the window."

"Do you have a pool of suspects?"

"We have an ocean of suspects. That's the problem." He took an enormous bite and mumbled around it. "Max Quiring had opinions. And not just about the theater production. He had opinions about everything." He paused to chew and swallow. "Not everyone he ran into on the streets and in the shelters wanted to hear them. But he couldn't keep his mouth shut."

I thought about Rick Rivers and his opinions. Then I recalled what he'd said about Mrs. Ballantine and how angry Jim had been. I guessed expressing unwanted opinions *could* be a motive for murder. "Any other motives?"

"Probably not money. Unless the guy is an heir to a fortune we haven't learned about left to him by a family member we haven't found. And I doubt love or jealousy were motives. Judging by what the women at the theater said about his hygiene, no one wanted to snuggle up to him."

"That doesn't mean there wasn't someone *he* wanted to get close to. Somebody who objected to that. Seriously objected."

180

"It's possible," Dave admitted. "But if there was, we haven't found her yet."

"Her?"

"Or him." He licked oozing sauce from the edge of his slice. "Unless a witness comes forward, we get a hot lead, or someone walks in and confesses, I won't be on the plane Wednesday when you leave for Las Vegas. I owe it to Chuck not to leave him holding the bag on his own."

Sunday morning at 10:00, after trying in vain to wake Dave, I plucked the list from the refrigerator door and headed out for the supermarket with the goal of buying only enough to tide us over until Wednesday morning. As I drove, I toyed with the idea of stocking a supply of frozen meals, sandwich meat, and salad in a sack for Dave in case he had to stay behind. Then I abandoned the plan. He'd accuse me of assuming he was incapable of fending for himself. The art of self-fending, at least in the past, hadn't included healthy meals. What it had included was pizza, spicy Chinese food, and even spicier Mexican dishes covered with melted cheese and sour cream and doused with hot sauce. Unless it was chopped and stuffed in a taco shell, I doubted a leaf of lettuce would pass his lips until I returned.

After finding a basket with four wheels that rolled and could be convinced to do that in the same direction at the same time, I took a gander at the grocery list. It was always a challenge to make sense of Allison's spelling (atrocious enough to make me wonder if the words were indeed in English) and Dave's handwriting (slipshod, slapdash, and spiky), but this morning I saw no reason to try to meet the challenge. Honestly, where's the lesson to be learned? When it appears that someone has written slammy, tirquee, and minoise, and I bring home salami, turkey, and mayonnaise, then I'm an enabler, right?

So I picked up baloney, the smallest turnip in the bin, and a squeeze bottle of mustard. After the turnip did its part toward making a point about handwriting and spelling, I'd chop it up for the squirrels and rabbits that hung around the trail along the river. I had no idea whether they'd eat it, but I was certain Dave and Allison wouldn't.

After I'd made my way down every aisle, my basket was still nearly empty. I'd selected a couple of frozen meals for school, and got a carton of OJ, a few bananas, a sack of salad, and a bag of walnuts. It all fit in one of the two cloth bags I'd brought. To reward myself for not overbuying and for taking a stand for penmanship and education, I decided to swing by a deli on the way home and pick up a few onion bagels. After all, there was half a package of cream cheese in the refrigerator and its use-by date was fast approaching.

My fat cells were singing and my salivary glands doing their thing when I spotted a disreputable brown van parked in the row across from mine.

Chapter 21

The sight of that van took the edge off my appetite. It also acted to slow my pace from brisk to foot-dragging.

Focusing on the pavement, I dug for my keys, hoping the see-no-evil approach would work. With any luck I could make my escape before Iz leaped from her hiding place and accosted me.

"Psssttt."

I pretended I didn't hear. No easy task considering Iz's attempt to get my attention was a lot like the sound you'd get if a balloon the size of a bathtub escaped before you could tie it off.

"Pssssttttt."

I glanced around. But not all the way around. Not in the direction of the van.

"Over here," Iz bellowed.

No way could I pretend I hadn't heard.

I turned toward the van.

A hand encased in a yellow rubber glove emerged from the driver's window. Its fingers waggled. "Over here."

For a fleeting moment I considered tossing the groceries in my car and making a break for it. But Iz was in position to block me as I backed out of my space.

Accepting my fate, I trudged to the van, pausing only to wish that sliding the unused cloth bag over my head would make me invisible. "Hey."

"I'm hungry. What did you buy?"

"Sandwich meat, frozen meals, bananas, and a turnip."

"No potato chips?"

"Not a one?"

"Tortilla chips?"

"Nope."

"Cola."

"Not a drop."

"You're lying. I can tell. Especially about the turnip."

As a long-time participant in sibling squabbles, I was tempted to deny that, but I knew Iz would only call me a liar again. So, in the interest of cutting the conversation short, I held the bag open so she could see inside.

"What's under the bananas?"

"Walnuts."

Iz made a noise reminiscent of a cow in need of milking. "You know I don't like walnuts."

Several replies leaped to my lips, chief among them being, "Who cares?" What I said was, "Oh. I forgot." All the while I was making a mental note to buy them more often. "I also forgot I was shopping for you instead of myself."

Iz ignored my sarcasm, leaned out the window, and stirred the contents of the bag. When she squeezed the bananas—apparently acting on the theory that I'd hidden something inside the peels—I jerked the bag away.

"You're right," she admitted in a pained voice. "There's nothing I want in there."

"You know, there's an enormous supermarket about 50 feet from where your cheeks are planted. Within a few minutes you could be out of that sorry excuse for a vehicle and inside. They have a huge assortment of face-stuffing food items on their shelves."

"Can't shop. I'm on a stakeout." She pointed across the lot to a service station and the plumber's van parked beside it. "Go get me something."

"Can't. I'm on a mission."

Iz narrowed eyes already like slits. "What kind of a mission?"

"A *secret* mission. Why are you wearing rubber gloves?"

"So I don't leave fingerprints."

I laughed. "In your own van?"

"All right. I'm wearing them because my hands get cold and I can't find anything else."

"Turn the heater on."

"I'm low on gas."

"Get some."

"I'm low on money."

"Hit your client for another advance."

Iz gaped as if I'd told her to walk on her hands across the river.

I felt another laugh bubbling up. "You didn't get an advance, did you?"

"I, uh, no. She said she'd pay me another hundred at the end if I waived the advance."

"And you got that in writing?"

"No. Uh, not yet."

Meaning it hadn't occurred to her. No big surprise. Iz's idea of managing money could be summarized as managing to spend all she made. "Be sure you don't give her proof of infidelity until she ponies up what she owes."

185

"I'm not sure I'll come up with any proof." My sister's face sagged into a frown. "All the guy does is unclog drains and fix leaks. If I don't get the goods on him before Wednesday morning, I'll have to drop this case."

"You could always drop out of going to Vegas," I suggested.

"You'd love that, wouldn't you? You'd love to go to without me."

You bet, I thought as I scurried to my car. I certainly would.

A trip to the deli was a now-more-than-ever deal. And, after a close encounter with Iz, I felt the need for more than a couple of bagels. So, laden with pasta salad and two slices of cake—one lemon, because everyone knows that balances the calories in chocolate—I returned home.

Jim and some of his crew were outside cleaning up discarded twist ties and bits of plastic wrapper, and hiding orange extension cords beneath green tarps and strategically placed evergreen boughs. Bernina, clad in her puffy coat and a scarf the color of boiled shrimp, alternately shouted, pointed, and wrung her hands. Neither Jim nor any of his cronies paid the least bit of attention.

As I came up the walk, Josh burst from our unit, slammed the door behind him, and leaped from the steps. He wore an expression that was one part anger, one part regret, one part confusion, and one part sheer relief.

"Won't be going to Las Vegas," he said as he trotted past. "See you around school."

Yikes.

I hoped Dave had peeled himself from between the sheets and was awake enough to deal with his daughter. But in case he hadn't, I lingered on the walk, watching Josh as he loped to the

186

visitors' lot, hurled himself into his beater of a car, and drove away, tires screeching.

Raindrops spattered my glasses.

Wind swirled around my ankles and found its way up my jeans, chilling my knees.

Jim raised an eyebrow as he passed on his way to the trash bins. "You posing for a sculptor?"

I forced a laugh, squared my shoulders, and marched to the door. The sound of whining engulfed me as soon as I opened it. I crept along the hallway, bracing for a full-bore drama queen meltdown.

"All I said was he had to wait because my hair wasn't doing what it should and I had to wash it again and start over," Allison blubbered. "And he said he was tired of waiting for me all the time and always being late and apologizing to people."

Dave emitted a high-pitched grunt. It was, I supposed, meant to convey sympathy, but it stuck me as being the sound of patience, worn thin by past events, ripping into shreds. "Well, uh, do you think it's possible that you might, um, sometimes, take longer than you, ah, said you would?"

The silence that followed Dave's timid question was so chilly I expected to see snowflakes drifting from the ceiling. To head off the explosion that was bound to follow the chill, I made my entrance, pretending I'd heard nothing.

"I'm back from the store. The list was a little confusing so I—"

Feigning surprise, I skidded to a stop by the dining room table and surveyed the scene. Allison, a wad of tissues in her hand, her face red and streaked with tears, loomed over Dave who had assumed a trapped-animal posture in the corner of the sofa. He was barefooted and wore the same jeans and T-shirt he'd had on last night. I guessed he'd been in bed when Allison's romance went up—or perhaps down—in flames.

Cheese Puff had burrowed into the crevice in his favorite chair. Lola had done all she could to hide behind the curtain screening the door to the deck.

"Something wrong?" I asked in a voice as phony as a three-dollar bill sporting a picture of Davy Crockett carrying an assault rifle and wearing flip-flops.

"No," Allison snarled. "Except my life is over and Dad doesn't care."

Dave raised his hands. "I—"

"You don't." Allison raged. "You like Josh better than me. You like *everyone* better than me."

And she was gone, taking the stairs two at a time, wailing like an air raid siren.

"How much did you hear?" Dave lofted his question into the deafening silence that followed the slam of her bedroom door.

"Only the part about having to wash her hair again." I unpacked my bags. "And the part where you tried to speak to her in a rational manner."

"Yeah." He pried himself off the sofa and got a bottle of beer from the refrigerator. "Big mistake." He glanced at the clock, then shrugged, opened the bottle, and took a long swallow. "I should have learned from the breakup in the fall."

"And the breakdown that followed," I added as I stowed groceries.

"I can't go through that again—at least not the way I did before." He cringed and slunk back to the sofa, shooting me a pleading look worthy of someone headed for the guillotine. "I can't commit to shopping trips and movies and card games. Not in the middle of a homicide investigation."

"I don't think you should have to."

He halted and raised his eyebrows. "You don't?"

188

"No. You made a Herculean effort then. And you already signaled that you didn't intend to do it again."

"I did?"

"Yes, you did. When you tried to get her to see Josh's side of it, you were telling her she needs to grow up."

"Oh."

Dave finished the beer and studied the empty bottle while I sliced and toasted a bagel. Finally he asked in a small voice, "Am I a bad father?"

"No." At least not compared to some. "What makes you ask that?"

"Because there's a part of me that's relieved Josh won't be in the same house with my daughter for a week. I mean, he's a responsible kid, but teenage hormones—"

"Are in the same power league with an atomic bomb?"

"Just about." He picked at the beer label and cast his gaze toward Allison's room. "What should I do now?"

"Leave her alone and let her think about it." I spread a thick layer of cream cheese on my bagel.

(For the record, I'm pretty sure everyone knows you don't count calories in the middle of a crisis. Even if it isn't *your* crisis.)

"Thinking isn't exactly Allison's strong suit," Dave ventured.

"I'm well aware."

He glanced at the staircase and shuffled his feet on the carpet. "Maybe I should go up there."

"No."

"You're sure?"

"Positive." I sat beside him. "Of course, she'll probably do far more stewing than thinking. She'll call her friends. She'll cry. But in abut an hour she'll come downstairs."

"An hour? You're sure?"

189

"Absolutely. Give or take ten minutes."

"How do you know?"

I pointed to the counter. "I don't see an empty juice glass or a trail of crumbs or an open jar of jelly or peanut butter."

"So?"

"So I don't have your training as an investigator, but I've spent many hours honing my powers of observation and reasoning while cleaning up after you and Allison. I can draw certain conclusions."

Dave rolled his eyes. "There's an insult in there somewhere, isn't there?"

"Can't get anything by you, can I? Anyway, it appears she didn't have breakfast before Josh came to get her. And that will make her a sucker for the aroma of peanut butter cookies baking to golden perfection."

"Peanut butter cookies have more appeal than chocolate chips?"

"Probably not, but someone wiped out the bag of chips I bought last week."

He glanced upward as if considering a lie, then met my gaze. "I admit I opened the bag. But I ate only a handful." He held out his hand and cupped it. "A little handful."

By my estimate, that would have been about half a cup.

"Except, okay, last night I had a few more. Ten. Or so. Allison must have eaten the rest. The bag was almost empty when I got to it."

"Whatever. Whether you're guilty doesn't matter if . . ."

He winced. "If what?"

"If you're willing to make a run to the store for chips while I get the other ingredients mixed."

"Done."

He dug a pair of running shoes from beneath the sofa—a place he referred to as "temporary storage." With a sickly grin he said, "I meant to put them outside to air."

"You always do," I assured him in a sweet voice.

He wedged his feet in the shoes without untying them, grabbed his jacket from the closet, and headed for the door. "I promise to do better."

"You always do," I repeated, knowing the promise was worth as much as that three-dollar bill mentioned earlier.

Chapter 22

And so it came to pass that, as I was transferring golden brown cookies from the fourth pan to a cooling rack on the dining room table, and as Dave was taste testing cookie number six, I heard footsteps on the stairs. Allison joined us, her eyes puffy, her face blotchy, and her lips pouty. Her hair, the source of the earlier dispute with Josh, had been chopped to within two inches of her scalp.

Dave's eyes widened. He opened his mouth.

I put a finger to my lips.

He swallowed and clenched his jaw.

When we decided on the silent approach, we hadn't foreseen anything as radical as a haircut bordering on mutilation. Still, we stuck to the plan of making her come to us and open a dialogue.

With an enormous sigh, she plopped in a chair and stared at the cookies. She stared so long I was about ready to scrap the plan. Then she reached for the smallest cookie and nibbled at it.

Interpreting that as evidence of a will to live—or at least not to go on a hunger strike—I got a carton of milk from the refrigerator, filled a glass, and set it within reach. Dave poured himself a cup of coffee and sat across from her, the morning

192

paper open to the crossword puzzle. He tapped the eraser end of his pencil against it. "This has me stumped. What's a four-letter word for a low mood?"

"Funk?" I suggested, taking a wild guess that "low mood" wasn't an actual clue.

"Possibly." He penciled it in. "How about a ten-letter word for grieving?"

"Hmmm." I placed dollops of dough in rows, filling the cookie sheet. "Despondent?"

"Could be." He chewed the eraser.

"Dispirited," I suggested. "Melan—"

"All the girls said I should make Josh wait and stuff." Allison spoke in a tiny voice and kept her head tucked, her body language indicating she knew she shouldn't have gone along with their suggestions. "They said he should prove he really, really cared."

I said nothing as I slid the cookie sheet into the oven, a blast of hot, moist air steaming up my glasses. Dave made a noise so soft it might have come from something the size of a hamster. He said nothing as he filled in a few squares on the puzzle.

"I shouldn't have listened to them, huh?"

Dave grunted again, this time with more force. And a faint undertone of sarcasm.

Allison raised her head. "I should be myself, right?" she asked in a wispy voice.

I scraped the last of the dough into a ball in the center of the bowl and nodded in a way I hoped demonstrated I was considering but not judging.

"I know I should. I know I should be myself." A sob caught in Allison's throat and she paused to swallow before continuing with the kind of keening wail usually reserved for funerals and the moments following the posting of election results. "But I don't know how to be myself because . . . because I don't know who I am."

Uh-oh.

The dreaded teen identity crisis.

Being, as you know, a high school substitute teacher, this was nothing I hadn't seen before. I was especially familiar with crises centering on the question "Who am I without so-and-so?" But being experienced didn't mean I wasn't trembling in my boots. Uh, make that moccasins. Getting through an identity crisis involved using insight, introspection, and honesty. These abilities weren't exactly in Allison's wheelhouse.

Dave set the puzzle aside. "Maybe you could start by making a list of who you're not."

Eeek.

I wanted to leap across the room and shove the words down his throat.

"That's easy," Allison blubbered. "I'm not Josh's girlfriend. Not anymore."

Dave turned to me with the kind of an expression a mouse might have in the second after the trap springs shut on its tail.

I pointed to the oven and hissed, "Take over."

"That's only one thing you're not," I told Allison as I plopped in Dave's chair. "You're also not a gang member or pregnant. You're not a brain surgeon or President. You're not living under a bridge or trying to make a living fishing in the Arctic Ocean."

Allison wiped her eyes on the hem of her T-shirt and skewered me with an icy gaze. "So what?"

"So you're not a whole bunch of things. Hundreds of things. Thousands of things. And neither am I."

Dave pulled a pan of cookies from the oven. "I'm not, either."

"And we don't beat ourselves up over what we're not."

At least not all the time. Usually only when I try on clothing in one of those three-mirror dressing rooms. Or when I come across the skinny jeans at the end of the rail in my closet. What was I thinking when I bought those?

"I'm no scientist, but I think we're hardwired to want more," Dave said. "And to compare ourselves to others."

"For better or for worse," I added. "There are plenty of people who don't have the advantages we do. And plenty who are smarter and richer and better looking."

"So I shouldn't do that?" Allison asked.

"Right." Dave wielded a spatula, lifting cookies from the pan and tossing them in the general direction of the cooling racks. "But it's kind of like trying not to breathe."

"You're not much help." Allison wiped her eyes once more.

"Unfortunately, that's the way it is." I scooted around the table and hugged her. "We can offer ideas, we can find a counselor if you want, we can be here to listen, but self-examination is lonely work."

"Then I better get started." Allison hugged me, hugged Dave, and scooped up the milk and a handful of cookies. "I'll be in my room."

"And I'll be at the cop shop." Dave snatched a few more cookies and kissed the nape of my neck.

"When will you be back?" I asked with a meaningful glance toward Allison's room.

"Uh, later," he responded in an evasive tone.

I nailed him with substitute-teacher glare number three, the one I reserved for kids who dropped the F-bomb. "Would you accept that answer from a suspect?"

"Uh, no."

"So?"

"I'll be back around 5:00?"

"Around?" I pinched my lips together.

195

"Close to 5:00," he amended. "Really close."

"Hmmm."

"I'll bring dinner. From your favorite Mexican place."

Music to my ears. *And* to my fat cells. "Deal."

He'd been gone only a few minutes when Verna and Sybil let themselves in through the sliding glass door. Like most members of the Committee, they hadn't called ahead or bothered to knock. On one hand, I was delighted that I had friends and neighbors who felt comfortable enough to drop by without calling first. But there were times—like now—when I felt the open-door policy needed a little tweaking and tightening.

"Cookies!" Sybil clapped her hands. Rubber boots squeaking on the linoleum, she closed on the cooling racks.

"Ask first," Verna ordered as she furled her umbrella. "You always—"

"Have some," I offered, cutting off a lecture on manners. If Verna couldn't bother to knock, I saw no reason why she should carp at Sybil to toe the etiquette line. "Have all you want. I can make coffee if you like."

Sybil picked out two cookies that had run together into one misshapen mass, broke them apart, and leaned against the counter. While her orange raincoat dripped on the linoleum, she nibbled on one and then the other as if she'd been asked to determine which tasted better.

"We can't stay long." Verna pulled off her plastic rain bonnet, selected a large, thick cookie with an abundance of chips, and took a seat at the table. "We came to see if you could settle an argument."

Uh oh.

As you know from my previous close encounters with these two, trying to settle an argument between them was as

196

thankless as it was perilous. In short, it was a task even a seasoned hostage negotiator would steer clear of. But, over the past year, I'd developed some techniques. The first line of defense, of course, was avoidance, but it was too late for that. So I'd have to skate along the edges of the argument and stay out of the middle. And while I was skating, I'd have to dodge and deflect efforts to get drawn in. Hard to do because their arguments were like swirling, sucking black holes.

"Could Penelope rewire a slot machine?" Sybil asked before I could plead an urgent appointment elsewhere or claim to have developed severe hearing loss or come down with a rare disease that affected the part of the brain that controlled decision-making. "Could she fix it so it paid off? Paid off thousands and thousands?"

"You know she could. Penelope is an electrical genius." Verna rotated her cookie, possibly searching for the best place to plant her teeth. "The question is whether she could do it without anyone noticing. There are cameras everywhere in those casinos. And guards watching video screens. And more guards walking around all the time."

"Well, what if Penelope could do it real fast?" Sybil turned her back on her friend and waved her cookies like semaphore flags. "And what if, maybe your sister and I created a diversion and distracted the guards so no one would see her?"

A kaleidoscope of images churned and crashed in my brain, images of the types of diversions Sybil and Iz might create. I conjured up diversions involving nudity, illusions, exotic animals, fist fights, fire, and feigned medical emergencies with gallons of fake blood. "Um, well—"

"I say it will never work. It's Vegas," Verna pointed out before I rained on Sybil's parade. "I bet there's not much the guys in charge of security haven't seen and aren't ready for." She turned to me. "Right?"

197

"Um, well—"

"I bet they're not ready for *everything*." Sybil took a few more nibbles.

Wondering what "everything" might encompass and telling myself not to inquire, I dumped the cookie tins in the sink and, keeping my head down, scrubbed them with enough vigor to work up a sweat. Okay, it was only a light sweat, but still . . .

"What do you think?" Verna and Sybil asked simultaneously.

Desperate to escape the vortex, I made a Hail Mary pass, tossing the ball in the direction of Mrs. Ballantine. "I think you should ask someone who knows a lot more about Las Vegas than I do." I lifted my chin and aimed it toward the condo next door. "I've never been. I only know what I've read and seen on TV. Mrs. B lived and worked there."

"A long time ago." Sybil slapped my figurative ball to the ground.

"Before video cameras and electronic security and alarms," Verna added.

I felt myself circling the drain. Then the forces of self-preservation kicked my brain into gear. "Why don't you call Dario and ask him what he thinks?"

Their silence was so intense I could hear it above the sounds made by the scrubby sponge. I waited a ten count, then glanced up from the sink. Verna's lips were pressed in a tight line. Sybil had stopped nibbling and stared at her cookies as if she suspected them of harboring some form of virulent bacteria that would necessitate stomach pumping and a month of antibiotics. "Dario doesn't take us seriously," she said after a moment.

"And between you and me," Verna said with a glance toward the door, "I often find him, well, more than a little scary."

Good to know.

I resumed my scrubbing and made a mental note to invoke his name if I found myself being drawn into another argument.

"So what do you think?" Sybil asked.

"I think Dario is the authority," I said, scrubbing up a storm to hide the quaver in my voice. "He's the one you should ask."

"But what do *you* think?" Sybil persisted.

I clattered cookie pans and pretended not to hear.

"Forget it." Verna stood and headed for the door. "Let's go find a happy hour. It's obvious Barbara isn't interested in helping us settle this."

"And we thought she was our friend." Sybil tossed the remains of her cookies in the trash.

In a moment they departed, leaving by the door to the parking lot with much squeaking of rubber boots and rustling of rain gear.

Feeling as if I'd dodged a bullet the size of a locomotive, I rinsed the cookie pans and was about to wipe the counter when the door slid open and Mrs. B poked her head in. Her silvery hair sparkled with rain drops and the shoulders of her green silk blouse were wet. "They're gone?"

"Gnashing their teeth all the way to the door. I refused to get drawn into their latest argument."

"I know. I overheard the last part. I love them both dearly, but . . ."

She bent to scratch the ears of the dog that had come to greet her—the ever-faithful Lola. Cheese Puff, meanwhile, shot her a baleful glare and, when she approached his chair, rearranged himself to offer a view of his backside.

Lola whined and gimped about to look at me with her liquid brown eyes as if to say she found his behavior reprehensible.

199

"That's rude," I told my scruffy mutt. "You're sadly in need of some discipline."

Cheese Puff snorted as if to say discipline would have no effect, but it would be amusing to watch me try. And, honestly, he had a point. By coddling and catering to him, Mrs. B and members of the Committee had created a monster.

"Now, dear," Mrs. B said. "The little prince is simply making it clear he has no intention of rehearsing today. And he's exactly right. We need to rest and rejuvenate our bodies and our minds."

Despite her upbeat tone, her shoulders slumped. She paced to the cooling racks, reached for a cookie, but then turned aside. "Mustn't do that. Must stop stress eating or I won't fit in my costumes. I gained a pound over the weekend."

I surveyed her trim waist, slim hips, and slender ankles. "And where might you be keeping that pound? Downtown in your safe deposit box?"

She flashed a simpering smile. "It's kind of you to say that, dear. But I believe it's stuck to my bottom. Thank goodness the costumes have a little stretch built in. Otherwise I could suffer enough embarrassment to last the rest of my life."

"Thirty years worth?" I asked innocently.

She rewarded me with another smile, a faded version of the first. Then she dropped into a chair at the dining room table.

"I hope you're not having another crisis of faith in yourself." I crammed cookies in a plastic bag. "And I really hope you haven't been talking with Glorree Morning again. And I really, really hope you aren't thinking about pulling out of the competition."

She paused half a minute before answering, tracing a figure eight on the table. "I talked with her this morning," she said without meeting my gaze.

"And?"

"And she says her ankle is about the same. She can put only half her weight on it."

"Hmmm." I zipped the bag closed and stuck it in the freezer. The cookies wouldn't last long enough to go stale if I put them in the cookie jar shaped like a cop car Allison had given Dave for his last birthday. But opening the freezer door was one more step I'd have to take before I pigged out. The few seconds it took to unzip the bag and nuke a cookie so I didn't break a tooth could give my brain time to overrule my stomach. Maybe. "Do you believe her?"

Mrs. B drew another figure eight, then said in a wistful tone. "I want to."

And I wanted to believe that when Allison came downstairs she'd be far closer to adulthood than she'd been a few hours ago. "But?"

She shrugged again. "But I keep thinking about the old Glorree and wondering if she's changed. I wonder if she's just talking the talk."

"And there's no way to know without X-rays and a note from her doctor."

"Yes." She glanced at Cheese Puff's orange bottom and frowned.

I got the unspoken message. "And you're worried Cheese Puff won't end his strike and your routine will be ruined."

"No. Not at all. I have complete confidence in the little prince."

Thanks to my subbing experience, I recognized that as a fib right up there with the time-honored dog-ate-my-homework excuse. I wished I could assure her that Cheese Puff would never let her down, but that would be another fib. He was stubborn. If he'd decided his dancing days were over, no amount of threats or treats would change his course.

NO SUBSTITUTE FOR MISINFORMATION

I pushed aside the image of Mrs. B going on alone, trying to improvise and make her routine seem as if she'd always intended it to be a solo act. Blinking aside tears, I conjured a vision of Cheese Puff trotting onstage with his little head held high, taking his mark, and executing each move flawlessly.

"I know he'll come through for me," Mrs. B said. "He's a performer at heart."

The first statement sounded a lot like a hopeful prayer, but the second was fact. Cheese Puff loved an audience. And when we got to Las Vegas, he'd have the biggest audience of his little life.

Chapter 23

Dave did, indeed, return around the stated time. And he carried a huge brown paper sack filled to the top with assorted Mexican treats—many more than we could consume at a single sitting.

"I got extra so we'd have leftovers to hold us until we leave for Las Vegas," he said.

"The 'we' in that sentence sounds like you're making fast progress on the case and will be on the plane."

He scuffed the toe of one running shoe on the linoleum. "We're making progress. But I wouldn't call it fast."

"Meaning you won't make an arrest before Wednesday morning?"

He shifted from foot to foot before admitting that was unlikely.

I unpacked the bag and set the contents on the counter, inhaling the mouth-watering scents of warm corn chips, hot salsa, onions, and peppers. I swallowed saliva along with my disappointment.

"If we get a break, I'll be on the first commercial flight with an empty seat," Dave said.

If.

As I folded the bag and placed it with others in the pantry, I noticed Dave was still shifting. "Let me guess—you have to go back to the cop shop."

"Yeah. Can't even stay for dinner. Got mine to go. It's in the car." He glanced over his shoulder toward the parking lot. "Sorry, but Chuck—"

I made the sign of a cross with my fingers, warding off bad memories that accompanied seeing Detective Charles Atwell or hearing his name. The sign also warded off the temptation to let those memories darken my mood and draw me into a crevasse of crabbiness. "It's okay. Go."

"It's not really okay, is it? You're lying, right?" He pulled me against his chest and kissed the top of my head.

"You think?"

His nuzzled my neck. "I'll make it up to you."

My breath caught in my throat. "Often?"

"So often you beg me to stop," he whispered.

That was worth a shot.

I kissed his chin. "Deal. Now go before I change my mind. And don't wake me up when you come home."

Dave didn't wake me during the night and my alarm didn't wake him before dawn when it beckoned me toward another day of subbing. I showered, dressed, and left him snuffling, snoring, and snoozing. When I reached the kitchen, the dogs at my heels, I found Allison making a meal of reheated nachos. "You're up early."

"*And* I did my homework." She hooked a thumb toward the backpack in the hall. "*All* of it. Even an essay that isn't due until tomorrow."

I bit back expressions of amazement or disbelief and responded without a trace of sarcasm. "Good going."

204

She stuffed a limp, cheese-laden corn chip in her mouth and mumbled around it. "And I'm never going to be late again. For anything."

I poured a glass of orange juice and put the carton back where it would screen my view of that pesky white take-out box still lurking at the rear of the refrigerator. "Good."

"Except when it's not my fault."

Ah, as I suspected, an amendment to her vow. Probably the first of many.

"Like when I really can't help it that I'm late. Like if you drive too slow on the way to school or rehearsal or someplace."

I rolled my eyes at the microwave as I nuked water for instant coffee.

"Or if Dad forgets to put my lunch money on the counter and I have to wake him up." Allison stuffed another chip in her mouth. "Like now."

"Don't wake him." I whistled to the dogs and headed for the door. "He was up late. Take money from the stash in my car."

Even over the sounds of the lock clicking, the door sliding open, and seven paws and a cast hitting the floor, there was no mistaking the intensity of Allison's silence. There was also no mistaking its meaning. She'd looted the collection of coins I kept in an old vitamin bottle in the glove box. My bet was she'd left enough coins to rattle, but not enough to cover a school lunch. "If there's something you want to tell me," I said in a neutral tone, "I'll be back in a few minutes."

More silence.

Sipping my orange juice, I shuffled across the slick deck and opened the gate for the dogs. It was as fine a morning as November brings to the Pacific Northwest, meaning the temperature was above freezing, it wasn't raining, the fog was lifting, and a pinkish blotch in the eastern sky hinted that the sun might appear. Cheese Puff and Lola descended the steps to the miniscule rose garden and left their deposits, then scrambled up the steps and across the deck.

By the time I reached the condo, they were shoving their food bowls around the perimeter of the kitchen. I served their rations of kibble, spooned instant coffee in the mug of steaming water, and dropped a slice of bread in the toaster, glancing now and then at Allison. Her right hand transferred nachos to her mouth at a rapid rate. Her left hand twisted a tuft of hair. Both signs of stress. Stress that would only be exacerbated by a stomach full of greasy cheese and chips.

I took pity on her. "Did you borrow from my stash and forget to pay it back?"

"Yes." She released the hair and dropped the chip. "I, uh, gave a kid five dollars. He was collecting for, um, some important charity."

It was possible Allison had actually donated money to a good cause. Kids were often collecting for sports teams, food drives, or families displaced by fire. It was also possible she'd socked the money in one of the many vending machines that supplemented school lunch offerings. If that was the case, the new and improved Allison needed to be called out for fibbing.

I spread peanut butter on my toast, carried it and my coffee to the table, and sat across from her. Keeping my focus on my food, I said, "If you can remember the name of the charity he was collecting for, I'll forgive the 'loan' of the money."

Allison reached for a chip, then pushed away from the table and folded her hands in her lap. "I made up the charity thing," she said, her head tucked against her chest. "I looted your stash to buy coffee before rehearsal. I'll pay it back when Bernina pays me for the decorating."

"Fair enough."

"Next time I'll ask."

"Great."

She reached for another chip, then clenched her hand into a fist. "It felt scary to tell you the truth. But it felt good, too."

"That's terrific."

"Change is hard."

"That's why lots of people don't change." I stood, folded the last bit of toast, crammed it in my mouth, and washed it down with the remaining coffee. "We better get going."

Allison smoothed crumpled aluminum foil over the bowl of nachos and stashed it in the refrigerator, then put her milk glass in the dishwasher with my coffee mug beside it. Unprecedented behavior. When Jim arrived to clean up he'd think he was in the wrong condo.

There was no crisis underway when I reached Captain Meriwether High School. Not only that, the history teacher I was subbing for had left clear instructions for his classes to continue work on a huge packet on the Civil War. Except for a few scholars who had all the control of loose cannons, most kids were on board with the assignment.

When I returned home, I discovered that Jim had gotten on board with his mission to clean and straighten. In fact, he'd gone above and beyond. The countertop gleamed, not a single fingerprint marred the surface of the microwave, the drift of dog hair was gone from beside the door to the pantry, and the carpet nap stood at attention.

Unfortunately, as I noticed when I escorted the dogs in from their duties, in the process of vacuuming, he'd moved every piece of furniture. And hadn't moved things back. Odd behavior for Jim. So odd it led me to assume he'd decided a redecorating shift was in order.

Granted, except for the dining room table, which now sat at an angle, most pieces had been relocated by only a few inches.

But those few inches would be enough to throw my friend Paulette, who had placed every stick of furniture, into a world-class tizzy.

I nudged the sofa a shade to the left, then paused, recognizing my perilous position between the rock named Paulette and the hard spot named Jim. I was damned if I moved the furniture to where it had been. And I was damned if I didn't.

Paralyzed with indecision I stood for a long moment considering my options. The list looked like this: 1) Leave things as they were and hope Paulette didn't notice. 2) Leave things as they were and tell her a minor earthquake was responsible for the shifting. 3) Leave things as they were and claim the shifting was the work of burglars or police zealously executing a search warrant on the wrong condo. 4) Move everything back and try the excuses detailed in options 2 and 3 on Jim instead of Paulette. 5) Move everything back and confess to Jim that I was less terrified of him than of Paulette. She was half his weight but had more attitude and longer and sharper fingernails. 6) Get the dogs and vital possessions out of the condo, siphon gasoline from my car, sprinkle it liberally about the premises, apply a match, and run.

Weighed against the others, option 6 looked pretty darn good.

But then I hit on option 7—leave things as they were and pretend I hadn't noticed. Weeks might pass before Paulette dropped in and saw what Jim had done. Jim, on the other hand, would come by tomorrow.

As you've surmised, option 7 merely delayed the inevitable. But delaying, postponing, and putting off were, as you've probably also surmised, pretty much the course I charted in life.

I was popping a diet cola when Allison, who had spotted Bernina Burke locking up her office and leaped from the car in order to make a plea for getting paid, charged in. She had a check in her hand, but a scowl on her face.

My first thought was that Bernina had stiffed her. In a rush, I examined mixed feelings. True, Allison hadn't exactly worked hard and had displayed the kind of attitude I don't have much tolerance for in a classroom. On the other hand, Bernina was a lousy leader who wouldn't recognize a work ethic if it bit her in her posterior. I doubted she could motivate rats to leave a sinking ship. If Allison asked me to go to bat for a bigger chunk of change, I'd be stuck between yet another rock and yet another hard place.

Allison scuffed her feet along the carpet and flopped on the sofa, making the cushions gasp. Unlike the problem presented by the relocated furniture, I couldn't pretend I didn't notice her distress. "Something wrong?"

"Why didn't anyone tell me I won't be able to play the slot machines with everybody else?"

To be honest, it hadn't occurred to me that Allison would assume there would be no rules about minors gambling in Las Vegas.

"What's the point of even going if I have to stay in some kids' area and play stupid video games? I can do that at home."

She pounded her fists on the sofa raising, to my delight, no cloud of dust and dog hair. Jim, bless his heart, must have vacuumed the cushions. Terrified as I was of Paulette's wrath, I felt my loyalty shift a few degrees toward Jim.

Cheese Puff and Lola, meanwhile, shifted their loyalty toward peace and quiet. With a lip lifted to show his disdain, the Puffster leaped from his favorite chair and raced upstairs. Lola clumped along in his wake.

"How come Dad didn't tell me? Or you? When I told Bernina I was going to get all quarters for my check and win lots of money, she said I'd been 'sadly misinformed.' How come I had to listen to her rub it in and be all superior and know-it-allish?"

Wondering if know-it-allish was an official word, and wishing Dave was around to handle the latest crisis, I took a long pull on the diet cola and waded in. "I'm sorry I didn't tell you. I assumed you already knew. I was wrong to do that because I know what they say about assumption." I sat beside her on the sofa, noting Jim had rearranged the throw pillows. "But I'm really, really sorry Bernina dumped on you."

Allison's scowl gave way to a pout and then an eye roll. "Yeah, well, I guess when you're Bernina you do anything you can to feel better about your so-called life. Even pick on a dumb kid."

"You're not a dumb kid. You weren't aware of the rules," I consoled her.

"I thought the rules didn't matter in Las Vegas. I thought I could play any of the games I wanted. Everybody says what happens there stays there."

"Well, that's the slogan."

"But it's a lie?"

"Well, not exactly a lie. Not across the board."

"What does *that* mean?" Allison asked in a voice so sharp I could have used it to grate cheese—dried out cheese the consistency of, say, concrete.

"It means the people who came up with the slogan want you to believe no one will find out you did something you, um, wouldn't have done at home. It means even though a lot of people love to gossip, they want you to think people don't gossip about what happens there."

"Right. If they're like the girls at school, they can't keep a secret for more than five minutes." Allison sighed. "I really wanted to play the slot machines with Sybil. I knew I'd win a whole bunch."

Exactly the way I felt when I approached a slot machine. That conviction was why casinos made their profits.

"I really want to play the one with all the jewels. And the one that has the ancient Egypt stuff. But I can't, because I'm not old enough."

I remembered my own powerful feelings about having to wait to grow up, feeling that my life was on hold, that I'd never be free of petty, arbitrary restrictions that had nothing to do with anything except my age.

"Maybe I can get a fake ID." Allison brightened. "Or borrow one from somebody."

Eeeekkk!!!

I stuck my fingers in my ears. "I'm going to pretend I didn't hear that. Meanwhile, you should recall the fact that your father is a police officer."

"He wouldn't arrest me." She frowned. "Would he?"

The disbelief and dismay in her voice came through my impromptu earplugs loud and clear. "I don't know if he'd go that far, but I bet he'd consider it."

Allison pounded the sofa as if it contained a hundred spiders set on breaking through the seams and biting her earlobes. "It's not fair," she screeched. "Other kids get away with stuff all the time. Other kids don't have to follow every stupid law there is."

Ah, the "other kids" defense. How often had I heard that one in the classroom?

Fingers still in my ears, I leaned back and closed my eyes. Facing potential parental wrath, Allison would abandon the phony-ID plan—a plan that, since she looked more like 14 than

16, was doomed. She'd have to abandon her dreams of parlaying her paycheck into a fortune in slot-machine winnings at a casino. She'd miss out on the spinning wheels, the lights and music. Unless . . .

I glanced toward Mrs. B's condo. Unless someone—someone with money and connections—somehow found a way around the problem. Perhaps that someone could arrange for a few slot machines to be set up in a private residence.

Chapter 24

Sometimes I think of my life as a three-ring circus. I'm the ringmaster, plunked down in the center ring without a bit of training, a shred of information about the next act, a flashy outfit, or one of those long whips I can crack. What I mean is, I'm used to feeling unprepared and as if I have no control over events. So I took it in stride when Dave swooped in to take Allison to rehearsal, gave me a long kiss, and pasted on a pleading expression.

"You look like a kid defending a ten-page Christmas wish list," I said. "What do you want?"

"We've got a lead on a guy who had an argument with the vic," he said as he loaded up a bowl with day-old Mexican food, splashed on salsa, and stuck it in the microwave. "Now all we have to do is find him. Chuck and I are hitting every shelter in town and every squat along the greenbelt this evening."

I mopped up a trail of salsa beside the microwave. "And you want me to ferry Allison home." Ferry being the operative word since the forecast called for rain, rain, and more rain.

"Please."

"I'll do it if you promise to be careful. Some of that terrain along the greenbelt is steep and rocky and full of tangled vines. And you're, well, plastered."

"Ha ha ha." Dave tapped his cast on the counter. "I'll let Chuck go first and try to fall on him."

Knowing Detective Charles Atwell as I did, I suspected *he* planned to use Dave to break *his* fall. But, in the interest of domestic tranquility, I didn't bring that up. What I did was mentally reserve the right to make I-knew-it comments in a snarky voice later on. "You think the guy you're looking for is the killer?"

"I *hope* he's the killer." Dave pulled his steaming bowl from the microwave. "And I hope we can find him. I want to be on that plane to Las Vegas Wednesday morning."

"Speaking of Vegas." I took a chair on the opposite side of the table and filled him in on Allison's meltdown.

"It's always something." He shoveled steaming rice, beans, and shredded pork in his mouth, winced, and grabbed for his water glass. "At least she pried a check out of Bernina. I was afraid one of us would have to go to the beast's lair and do battle for a few bucks."

"One of us meaning you," I said in my most severe no-nonsense voice. "I've had my quota of that woman for the year."

"There's a quota?"

"There should be. And she should be required to wear a warning label. One with a skull and crossbones."

Allison shot down the stairs, flip-flops thwapping. Never mind the date on the calendar, the need to be on the same fashion page with others her age trumped the need to be warm and dry. "I picked out all the clothes I want to take." She zipped past me to grab a cola from the refrigerator. "They're on my bed. Can you pack them so they don't get all wrinkled?"

214

A vision of Allison's room unfolded in my mind. Generally there were more clothes on the bed than in the closet or dresser drawers. How would I know which were destined for Vegas and which would stay behind?

I opened my mouth to ask, but she was already out of the kitchen and in the hallway. "Come on, Dad."

Dave brought the loaded fork to his lips and blew on it.

"Come on. If I'm late again Frankie will have a cow and give me the worst clean-up job on the list—the restrooms."

"But you won't argue." Dave winked at me. "You'll scrub that porcelain until it shines because show business is your life, right?"

"Gag me." Allison headed for the door. "Come onnnnnnn!"

Dave filled his mouth and cast a longing glance at what remained in the bowl.

"That's a mismatched bowl I use for school lunches. If it gets lost or broken it's no big deal." I got a roll of foil from a drawer. "I'll slap a cover on it and you can take it with you—as long as you let me trade you for another fork."

Dave eyed the fork. "Something wrong with this one?"

"No. There's something *right* with that one." I snatched it from his hand. "It matches the others in the drawer. It's part of a set."

"Part of a set. Got it." Dave nodded in that annoying way that told me he didn't understand what I meant, but was going along in order to end the discussion before I elaborated further and his head spun around backwards.

Honestly. Why was the concept of owning a set of stainless-steel utensils and wanting to keep that set intact so difficult for this man to comprehend?

I ripped off a sheet of aluminum foil and slapped it on the bowl.

"Daaaddddd. Come onnnnnnn," Allison screeched.

I stuck the bowl and a plastic fork in a paper bag, stuck the bag in Dave's hand, kissed his chin, and sent him on his way.

After water aerobics, I went upstairs to do some preliminary packing. Step one was to ponder the few elements of my wardrobe worthy of coming along to Las Vegas and attending the taping of *Still Got That Strut*. Thanks to Mrs. B's penchant for hitting sales and buying "a little something" for many of her friends, I had enough to get by—black slacks and heels, a few silky blouses, a couple of long sweaters, and a gray raincoat with a hood *and* all its original buttons. Step two was to sort through the clothing hanging in Dave's side of the closet.

(For the record, I use the word "hanging" loosely. Thanks to Dave's grab-and-go method of selecting his outfits and his stuff-it-anywhere approach to putting clean items away, several shirts were clinging to hangers by a single sleeve. Others were suspended from a lone button caught in the corner of a wire triangle. Many items shared hangers and a few had given up the effort to remain suspended and draped themselves over shoes in the rack on the floor of the closet. Still others lay crumpled behind the rack.)

A quick survey revealed two shirts that hadn't been washed to a limp death, one navy blue jacket less out of style than its kin, one tie without wrinkles or soup stains, and a single pair of gray slacks with only one dark smudge. I was pretty certain I could get that out with a spritz of pre-treating solution and a little scrubbing. As for shoes, well, after a search beneath the bed and behind the clothes hamper, I located one pair that a liberal application of polish and half an hour of buffing might salvage.

Shoes in hand, I sat on the bed, pondering Dave's wardrobe and whether I bore any responsibility for bringing it up to snuff and spiffing him up. Not, you understand, whether I *wanted* to make the effort to do that, but whether I *should*.

216

After all, we weren't married. Or engaged. Or engaged to be engaged. And even if we were, should I impose my preferences on his wardrobe?

Because of his personality and the nature of his work as a drug cop, Dave was a T-shirt and jeans kind of guy. I liked that. I respected that. It meshed with my own comfort-clothing choices. Dave was who he was. And I didn't want to change that. Except maybe for a few hours now and then when I wanted to dress up a little.

The problem, I decided after a few soul-searching moments, was all mine.

So I'd own it.

And I'd do my best to move past it.

What did it matter if the man by my side at Mrs. B's event was attired in an outfit that wouldn't pass muster on casual Friday in an abandoned office building on the seamy side of a run-down town? What did it matter if we were the recipients of raised-eyebrow glances and disapproving looks? What we had and what we were ran deeper than what we wore.

Did I believe that with all my heart?

Not quite.

But I had enough conviction that I stowed the shoes back where I found them. Then I concentrated on picking and packing for myself and moved on to Allison's room. Once I decided that the towering heap at the foot of the bed was destined for Vegas, the task became easier. And once I realized that every article of clothing had been tossed on the heap with no concern about wrinkling, the task became a snap.

In ten minutes I had her suitcase packed, zipped, and downstairs in the hallway.

Rain outpaced the windshield wipers and rivers ran in the gutters when I pulled up in front of the theater. Allison hurtled from the shelter of the awning, jerked open the passenger door, and threw herself inside, talking so fast and at such a high pitch that a bat might have been challenged to make sense of it. As for me, what with the wipers slapping, tires hissing, and defroster blasting, I was able to glean only a few words: "rehearsal, tomorrow, star, Dad, everyone."

Once we were out of the downtown core and on roads less traveled and more familiar, I turned the fan down a notch and switched the wipers to medium speed. "I didn't get all of that. What about tomorrow's rehearsal?"

"It's a whole run-through and Audrey has a cold. Well, she doesn't *really* have a cold. She has an audition for a play over in Portland. But Frankie DeMille doesn't know that. So, anyway, I get to be Audrey and sing all the songs and everything."

I gripped the wheel tighter. Have I mentioned that Allison's singing voice was a whole lot like the sound of fingernails on a chalkboard?

"And Frankie says I can invite you and Dad to watch. And you've got to come because it might be the only time I get to be the star."

That accounted for several of the words I'd grasped. But not all of them. "Just me and your father?"

"Well, yeah, that's what she said. But I'm gonna ask Mrs. B. And Verna and Sybil. And Jim. And some of the kids from school."

"And Frankie DeMille won't mind that many people in the audience?"

"It's not *that* many. I'm not inviting *everyone*," she explained. "I'm not gonna invite Bernina. It would be cool if Penelope came, but then . . ."

She didn't finish that sentence. She didn't have to. If she invited Penelope, good manners would call for her to invite Iz as well. And if she didn't, bad manners would result in Iz tagging along, invited or not.

I understood Allison's dilemma. There were times when my critical and overbearing sister had to be included. After all, she was family. But if it wasn't for that, I wouldn't invite Iz to much beyond a few hours of swimming in shark-infested waters while wearing a bacon bathing suit.

"Anyway," Allison went on, "you and Dad have to come."

"I'll be there," I said after a moment's hesitation spent contemplating the quality of the tones and phrasing I'd heard emanating from Allison's room. "But unless your father gets a break in the murder case tonight, he might not be able to make it."

"But he has to." Allison folded her arms across her chest. "Audrey won't miss a real performance unless she's like practically dead. This could be the only time Dad gets to see me sing. And dance."

"That's true," I said in a soothing voice with a core of steel. "And I know he won't want to miss it, but sometimes things are out of his control. If Detective Atwell says he has to work, he can't refuse, he can't even argue."

I stressed the last word, trying to make it clear she shouldn't argue, either.

Mumbling, Allison crossed her arms the other way, then spoke a clear sentence. "Detective Atwell's a jerk."

With a few exceptions, that was accurate. But, rather than defend him for the times he hadn't been 100% jerkified, I said nothing.

We reached the condo driveway and splashed along to my allotted space beneath the parking canopy.

"I won't nag or whine or anything," Allison said. "When Dad gets home I'll tell him it's really, really, really important to me."

"He's going to be out late. And he might not get home at all," I advised. "Maybe you should write a note."

She did.

When I woke up, it was on the pillow where Dave's head would have been if he'd come home. "Dad, pleeese come to rehersel tonite," it read in large black letters surrounded by bright red lip prints and hearts. "I reely want you their."

I found a second note on the dining room table, and a third taped to the refrigerator. The spelling wasn't a bit better. Nor were the errors consistent. No wonder Allison's grades in English were abysmal.

While the dogs did their thing in the rose garden, I composed a note of my own and taped it to the inside of the door to the parking lot. "Dave, it would mean a lot to Allison if you could make it to even a few minutes of tonight's rehearsal to see her in the starring role. Maybe you could work it in as a dinner break? Let me know and I'll bring something along for you to eat."

The opportunity to be a star, if only in a rehearsal, had lifted Allison's spirits. There wasn't, to my great joy, a single mention of how pitiful her life was without Josh. The conversation on the way to school was all about how fantastic she'd be tonight.

There was, however, nothing fantastic about the mood at Captain Meriwether High School.

"They had calendars in the Bronze Age," Aston Marsden groused to the grumbling group clustered outside Big Chill's office. "If they could master the concept back then, why can't the big brains at the main office figure it out in this day and age?"

I tugged on Doug Whitman's sleeve. "What happened?"

220

"Another faulty directive from on high came out late yesterday." He shifted his gaze to the ceiling. "It was loaded with misinformation about statewide math testing."

I glanced at Aston. "Including the wrong date?"

"A Sunday, no less. Apparently plucked from a three-year-old calendar. There was a lot of hair pulling and re-arranging of schedules until someone checked this year's calendar and spotted the error."

"Wow. Off by three years. That took effort."

"The Chillster's been using other words to describe the process." He grinned. "She's a scary woman. I wouldn't want her as an enemy, but I love it when she's on our side."

A receiver thwumped in a cradle.

Teachers jumped away from the door to the head secretary's office.

"Shouldn't you all be in your classrooms?" Big Chill asked in a tone that was more command than question. She slammed the phone in the cradle once more for emphasis. "Shouldn't you be earning your paychecks by preparing to pour knowledge into young minds?"

Teachers scattered, bumping against me, spinning me like a top to Big Chill's office. She glowered and pointed a forefinger at me. The shiny scarlet nail appeared sharp enough to make a surgical incision in my forehead. "And where are *you* supposed to be today?"

Chapter 25

I curtseyed. "The assignment wasn't specific, so I will proceed posthaste to the destination of your choice, your Chillness."

"Don't get smart with me or I'll put you in the gym. The boys' gym."

Noting that the sparkle in her eyes didn't match her snippy tone, I bowed until my forehead touched her desk. "It will be as you command, great one."

"Don't push it."

I straightened. "No pushing. None, supreme ruler. I would never attempt to push a woman who single-handedly took on the main office."

She smiled and polished her fingernails on the sleeve of her golden brown sweater as if to say there was nothing to it.

"Can we expect heads to roll? Changes to be made near the top of the administrative pyramid?"

"Changes, yes. But I believe the particular head I wanted will remain attached—although the body it's attached to will be relocated to a position with less responsibility and authority. Probably a position at the warehouse."

I didn't burst her satisfaction bubble by mentioning that there would be plenty of opportunities to mess up at the warehouse. Anyone who couldn't check a calendar couldn't be counted on to ship the correct number of the correct textbooks to the correct school.

I smiled and hitched the strap of my briefcase farther along my shoulder. "So, where will I be today?"

"In the cafeteria."

I blinked. These were desperate times if Big Chill was tossing me in the food-preparation mix. "The cafeteria?"

"Did you forget? Today is the annual turkey feed."

Ah.

The turkey feed, held on the final school day before Thanksgiving, was a lot like the D-Day Invasion—although on a far smaller scale and without enemy fire. To get sliced turkey and all the traditional trimming on lunch trays took a whole lot of planning, coordination, and tedious prep work. But it was worth every minute of that to provide a special lunch, especially for kids from families struggling to put even basics on the table. The meal was extravagant compared to the usual fare, and the extra cost was borne by donations from staff and the community. I liked to think that my $20 contribution went toward the tiny pumpkin pies with whipped cream that my fat cells were so fond of.

"Just so you know," I told Big Chill, "I suck at mashing potatoes—unless you like lumps."

"No mashing. You're dishing up, and helping with crowd control and cleanup."

Those were big tasks, but they wouldn't eat up the entire day. "That's all?"

"You wish." She pointed to stacks of boxes lining the wall. "All those need to go up to the Family Support Room. There are a dozen more in the copier room."

223

She fished a key from her desk drawer; it hung from a fob that looked so much like a tiny chocolate-frosted cupcake it made my mouth water. "Gertrude would like you to sort and shelve the contents if you have time. I told her you'd be delighted to help out, and you'd stay until the job was done."

Delighted might be a stretch, but of course I'd see the job through. Far too many families in Reckless River were straining to make ends meet. And with cold weather looming, they'd need more help. Everything donated to the school was doled out to families of enrolled student at no charge. And there were few questions asked besides, "What else do you need?"

I eyed the boxes. Most of them were bulging, so I doubted they were filled with sacks of marshmallows or puffed rice or rolls of toilet paper. More likely they held family-sized cans of beans and soup, or heavy blankets. By the end of the day I'd be sore from lifting and shoving. But, like the turkey feed, this would pay off with a warm feeling of accomplishment.

"A lot of kids won't leave campus for lunch like usual," Big Chill told me, "so the custodians are busy setting up tables for the overflow. They can't help truck boxes, but they'll loan you a dolly."

"One with two good wheels?" I asked, only half in jest.

"Don't demand the moon." Big Chill flipped her fingers. "Better hustle."

I saluted and went in search of the alleged dolly. And a few members of student government. Since their grades depended on volunteer activities and helping out in the school and community, and since I had a dozen mini chocolate bars in my briefcase, I felt confident I could round up some help.

But, as it turned out, help found me.

Help in the form of Josh.

He made a pretense of acting surprised to see me as I left the office area. "Hey, Ms. Reed. How are you?" He held the door and waved a piece of paper covered with numbers, letters, and graphs with curving and swooping lines. "I'm going to copy some physics stuff."

Although I suspected the "physics stuff" was bogus and he'd been lurking outside the office area in order to waylay me and talk about Allison, I played along. "I'm fine, Josh. And you?"

"Good. Um, yeah, good, fine." He bobbed his head as if to reinforce his statement, his eyes bright, his longish hair swaying. "Can I help you with anything? Make copies? Carry your briefcase?"

"No, but would you have time to commandeer a dolly from the custodians and truck some boxes from Ms. Frost's office to the Family Support Room?"

"You bet." Proving my lurking theory, he sailed the paper into a recycling bin beside the office door and took off for the head custodian's office. "Back in a flash. And I'll get a key to the elevator."

I liberated half a dozen chocolate bars, stashed my briefcase against the wall behind Big Chill's desk, and met Josh when he returned. He was pushing a dolly substantial enough to move a large refrigerator.

"Payment in advance." I offered the candy.

He waved it aside. "You don't have to bribe me."

"I know." I stuffed the chocolate in his backpack. "If you don't want it, share it with Al—" I caught myself. "Share it with all your friends."

He grimaced. "I know what you almost said."

"And I'm sorry. I guess I haven't adjusted to the . . . situation."

"Neither have I." He hung his head and scuffed his shoes on the industrial gray carpet. "I miss her. I don't miss all the drama, but I miss *her*. You know?"

I patted his shoulder. "I know. She can be a lot of fun. When she's not acting like a human version of Cheese Puff."

His lips twitched into a smile. It collapsed in a second.

"Did she cut off her hair on account of me?" he asked in a whisper.

I thought about that for a moment. "I think that when she examines her motives she'll realize she did it because she was angry at herself—angrier than she was at you."

Josh's eyes showed doubt and confusion. "Maybe if I hadn't been so impatient. Maybe . . ."

"Don't go there!" I warned. "It's over. I don't blame you. Dave doesn't blame you. And you can't go back and do it over."

"I know." He scuffed the carpet again. "But I wish . . . I really wanted to go to Las Vegas. I wanted to see all the lights and glitter. I wanted to see Cheese Puff dance with Mrs. B."

"*If* he dances. Lately he's been refusing to practice—or even go to her condo. She thinks he's tired and needs a rest, but I'm afraid it's more than that."

Josh said nothing but his worried expression mirrored my concerns. Once again I ran through a list of what might motivate Cheese Puff to abandon his strike.

Special treats? No, he got plenty of those simply for existing, and I doubted there was anything more special than the filet mignon or roasted Cornish game hen he'd been bribed with before. Besides, Mrs. B had already gone far down that road, and to no avail.

A liberal application of guilt? No, he'd displayed a remarkable immunity to guilt in the past and I doubted his resistance had weakened.

Jealousy? No, even when Mrs. B danced with the cat from next door he hadn't been moved.

Punitive measures? No, I'd never given Cheese Puff more than a light smack on his bottom to let him know his behavior

226

was putting him in danger or he'd crossed a line too far. Those smacks, which probably wouldn't be condoned by training experts, had been immediate knee-jerk responses to his actions. And he'd gotten the message. He no longer bolted out the door to the parking lot or dumped the wastebasket in the bathroom. But his refusal to dance was his own brand of passive resistance. Punishment, I suspected, would only serve to harden his position.

"We better get those boxes on the dolly." Josh interrupted my morose thoughts. "Maybe we can get the first load upstairs before the bell."

Motivational words. When the bell rang, the halls would be packed with kids shoving and shuffling, sniffling and scuffling.

We stacked four boxes on the dolly and headed for the elevator at a pace that made the wheels wobble and squeak in protest. With a minute to spare, we reached the Family Support Room. I unlocked the door, and we rolled our load inside.

"Where do you want them?"

"Against the far wall. I'll unpack when we've got them all up here."

"I can help. Second period. It's Film Studies and I already saw *Citizen Kane* twice."

"I'd love to have some help." I fixed him with the substitute teacher expression that made it clear there were rules and I intended to follow them. "But only if you bring a pass from your teacher."

"I will." He wiggled the dolly from beneath the stack. "Are you all ready to go to Vegas?"

I thought of Dave's clothing. "It depends on how you define 'ready.'"

Josh did the head bobbing thing again. "I didn't see anything in the paper about an arrest in that case Mr. Martin's working. Will he get to go?"

"Maybe. But he probably won't leave with us tomorrow. Not unless there's a break."

He straightened a box, then showed me crossed fingers. "I'm pulling for him. And for Mrs. Ballantine. And I hope everyone has a great time." His smile crumpled. "Even Allison. Really. I hope she has a lot of fun. And I hope she gets a chance to be the star of that show at the amateur theater."

I wanted to hug him.

He sniffed the way you do when you're holding back tears.

I *really* wanted to hug him.

But he was, after all, a student under my supervision.

And he was a guy. And easily embarrassed.

So I patted his shoulder. "I know she won't have as much fun in Las Vegas as she'd have if you were along with us."

"Thanks."

"As far as the play is concerned . . ."

I paused, picking at a loose edge of the tape securing the lid of a box. Should I tell him about tonight's rehearsal? Would he want to come? Would Allison want him there? Would Dave accuse me of meddling? Would the whole thing blow up in my face?

I didn't have to mull that last question long to know the answer.

But it wouldn't be the first thing that blew up in my face. And it wouldn't be the last.

I hauled in a breath and plunged in. "Allison's pretty sure the actress playing Audrey will go on every night even if she's in traction. But she has a conflict tonight, so Allison will get to play the part in a full rehearsal. It starts at 7:00. She's inviting some of the neighbors. And her friends."

I left it there. If Josh wanted to take the bait, he would.

He shoved the stack of boxes tighter against the wall. "Any chance I could sneak in for a few minutes? I'd come in after the show started. I'd sit way in the back in a dark spot. I'd keep my hood up."

He demonstrated, pulling his hoodie across his head, tugging it to cover his eyes, and tucking his chin so his face was in shadow. "I'd leave before the show was over. And if she found out I was there, I'll say I heard some of her friends talking about it in the hall."

A lie.

But a lie that could fly.

"It's your decision." I turned the dolly and aimed it toward the doorway. "Now you better get to class before the final bell."

Josh slipped ahead and turned to look at me. "Do you think she'd be mad?"

Would she be?

Would I have been?

No, I might have felt pangs of loss and remorse and a whole lot more. But I couldn't speak for Allison's feelings. I wheeled the dolly into the hallway and closed the door behind us. "I don't have an answer to that."

Josh caught up with me again downstairs, displayed passes from both his first- and second-period teachers, and helped cart the rest of the boxes. He was quiet except for uttering a few brief sentences: "You're welcome. Watch your foot. Is this the last one? See you later."

When time came to report to the cafeteria, I had half the boxes unpacked and donations lined up neatly on the shelves, separated into sections of meat, fruit, vegetables, clothing, blankets etc. My arms and back were already sore, but I had that good-deed-done glow.

The feeling got warmer when the turkey feed began— although part of that might have been because I was stationed at a steam table. My mission was to scoop mashed potatoes and gravy into the correct compartment in each tray, and pass those trays along to the stuffing scooper, a.k.a. the library clerk. Like me, she wore glasses. And, like me, she often pushed them up with a knuckle in order to see out from beneath them.

As the ache in my scooping arm intensified, the aroma of turkey and gravy reminded my stomach it was empty. In turn, it chastised my brain for not considering the needs of the digestive system and failing to send a little something down the esophagus before lunch began. As saliva pooled under my tongue, my stomach lobbied hard for me to snatch up a plastic spoon and shovel in half a pound of potatoes.

I swallowed and shook off the demand. No one else on the turkey feed serving line was snacking.

My stomach upped its game and rumbled a new demand. "Forget the spoon. Use your fingers."

"No."

"Just one finger."

"No."

"Your little finger."

"No. Definitely not."

I didn't realize I was holding up my end of the conversation out loud until I noticed the library clerk squinting at me through steam rising from her vast vat of stuffing. "Were you talking to me?"

"No. Uh, yes. I uh, um, was saying there's no end in sight yet." I stood on tiptoe and peered along the line of students coming our way. Brenda Waring, her magenta hair showing patches of traffic-cone orange, handed out trays and plastic utensils at the top of the line. Beyond her at least a hundred students shuffled our way. "Definitely no end yet."

"I think almost all the kids in school are taking part," she said. "I'm glad I had a snack before I came down, otherwise my stomach would be growling like a wolf."

I nodded, hoping she couldn't hear my grumbling gut over the clatter of utensils and conversations of students. It had given up on growling and rumbling and was making a sound like rolling thunder emanating from one of those towering clouds that build up over the Great Plains in the spring and summer. You know, the ones that spawn enormous tornadoes.

"Stop it," I ordered through clenched teeth. "You don't have the first idea what real hunger feels like."

"Excuse me," the library clerk said.

"Sorry. I was, um, reminding myself how good I have it."

"I know what you mean." She scraped the last bit of stuffing from a corner of the metal pan and stepped aside so two women in white smocks could lift the pan out and replace it with a full one. "When I was a kid my family was barely clinging to the bottom rung of the middle-class ladder. We didn't have much, but there was always food on the table. Sometimes it wasn't great, but it was filling."

I thought of those meals Iz had thrown together for me and the ones I'd provided and nuked for myself when I was old enough to drive. "Same here."

That didn't shut my stomach up, but it gave me the strength to ignore its demands and to threaten it—silently—with a cheesy-snack ban for the next several weeks. The grumbling subsided.

As soon as the last kids came through the line, however, I split a dinner roll with my fingers, scooped on mashed potatoes and a little gravy, and stuffed my mouth. What can I say? It was bliss. A second sandwich, this time with a turkey and stuffing filling, sustained me through the long hour of cleaning up. Then, thanks to powering up with a few tiny pumpkin pies that amazingly were left over, I finished unpacking boxes and organizing the Family Support Room.

231

All in all, I was feeling pretty positive when I unlocked my car.

Given my history, I should have known that wouldn't last.

Chapter 26

Allison plopped herself in the passenger seat and shifted into rant overdrive. "I hate her. I hate her. I hate her."

"Who?"

Dang it.

I hadn't intended to ask that. I'd meant to nod in a vague way and then pretend to be so occupied backing out of my parking space that I couldn't respond. Instead, with a single word, I'd launched myself into a black hole.

"Her!" Allison waved her phone in my face.

Vision impaired, I hit the brake.

"Why are you stopping?"

"Because I can't see with a phone in my face."

Allison snatched the phone away and burst into tears. "Why is everything my fault?"

Gritting my teeth, I tapped the gas pedal and eased out of the lot and into a line of cars filled with teachers and students impatient to begin the long weekend.

"I'm soorrrrrry," Allison wailed a few minutes later. "I'm just so mad about Audrey." Keeping it on her side of the car, she waved the phone again. "She texted me that she's coming to the theater after her audition and she'll give me notes on my performance when rehearsal's over."

I thought of those scraps of paper in Max Quiring's pockets. "Notes?"

"Comments. Ideas about what worked and what didn't. And how to make things better."

I stuck with the faintest of acknowledgments. "Ah."

"Like she's the greatest actress in the world. It's not like she really cares about the show. She ignored all the notes she got from everyone else, especially the dead wino guy. And he had some good ideas, too. And she was the one who was gonna call in sick if Seymour did so she wouldn't have to kiss the smelly understudy wino guy." Allison shuddered dramatically. "And now she's *hoping* Seymour has to miss a show so she can slime herself all over Jake. And I bet if *he* makes suggestions she won't go all nuclear on him."

That was a tad hard to follow, but I got the gist of it.

"And if they're both sick and *I* have to kiss Jake I'm not gonna do it." Allison made a gag-me gesture. "Ewwww. You were married to him. It's just wrong."

True. It was wrong. Whether she was talking about stage kissing Jake, or my brief marriage to the smarmy con man.

Allison went on with her rant, and I went on trying to stay as uninvolved as possible—getting me warmed up, although I didn't know it at the time, for what I'd find at home.

As I closed the door behind me, I spotted a scrawl from Dave on the bottom of the note I'd left about Allison's rehearsal. "I'll try."

I tore down the note and stuffed it in my briefcase so Allison wouldn't see it. In her present mood, a promise to try wouldn't cut it.

When I reached the end of the hall, I saw Mrs. B on the sofa, her gaze locked on Cheese Puff. He crouched in the center of his favorite chair, his unblinking eyes aimed at hers, his lower jaw thrust out to reveal his bottom teeth, a demonstration of disdain.

Neither moved as Allison and I entered the room. Neither moved as she liberated a cola from the refrigerator and popped it open. Neither moved as I stashed my briefcase in the hall closet.

Only Lola raised her head from a spot by the door to the deck. She thumped her tail once, then turned toward Cheese Puff and raised her upper lip in a silent snarl. I'm not an expert on the body language of dogs, but it appeared she was growing tired of his attitude.

"What are they doing?" Allison whispered.

"I think it's a silent battle of wills."

"How long have they been doing it?"

I studied the combatants. Her drooping shoulders indicated Mrs. B's usual perfect posture was failing. As I watched, she flexed her ankles, perhaps out of concern for the circulation in her legs and the possibility of blood clots. Cheese Puff, however, appeared as immobile as one of those marble animals that occasionally adorn public buildings. A round of pepperoni, curling a little, lay on a napkin at the edge of his chair, a chunk of cheese beside it. Bribes apparently had gotten Mrs. B nowhere, so she'd employed the force of her personality.

"I don't know," I told Allison, "but it appears they've been like this for an hour or more."

"Who's winning?"

"It looks like a tie."

But my money was on Cheese Puff wearing Mrs. B down. He always had.

"Will they be done before it's time to go to rehearsal?"

"I don't know."

"They better." Allison headed up the stairs to her room. "Because if she can't come, I'll be really, really mad."

Alert the media.

"I mean it."

Take cover.

"Everybody better be there or . . . or we won't be friends anymore."

The slamming of her door punctuated the threat.

I snagged a diet cola from the refrigerator, noting that Jim had wiped down the shelves, polished the glass, and lined the vegetable bins with paper towels. The white take-out box was still there, but he'd stuck a note on it that read, "Is this for real? What are you going to do?"

"You bet it's real," I muttered. "The decaying crud in that box is a symbol of what I'm up against. And what I'm going to do is nothing. I refuse to be the only one who checks containers and disposes of spoiled food."

I ripped off the note and tossed it in the trash. I left the box where it was.

Popping the cola, I plopped on the sofa near Mrs. B. "Don't mind me." I kicked off my shoes and rested my feet on the coffee table. "Carry on."

"I'm not sure I can for much longer." Mrs. B spoke from the side of her mouth. "My feet are numb and a muscle in my back is starting to spasm."

"I can turn the heat up. And get you a heating pad."

"I don't want to appear weak."

"But weak of mind is okay?"

"What do you mean by that?"

"That's an odd question coming from the woman who's having a staring contest with a dog." I sipped cola. "If you keep this up much longer your joints will lock up and you'll never be limber enough to perform."

236

"You're right!" Mrs. B said after a moment.

She rolled her shoulders, stood, and stomped around the dining room table, shaking her legs between steps.

Cheese Puff, meanwhile, maintained his position for a full minute by the kitchen clock, then scarfed up his goodies, turned his back, and wedged himself between the cushion and the chair arm.

Lola lifted her lip in another silent snarl and—I swear—rolled her eyes. Definitely tiring of the little prince's snit.

"I had an idea for a wonderful new move this morning." Mrs. B demonstrated, humming a tune while she dipped and turned and her shoes tapped a pattern on the kitchen linoleum.

(For the record, I was born with two left feet and no ear for music. I have all the dancing ability of a block of granite, and I don't doubt that if garden slugs had hands they could clap to the beat better than I can. In other words, don't expect me to plug in a more complete description of her movements.)

"Ta-da." She wound up and took a bow. "What do you think?"

"Impressive."

An accurate statement. To me, any athletic dance move that ended with the person still standing and uninjured was impressive.

"*I* thought so." She poured herself a small glass of orange juice. "But the little prince refused to so much as watch, let alone allow me to show him his part."

"Hence the staring contest?"

"Hence." She sighed and dropped beside me on the sofa. "I tried sweet talk and treats first, but his will power far surpasses my own."

I clinked my can against her glass. "And mine."

"Do you really think he'll come around?"

"Yes. Of course he will."

237

Her sapphire eyes, usually so sparkly, were dull. "I wish I believed that."

"You have to. At least you have to try."

"Wise words."

I heard a faint note of surprise but didn't fault her for it. After all, I was usually the one carting problems over to her place, and she was the one serving up words of wisdom along with snacks and drinks.

She finished her juice and carried the glass to the dishwasher. "The kitchen is . . . remarkably neat and clean."

Although her tone was light, I caught the hesitation in the middle of that sentence and heard the emphasis on the adverb. "We hired Jim to come in an hour or so a day and do a little policing."

"Well, he's doing a great job. In fact, he seems to be going above and beyond."

"He certainly is." I pointed to the dining room table set at a slant and the TV stand which had been shifted another few inches. "He's moving furniture. And that's setting him up for a showdown with Paulette."

"Oh my." Mrs. B pressed her hands to her cheeks. "That will be interesting."

Personally, I would have used descriptive words like explosive or incendiary.

With a final glance at my entitled little mutt, she headed for the door to the deck. "Must finish packing. See you at the theater?"

"Wouldn't miss it."

She glanced toward Allison's room. "Unless you want to pay the price." She flashed a smile and was gone.

I shuddered at the idea of what forms of torture the evening had in store for me. Then I shuddered again at the high price of skipping Allison's performance—with or without a valid excuse.

No, I'd have to endure this one evening of misery in order to avoid *many days* of misery.

With a sigh, I toddled off to gather the dogs' vaccination papers, leashes, food, toys, treats, and brushes. When they were stowed in a bag beside our suitcases, I sent a text to Dave asking if he thought he'd make it.

No reply.

I went through the heap of mail in the office and found a utility bill teetering on the rim of past-due canyon. To my great delight, I also discovered my stamps. Granted, half of one was stuck to the slick paper it came on and half to a ruler someone had wedged in the drawer, but with a little careful peeling and a spot of glue, I made it work. Then I sent Dave another text.

No reply.

Hoping he was too busy arresting a suspect to get back to me, I climbed the stairs and prowled through his wardrobe again. Nothing newer, cleaner, or less wrinkled had magically appeared. I wrestled again with the idea of packing for him, won the match, and took a nap instead.

The sound of Allison warming up woke me. I folded the pillow around my head, but it was no good. Her voice leaked through, assaulting my eardrums with the force of an ice pick. Imagine a male cat in a narrow alley crying out that he was in the mood for love. Imagine his rusty yowl echoing off the sides of buildings. Imagine you're chained to a drainpipe and can't escape from the alley.

And this was only the warm-up.

I splashed cold water on my face, changed to a clean T-shirt and a warm sweater, and shot downstairs where I turned on the TV. It was set to a sports-talk channel. No matter. All I needed was some noise to cover Allison's yowling.

I zipped to the kitchen, flipped on the small radio at the back of the counter and got a twang of Country Music. Jim's selection, obviously. What the heck, I was using it only to block the sound from upstairs. I increased the volume and warmed up a chicken burrito while I checked my phone.

Nothing from Dave.

Sticking to my no-news-is-good-news optimism, I made him a baloney sandwich with cheese and pickles and stuck it in a bag with a can of cola and the last two cookies in the freezer.

Allison thundered down the stairs almost a full hour before rehearsal was set to begin. "I'm ready."

Her spiky hair sparkled with glitter. She wore a pair of dangly earrings I'd searched for in vain a few weeks ago and the little black dress she'd borrowed from Mrs. B in the spring. The dress seemed shorter—a whole lot shorter. Squinting, I detected a line of amateur stitching along the uneven hem. Fishnet pantyhose and gold high-heeled sandals completed her outfit. "How do I look?"

Where to begin?

I went with nonchalant blandness. "Stylish."

Allison twirled. The skirt lifted to reveal, beneath the fishnet stockings, a pair of red thong panties.

No. No. No. No. No.

Not unless she wanted her father to have a stroke.

But expressing *my* concerns about *his* concerns would launch a storm of outrage of the I'm-not-a-baby variety. Fortunately, I came up with an on-the-spot cunning plan.

"It seems to me that Audrey would wear a sweater."

Allison frowned.

I rushed on. "Not a big sweater. One of those short tight ones. A bolero style. Mrs. B has several."

The frown gave way to a look of skeptical consideration.

240

I pretended I didn't have a dog in this fight. Then, speaking of dogs, I called for Cheese Puff and Lola. Telling them to ignore the steady rain, I ordered them to go out and do their thing.

Allison followed us and traipsed over to Mrs. B's condo. She returned as I was ushering the dogs inside, a fuzzy black sweater with gold trim on her shoulders, another frown on her face. "I'm going to change," she snarled. "I'll be down in five minutes. Five. Minutes."

Meaning "Be ready, or else."

I didn't respond. As soon as I heard the door to her room slam, I nipped to the deck. Mrs. B was waiting. "The thong is history?" I asked.

"Yes. And I hope history that will never repeat itself."

We exchanged a high five. "How did you do it?"

"Head-on assault. It appeared we had no time for subtlety so I simply told her the panties were trashy, tawdry, and a tragic bid for attention that I wanted to believe was beneath her. Then I said it was, of course, up to her whether she changed or not, but I would be sorely disappointed to learn she had so little faith in her acting ability that she felt she had to draw attention away from it with her wardrobe." She sniffed. "Or lack of a wardrobe."

"I'm glad you're on my team." I gave her a quick hug, darted inside, locked up, grabbed the sack for Dave, and shrugged on a hooded raincoat. I was waiting at the door to the parking lot when Allison came down.

"These make me look fat." She flipped up the front of the skirt to show me a pair of skimpy black satin running shorts. "Really fat."

I didn't bother to respond. No, I held the door and followed her through the downpour to my car. But, showing I can be a sympathetic and kind person, I let her off in front of the theater and cruised the area in widening circles until I found a parking space a mere three blocks away. It wasn't in the middle of a puddle, it was large enough for me to slide my car in easily, and it was beside a business with a long awning I could duck beneath.

The only problem with the spot was its proximity to a van. A baby-poop brown van.

Chapter 27

Crud!

As I contemplated another tour of the area in order to avoid the van *and* my sister, the driver behind me tapped his horn. I glanced in the rearview mirror and saw him pointing at the spot.

Nothing makes an item as attractive as knowing someone else covets it. And a downburst helped my decision-making process along. I rolled down the window and waved him around. Sure, I'd risk a close encounter with Iz by taking this spot, but I'd cut a block or more from my trek to the theater.

I shuttled into the spot, waited for the shower to let up, raised my hood, stuffed Dave's goodie bag in my purse, and leaped out. To my delight, Iz didn't open her door and flag me down as I scurried past the van in the hunched-over position many of us in the Northwest—especially those of us who wear glasses—assume when it rains. I didn't see her as I trotted past a coffee shop, and she didn't pop out of the deep doorway of a wine bar. Feeling a sweet shot of joyful relief even more potent than learning I'd get a tax return, I charged along the last block. But as I passed a bus shelter, I crashed into the obstacle known as my sister.

As obstacles go, she wasn't of the worst variety—meaning she wasn't made of stone, electrified, or wrapped in barbed wire. In fact she was soft and spongy. She gave a little as we collided.

"Don't you ever watch where you're going?" she said by way of greeting me.

I abandoned any attempt at explanation or excuse. "Apparently not."

"I saw you drop Allison off for rehearsal. I yelled at her, but she didn't hear me."

Hah.

I bet Allison heard Iz's bellow loud and clear. And I bet she picked up the pace while making those intricate evil-begone finger moves.

Iz grabbed my sleeve and towed me into the bus shelter. Since one long side was open and the wind was coming from that direction, it didn't offer much to earn the right to be called a shelter. "Are you going to the theater?"

No point in lying. She'd follow. "Yes."

"Take me with you."

Not for a second did I think Iz had an interest in how the production of *Little Shop of Horrors* was coming together. "Why?"

"The plumber's in there fixing a toilet. And I'm sick of standing in the rain. My feet are freezing."

I glanced down and saw she was wearing a pair of pink slide slippers with low heels and striped faux fur across the arches. The fact that Iz's heels hung far over the backs told me the slippers belonged to Penelope.

"I came out in a hurry," she confessed. "Thought my boots were in the van."

Before you accuse me of feeling sorry for my sister, let me make it clear that any sorrow I felt was for the slippers and their owner. They didn't look comfortable. But they were definitely what I'd call "cute." And in my experience with footwear, that probably meant Penelope had paid more for them than I'd ever dream of forking out. Granted, she loved my sister. But, even if she could easily afford to replace them, would that love stand up to the test of having her slippers rained on, stretched out, and ruined?

"All right. Come on." I darted into a narrow space between the theater and the building beside it and hustled along to the alley. There, we squeezed past the plumber's van and climbed three steps to the stage door. It was locked, but Allison had sworn if I tapped out the opening bars to "Smoke on the Water" she'd hear and open the door.

She did.

And immediately tried to close the door on Iz.

"Frankie's all in a snit," she whispered. "She says I asked too many people."

"Then one more won't make a difference." Iz shouldered through the doorway and into a long and narrow space behind a canvas and wood scenery flat.

"It will matter if it's you," Allison shot back, her voice rising.

"Well, I'm not here to watch your play."

"It's a musical."

A muffled conversation on the other side of the flat came to a halt. Allison put her finger to her lips. "Sssshhhhh."

"Ask me if I care whether it's a play or a musical or a puppet show," Iz growled. "Which way to the restroom?"

"Which one?"

Iz scowled. "The one they called a plumber for."

Allison pointed along a skimpy passageway between more canvas flats, stacks of chairs and tables, a piano, a refrigerator, and a phone booth. "Go through there and down the stairs. It's the restroom by the dressing room."

I plucked at the sleeve of her dripping coat as my sister started that way. "Won't he see you if you get too close?"

"So? He hasn't spotted me following him so far. And if he sees me down there he'll think I'm an actress."

Allison whooped out a laugh and covered her mouth again.

I did the same. But for a different reason. I knew diddlysquat about this plumber, but unless he was oblivious and visually impaired, he *must* have spotted Iz.

"Gotta make sure he's working on the plumbing," Iz insisted. "Instead of up to some hanky-panky."

"Hanky-panky?" Allison echoed.

"Fooling around," I clarified.

"In a place that got all flooded with poop when the toilet backed up?" Allison made the gag-me sign. "That's just . . . just icky."

Iz shrugged, but didn't respond. She moved through the stored scenery and props with all the stealth of John Belushi sneaking up to spy on the sorority girls in *Animal House*.

I changed the subject before Allison could ask me questions I couldn't answer. "Don't you need to go over your lines? Or get on the stage? Or something? Before Frankie gets mad?"

"Oh. Yeah." She made a fluttery motion with both hands. "Stay here. Open the door for the others." She pointed in the opposite direction Iz had gone, past dangling ropes, a couple of chairs, and a table with a jug of water and a platoon of paper cups. "Tell them to go down those stairs and back up the ones to the lobby and to the theater that way. Tell them to sit way in the back with the others and be real quiet."

I snapped off a salute and leaned against the wall.

246

In a moment Iz returned. She smelled faintly of— Well, trust me, you really don't want to know. Let me just say that the odor managed to triumph over dust and damp, mold and mildew. "He's in there. He'll have to come out this door when he's done so I'll wait here with you."

Great. My life was now complete.

She cast a longing glance at the water table. "Think they have any food around here?"

"They do during performances. But I doubt anyone will be working the snack bar during a rehearsal."

"That's stupid." Iz rubbed her stomach. "I'm starving."

Recalling the sandwich I'd brought along for Dave, I launched negotiations. "If I give you a sandwich, will you watch the door so I can watch the show?"

"What kind of a sandwich?"

"Baloney."

Iz grimaced, making me wonder if she'd ever heard the expression "Beggars can't be choosers."

"With cheese. And mustard and mayo. And pickles."

"On rye?"

"Whole wheat."

She frowned.

I sweetened the deal. After all, Dave might never show. And if he did, I'd offer the emergency bag of peanuts that surfaced in my purse two days ago. The sell-by date was in September, but the plastic bag was intact so the nuts probably weren't too stale. "A cola and two cookies go with the sandwich."

"Deal. But if the plumber leaves, I'll be right behind him."

From Allison's description of the restroom, I doubted he'd be leaving soon. "No problem."

I handed over the paper sack and, before Iz could change her mind, hustled to the staircase and descended to the lower level. The low-ceilinged space gave new meaning to the word "cluttered." Racks of costumes, boxes of props, and piles of furniture left little room for actors. Most were rehearsing their lines complete with gestures and movements. Others were warming up for their musical numbers by singing scales or snatches of songs. The rest—all females—were clustered around my ex-husband who was demonstrating a range of facial expressions designed to convey a fleet of emotions. I doubted he'd explained that he developed most of those expressions with one goal in mind—enticing women of all ages to do his bidding.

Turning my head, I sidled past and shot up the stairs to the lobby. It was dark except for the light in the display case of the snack bar. A gaggle of girls—friends of Allison's—milled in the far corner, giggling, primping, and tapping their phones. Probably exchanging texts with each other. Two boys I recognized from Captain Meriwether leaned against a wall. They wore expressions of chronic boredom and indifference.

I clapped my hands to get their attention and repeated Allison's orders. "Go in quietly. Sit in the back rows. And, unless you want the director to toss you out, make a whole heck of a lot less noise than you ever have when I subbed in your classes."

One girl managed an innocent and offended look. The rest laughed and shuffled their way to the theater.

In a few minutes, Mrs. B, several members of the Committee, and a few more of Allison's friends emerged from the depths. Mrs. B carried a large canvas shopping bag with a suspicious bulge. "You brought Cheese Puff?"

"I thought perhaps a trip to the theater would inspire him."

I peered in the bag. Cheese Puff didn't peer back. His head remained tucked, his body curled in a tight ball on the cushion stuffed in the bottom of the bag. Still on strike.

"He used to love our trips to the theater," Mrs. B mourned, "but tonight he didn't want to get in the sack. Even though I brought him a nice piece of sirloin."

"Snarled at Muriel," Jim added with a mixture of disbelief and disgust. "After he ate the steak, of course."

"Maybe he's sick," she said. "Or has a toothache."

"He chewed the steak without a problem," Jim stated. "If you consider gobbling the same as chewing."

I slid my hand in the bag and felt Cheese Puff's nose. Damp and cool. I felt his belly. Warm but not hot. And tight as a drum. I prodded gently. He grunted. "How large was that chunk of sirloin?"

"Not large," Mrs. B said.

Jim measured air with his fingers, indicating the chunk had the circumference of a wineglass.

"Cheese Puff is fine," I pronounced. If your definition of "fine" was overfed and overindulged. "Ignore him."

Easy for me to say. Tough for Mrs. B to do.

I patted her arm and spouted a few platitudes meaning it would all be okay, then urged them to be quiet and unobtrusive and ushered them to seats in the rear of the theater. The three musicians at the side of the stage closest to the lobby door raised their eyebrows as we passed. But Frankie DeMille, yellow scarf fluttering and prairie skirt swirling as she flounced about the stage checking the lighting, didn't seem to notice. She didn't look our way, even when Mrs. B set Cheese Puff's sack on the seat beside her and rolled the sides down so he could see the performance if he got the urge.

When I returned to the lobby, Josh was there in dark jeans, an oversized hoodie, and a pair of gigantic sunglasses. "How do I look?"

"Like someone I'd avoid if I saw you in a dark alley."

He puffed himself up with pride.

"Slump," I ordered. "And shuffle."

He did and I escorted him in as the lights dimmed and the music began. I planted him in an aisle seat in front of Jim, and took a seat of my own lower down, closer to the door where I could watch for Dave. He hadn't sent a text and I'd given away his dinner, but I remained optimistic.

I couldn't use that word to describe my feelings about Allison's singing. When it came to hitting notes, she was no Annie Oakley. But she certainly could emote. No, make that over-emote. Emotion spilled from her like oil from a blown underwater well. In the same way the plant in the musical thrived on blood, she thrived on the spotlight.

Her buddies in the back rows, Mrs. B included, forgot all about their pledges to be quiet and unobtrusive. They applauded every minute or so, with occasional bursts of whooping, whistling, and stomping.

Meanwhile, a young woman who'd come in late, shrugged out of a silver-gray raincoat, and taken a seat in the center and two rows behind me, expressed a different opinion. She did that with exasperated sighs, groans, and whispered comments making it clear there was better acting to be seen in a kindergarten class. I decided she must be Allison's nemesis, Audrey. For a few moments I considered sliding in beside her and requesting she zip her lips, then decided this was a battle Allison would have to fight on her own.

The louder Audrey's comments were, the louder the group in the back became.

Frankie DeMille, seated in the center of the front row and armed with a clipboard, made copious notes, but never turned around to call for silence.

"What have I missed?" Dave dropped into the seat beside me.

"About half of it," I whispered.

"Timing is everything," he chortled.

"Did you make an arrest?"

"No."

"Are you close?"

He snorted. "About as close as I am to having a sandwich in my hand right now."

"Sorry." I offered the packet of peanuts. "I had to bribe Iz to watch the door so I could watch your daughter."

"You are an exceptional woman." Dave ripped open the bag and dumped half the contents in his mouth.

An exceptional woman who wished she'd had the foresight to bring along the industrial-strength earplugs she used for subbing in band class.

Dave finished crunching peanuts, crumpled the bag, and tucked it in the pocket of his windbreaker. I heard none of that because Allison was caterwauling her way through "Suddenly Seymour" and dancing with all the grace of a giraffe wearing roller skates.

"OMG," the woman two rows behind us groaned.

Dave turned to stare at her. I gripped his arm. "Don't get involved."

Chapter 28

Dave's arm muscles tightened. But in a moment he nodded and faced the front again.

"The woman behind us is the one who usually plays the part," I told him. "She's jealous."

Dave winced as his daughter missed another series of notes, serving up a snatch of song as sour as a rhubarb salad with a vinegar dressing. "If you say so."

"Puhleese," Audrey groused.

"Okay, maybe she's not jealous of Allison's talents," I told Dave. "But she's obviously insecure about Allison playing the part, even in a rehearsal."

"She's dreadful," Audrey complained.

"Sounds more like vindictiveness than jealousy," Dave said. "Allison's singing sounds like a car with a loose fan belt, but I thought they saved comments for after the production."

"My ears are bleeding," Audrey whimpered.

"Ignore her," I counseled.

"I'll try." Dave's hands rolled into fists.

Mrs. B, members of the Committee, and Allison's friends, however, met the critic's comments with waves of applause.

The critic raised her voice to meet their challenge.

They clapped harder.

Frankie DeMille turned in her seat and scowled.

The fans in the back stopped clapping.

"Get her off before her screeching cracks the windows," Audrey called.

Allison stopped singing, pushed Seymour aside, and stalked to the front of the stage. "Shut up, Audrey."

With a clash of notes, the band stopped playing.

"I won't," Audrey said. "And you can't make me."

Seymour herded the women playing Crystal, Ronette, and Chiffon to the rear of the stage.

"Save it for notes," Frankie said.

"Yeah," Allison said. "Save it for later."

"I can't," Audrey protested. "You're so terrible I have to speak out. I have to stop you. It's my obligation as a real actress."

"If you were a *real* actress," Allison sniped, "they would have asked you to do another reading and you'd still be in Portland at that audition."

"The audition went fine. And we're not talking about me." Audrey stood and leveled a finger at Allison. "We're talking about you."

Dave turned in his seat to get a better look at Audrey. Mrs. B and the group in the back leaned forward in their seats. Even Cheese Puff popped his head from his sack.

"Well, I'm not listening. Not to someone who talks about the 'integrity of the performance' and then says she'll fake being sick if Seymour has to miss a show. All so she won't have to kiss the wino."

"Me?" Jake appeared from backstage, his eyes wide with disbelief. "She doesn't want to kiss me?"

"Not you, Jake." Allison stomped her feet. "The *other* wino. The one who got killed. The one who was *talented*."

253

Jake put his hand over his heart and dropped to his knees as if he'd suffered a mortal blow. The girls playing Crystal, Ronette, and Chiffon trotted across the stage to console him.

"He was *not* talented," Audrey claimed. "He was dirty and stinky."

"Well, he was homeless, so he couldn't take a shower every day. He probably had to beg for his food and sometimes eat out of trash cans. But that didn't give you the right to be so mean to him, and tell him all the time that he should quit, and threaten to get him arrested."

Frankie DeMille turned to Audrey and shook her head. "Did you—?"

"You bet she did," Allison answered. "She told him she was gonna call the police and say he was stealing from the snack bar and taking stuff out of people's pockets and purses."

"He was," Audrey insisted.

"He wasn't. I asked everybody. He never took a dime."

The women playing Crystal, Ronette, and Chiffon nodded in agreement.

"Good girl," Dave murmured.

I squeezed his hand. I was proud of Allison for sticking up for herself, but mostly for defending Max Quiring.

Audrey didn't back down. "Well, he could have. He would have if he got the chance. That's what bums do."

"He wasn't a bum and he wasn't a thief. He was homeless. And he had more talent in his left little toe than you have in your entire pudgy body."

Audrey ran her hands down her sides and over her hips, smoothing her tight red dress. "I am *not* pudgy."

"Right." Allison laughed. "You're not pudgy. You're waaaayyyy past pudgy."

"Ladies." Frankie stood and smacked her clipboard on the edge of the stage. "End this petty squabble right—"

"Not until she apologizes," Allison said.

"Not until you toss her out of the cast," Audrey insisted. "Find another understudy. Anybody would be better. If something happens to me and she goes on, she'll murder the performance."

"I will not."

"You will so." Audrey put her hands to her throat. "You sing like you're being strangled."

"Oh, yeah. Well I bet that's what you did to the poor wino guy."

A gasp resonated from the back row.

The bass guitarist played the first four notes of the *Dragnet* theme.

Frankie turned to gape at Audrey whose hands remained at her throat.

"Was he strangled?" I asked Dave in a whisper.

"Yeah. Hit on the head with a brick, then strangled."

"You're not denying it," Allison taunted.

"I . . . I shouldn't have to. It's . . . it's ridiculous. Completely ridiculous. It's so ridiculous it's funny."

"Then why aren't you laughing?" Allison pointed at Dave. "I bet you think you have a great alibi, but my dad's a cop and he can break it."

Dave pulled a notebook from the pocket of his windbreaker and flipped through the pages.

"Audrey," I whispered. "Her name is Audrey. The same as the character."

He flipped more pages. Given the low light and his atrocious handwriting, I doubted he could make sense of the notes he'd taken when he interviewed her.

Audrey faced Dave and spread her hands in appeal. "How could anyone believe I'm a killer?" She turned to face the group in the back. "And why? Why would I kill him?"

"Because you love to pick at others." Allison stomped her feet, fast and hard. "You pick, pick, pick, pick, pick. But you can't stand it when someone criticizes you. And he did. And he was right."

"He was not! His ideas were stupid."

"If they were so stupid, how come everybody thought they were great?" Allison's eyes widened. "And how come you never wear that scarf anymore? The striped one that goes with your coat?"

The bass guitar sounded the theme from *Dragnet* once more.

Dave tucked his notebook in his pocket and stood.

Audrey ran.

Dave scrambled over me and took off in pursuit.

They barreled to the far aisle and onto the stage, scattering Jake and his covey of actresses, knocking over a table, bouncing off the plant, and disappearing from view.

Like everyone else, I rushed to the stage, listening to the sounds of running feet and toppling flats.

"Stop her," Dave yelled. "Police. Stop her."

A clanging clatter followed.

A round of cursing followed that. The curses were delivered by several voices. Male and female.

Then Dave emerged through the backdrop curtain. He had a firm grip on Audrey's left arm. My sister, minus one slipper, had a grip on her right. Behind them came a burly man holding a plunger like a sword.

Allison led the applause.

I wasn't at all surprised when Audrey tried to take a bow.

Neither was I surprised when Allison jumped from the stage and into Josh's open arms.

"Does this mean you'll be on the plane with us tomorrow," I asked after Dave called for Detective Atwell.

"If we get a confession. And finish all the paperwork. And Chuck doesn't need me to stay."

I groaned.

If our vacation was at the mercy of Detective Charles Atwell, it was toast.

"If I don't make it, I'll be on the first commercial flight I can find." Keeping a grip on Audrey, he dipped his head and kissed me. "Even if it's routed through Atlanta or Miami or Toronto. I promise."

The quality of the kiss weakened my resolve. "Want me to pack a suitcase for you?"

He laughed. "I don't think I have much worth packing. Toss a spare toothbrush in your bag. I'll pick up some gear when I get there."

Dave hadn't turned up by 10:00 the next morning when a small fleet of cabs pulled up at 90 Columbia Lane and we loaded up our gear. Mrs. B, of course, had half a dozen pieces of deep red matching luggage in various shapes and sizes. Jim had a faded green duffel bag. Verna and Sybil towed huge cases in pink and lime green. Josh brought a beige and brown plaid suitcase from bygone days, one without wheels or a pull-out handle. Allison, all about being a new and improved version of herself, pronounced it cool and retro.

Obedient Lola had ducked her head and raised her feet to help me get her into her harness, but Cheese Puff fought, flopping on his side and tucking his head against his chest. I'd persevered, not always in the gentlest manner. His next strategy had involved going limp and refusing to walk when I snapped on the leash. I'd given up and stuffed him under my arm. He emerged from the condo hind-end-first, feet paddling air as Lola trudged along beside us, her cast thumping the sidewalk. Inside the cab, he attempted to crawl beneath the front seat. I discouraged that with a jerk of his tail and set him on Mrs. B's lap.

She never once suggested I treat the little prince with more kindness and respect.

My sister and Penelope met us on the tarmac beside a gleaming white charter jet. Penelope sat on a silver hardside suitcase, filing her nails, her back to my sister. Iz, still wearing her disreputable trench coat, was telling the pilot how easy detecting was and how she'd captured a killer. The pilot, a wiry man with a weathered face and sandy gray hair, was looking everywhere but at Iz. He didn't appear to be swallowing her tale hook, line, *or* sinker.

When he spotted Mrs. B, he broke away and took charge of stowing our luggage. "Coffee and doughnuts and stuff in the galley," he said.

"Doughnuts!" Allison darted up the steps to the cabin, towing Josh behind her.

The others followed, leaving me with Lola and Cheese Puff. Knowing she'd follow, I unsnapped Lola's leash, then started up the narrow steps as the pilot watched.

The retractable leash unwound to the end.

Cheese Puff didn't budge.

I tugged.

He reared back and snapped at the leash.

Lola nudged him forward a foot.

I tugged again. "Come on, Cheese Puff."

Nails scraping, he turned and scrabbled at the tarmac, attempting to run off, but getting nowhere.

"All right. Be stubborn. Be an embarrassment to your species." I plodded down the steps. "If I have to carry you, I will."

But I didn't have to.

Lola growled, growled in a way that made Cheese Puff turn and look at her. She lowered her head and nudged him again.

He barked.

She growled.

He snarled.

She lunged and snapped at his back.

"Lola," I gasped.

She raised her head.

Cheese Puff dangled from her mouth, his harness clamped between her teeth.

He wiggled like an eel but, step by halting step, Lola followed me to the cabin.

She deposited him in a front-row seat beside Mrs. B, and growled at him once more.

Cheese Puff curled his lip, but didn't make a sound. Nor did he attempt to escape. When I unsnapped his leash, he crawled onto Mrs. B's lap, whining and pawing at her arm as he did when he wanted attention.

She raised a hand as if to pet him, then leaned over and scratched Lola's ears instead. "Good girl. Thank you for getting Cheese Puff on the plane. When we get to Las Vegas, you'll get a special treat."

Cheese Puff whined at the word "treat" and pawed her arm again.

Mrs. B made a show of placing her hands on the armrests. Then she fixed him with a steely gaze. "Lie down and be quiet. You'll get a treat when you deserve one, and not one minute before."

The sharp tone of her voice and his dismayed whimper told me a new day had dawned. For both of them.

Lola was stretched across two seats in the back and the pilot was about to pull up the steps when Dave came loping across the tarmac. His hair stood up in greasy tufts, his skin had a gray tinge, he sported dark bags beneath his eyes, and he wore the same jeans, T-shirt, and jacket he'd had on last night. He flung himself up the steps and entered the cabin to a round of applause. After a Rocky-style victory dance, he flopped into the seat beside mine.

"Coffee," he moaned.

Members of the Committee scrambled to supply him.

We'd left Mt. Hood behind us when Dave drained his second cup of coffee, brushed powdered sugar from his stubble, and pulled a box from his jacket pocket. "You forgot this."

I scowled at the white take-out box last seen at the rear of the refrigerator. "If you mean I forgot to throw it away, I didn't. I was hoping you'd dispose of it."

"So you never looked inside?" He balanced the box on his palm and inched it into my personal space.

I leaned away. "No."

"Why not?"

"Because the leftover whatever in that box is probably rotten or toxic or evolving into an alien life form. Or all three."

Dave shook his head and made with an expression of puzzled disbelief.

"What? What's with the head shake?"

"You're always so curious. I bet Chuck you'd have this box open within 24 hours of the minute I put it on the shelf."

"You bet . . . You put it . . . Wait! What are you talking about?" I stared at the little box, my mind swirling with questions. "And how would you know whether I opened it? Unless you happened to be there when I did."

260

"Oh, I'm pretty sure I'd know." He grinned. "If I wasn't home, I'd hear about it soon afterward."

I leaned farther away from the box. "Why? Is there a snake inside? One of those little ones with really strong venom?"

"Not the last time I looked."

He shook the box.

I heard a muffled thump. It wasn't followed by a hiss. If the box contained a snake, it was hibernating. Or sedated. Or dead.

But, dead, alive, or sedated, I wanted nothing to do with a snake.

"It's not a snake," Dave assured me. "Or a spider. Or a mouse. It's not decaying. It doesn't stink."

"You swear?"

"I swear." He set the box on my lap.

I checked to make sure his fingers weren't crossed.

Then I opened the flaps.

Inside was a tiny velvet-covered box.

Inside that was a diamond ring.

Epilogue

In case you're wondering, I told Dave I'd marry him. But not at a wedding chapel in Las Vegas. And not soon. He was fine with that. He said he and Allison had a long way to go toward being ideal roommates. I assured him he excelled in a few select categories. Later, when we were alone, he proved it. After that I didn't much care what he wore to Mrs. B's competition.

In case you're wondering, Sybil played her seventh slot machine system and it paid off. Big time. The next day she lost it all playing roulette. I couldn't tell whether Verna was more upset by the win or by the loss.

In case you're wondering, Mrs. B and Glorree Morning wound up tied after the first round of competition. Glorree's second performance, although risk-free and uninspired, was flawless. My stomach was in knots and I was nibbling my nails when the curtain went up and Mrs. B tapped from the wings. She was dressed as a black cat, with bands of pearls around her neck, wrists, and ankles. Just when I thought Cheese Puff had left her in the lurch, he trotted out wearing a tiny tuxedo with a top hat tilted over one ear. The dance they did together blew everyone away.

262

When she was awarded the prize, however, Mrs. B called the judges' attention to a fine-print paragraph that stated contestants would perform without assistance. While judges scratched their heads, Mrs. B handed the prize to her rival.

In case you're wondering, while we were gone Frankie DeMille found another Audrey. Allison, meanwhile, realized Reckless River is pretty darn small compared to Las Vegas, not to mention the rest of the wide world. She returned home more determined to be a new and improved version of herself—starting with singing lessons.

And, in case you're wondering, while we were gone Bernina Burke got her hands on a sunbathing plastic Santa. Under cover of darkness, she added him to the display by the pool. The judges got wind of the rule violation and disqualified our condo complex.

While we were railing about wasted time, money, and effort, we learned the Shoalwater Bend manager intended to remain on the job for another year. Bernina, determined to impress the hiring committee and land the position, is already planning next winter's holiday display.

I wish I could say that was fake news, but it isn't.

NO SUBSTITUTE FOR MISINFORMATION

Also by Carolyn J. Rose

The Catskill Mountains Mysteries
Hemlock Lake
Through a Yellow Wood
The Devil's Tombstone

The Subbing isn't for Sissies series
No Substitute for Murder
No Substitute for Money
No Substitute for Maturity
No Substitute for Myth
No Substitute for Mistakes
No Substitute for Motives

And others
Nightfall Bay
An Uncertain Refuge
Sea of Regret
A Place of Forgetting

With Michael A. Nettleton
Death at Devil's Harbor
Deception at Devil's Harbor
The Hard Karma Shuffle
The Crushed Velvet Miasma
Drum Warrior
Sucker Punches

Carolyn J. grew up in New York's Catskill Mountains, graduated from the University of Arizona, logged two years in Arkansas with Volunteers in Service to America, and spent 25 years as a television news researcher, writer, producer, and assignment editor in Arkansas, New Mexico, Oregon, and Washington. She's now a substitute teacher in Vancouver, Washington, and her interests are reading, swimming, walking, gardening, and NOT cooking.

www.ingramcontent.com/pod-product-compliance
Lightning Source LLC
Chambersburg PA
CBHW061600170626
46811CB00001B/262